The Gisburn Witch
A Witches of Pendle Novel

Sarah L King

ACKNOWLEDGMENTS

I would like to thank my husband David who has supported me throughout this new and often daunting process of creating a novel. He has been at once my editor, agent and guide into the world of self-publishing, not to mention my biggest cheerleader! Without him this work wouldn't have made it beyond the lonely confines of my laptop.

I would also like to thank my beta readers, K.J Farnham and Deborah Lincoln, for their time, effort and feedback.

PENDLE AREA MAP

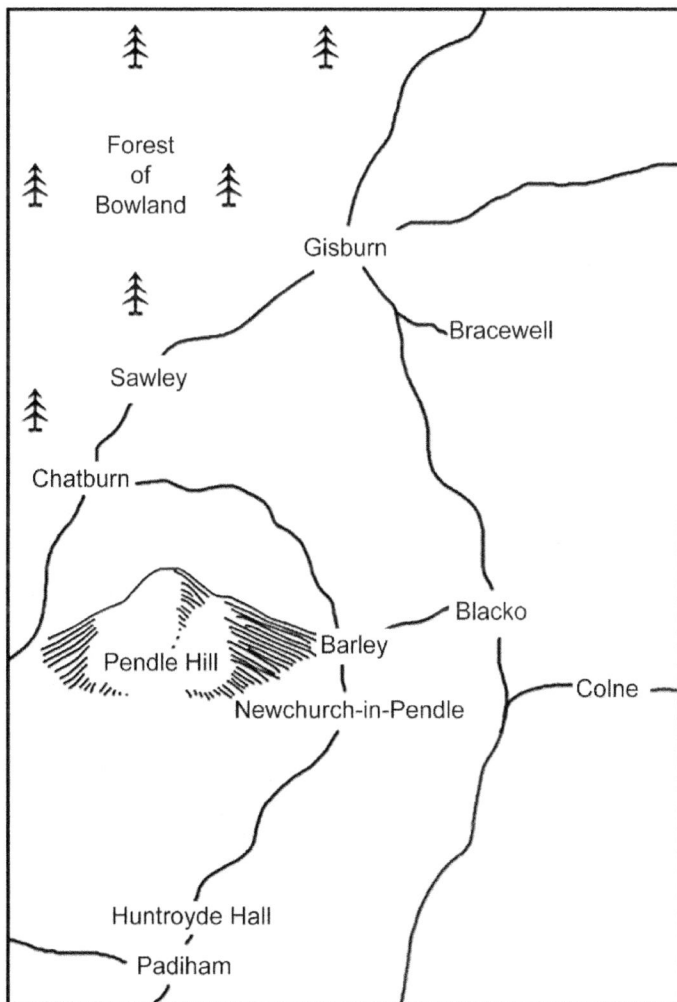

Part One

1585 - 1587

1

Westby Hall, Gisburn
January 1585

Jennet gazed out of the window. Outside, the light was dim and she reflected that it was so dull it barely seemed possible that it was approaching midday. Winter's days in Gisburn were short and mostly shrouded in dark clouds which seemed to hide the sun for months on end. It was a pity it was so dark, she thought, as it made it difficult to appreciate the picturesque character of the Westby estate: gently yielding curves interspersed with occasional clusters of trees, dwellings for the pigs or sporadic patches of fluffy white sheep. The air outside was damp but mild, preventing the arrival of snow. At the mere thought of snow, Jennet shivered. Beautiful as it was, blanketing the surrounding countryside in a shimmering sea of glistening white, nevertheless it made the business of work, of travel, not to mention keeping warm while sleeping, that bit more difficult. At this thought Jennet smiled, perhaps for the first time that day. At least she was warm now, one of the advantages of working in the kitchen at Westby next to the glowing open fire.

"Are you quite finished with those eggs?" a snappy voice interrupted Jennet's thoughts. "If you beat them any slower they will get up out of that bowl and walk away from you, girl."

"Sorry Goody Robinson," Jennet replied.

Goodwife Robinson gave the young girl a harsh stare, which then melted away to an affectionate smile. She couldn't help it; Jennet spent much of her day in a dream and more often than not worked at a pace all of her very own, but she was a delicate little thing and the work always got done.

"It's alright, lass. Though I would like to know what's going on in that head of yours sometimes, because I doubt very much that you are occupying your mind with thoughts of game pies and stews." Goody Robinson smiled. She had been joking, but the girl continued to stand seriously in front of her. She sighed. "Come on then, back to work lass. We're fortunate to have the luxury of time today anyway. No visitors again, only the family to cook for this afternoon; the Master, the Mistress and the children, and the younger ones don't eat much. Young Master Thomas is out on the estate, he's already taken some bread and meats out with him and won't require anything else until supper. We've the servants too, of course, but they'll be content with pottage this time of the year."

Goodwife Robinson's sentence trailed off as she realised she'd already lost Jennet's attention. The young girl had already returned to staring out of the window, gently caressing the eggs in the bowl, instead of giving them the vigorous beating required to bring them to the correct form. Goodwife Robinson sighed again. Jennet was so quiet, so reserved. The cook had never been able to relate easily to a person of Jennet's disposition; being somewhat of a brash and vocal character herself, she was forthcoming in letting someone know what she thought and how she was feeling. Jennet, on the other hand, could sometimes spend a full day in the kitchen with her and barely speak a word, other than to acknowledge her tasks or apologise in response to a scolding, and today was one such day. Goody Robinson had initially assumed that Jennet's reticence was due to the generational difference between the two of them, that Jennet felt uneasy and therefore assumed a demeanour of quiet deference. But then, having discussed the matter with her daughter Anne who also worked in the Lister household, it seemed that

Jennet was much the same with those of a similar age to herself, the only exception being the young master, Thomas Lister.

This was hardly surprising, Goodwife Robinson reflected. Despite the social difference which existed between them, there had been a long history of good relations between the Listers and the Balderstons. For almost one hundred years the Balderstons had had the tenure of a portion of the Lister estate and over the decades the Balderston family had come to be well-regarded by their landlords for their hard work and timely payment of rents. For generations, the children of the two families had grown up together, and young Master Thomas and Jennet were no exception. Goodwife Robinson pondered momentarily on how freely all the Lister children were allowed to mix with the village boys and girls, only to grow up and be separated from them by position for the rest of their lives. Position was exactly what separated young Master Thomas and Jennet now, not that either of them seemed to notice it much. The number of times that Goodwife Robinson could recall catching her young kitchen maid and Thomas Lister sharing a private joke or a whispered conversation! Each time the cook had been forced to gently remind Jennet of her position in the house, a position which in itself was something of a long tradition. Countless Balderston women before her had been sent to work at Westby; service in a large household acted as a convenient way to fill a girl's time between childhood and marriage, not to mention provide a useful wage. It was also a way to further a girl's skills in readiness for becoming a wife. Whilst their mothers had already taught them much, large country houses could teach them to cook, cure, pickle and bake on a far larger and grander scale, and those were just the skills learned in the kitchen. Although, Goodwife Robinson lamented, in many cases once married these young women would not have the fortune to cook in such a manner again, reduced instead to repetitions of the same pottages and stews or worse, trying to avert starvation in the winter. Goodwife Robinson sighed. She could only do her best to teach this girl everything she knew; the rest would be up to Jennet, and

God's will of course.

"Goody Robinson, I've finished the eggs. What would you like me to do next?" said a voice from across the kitchen.

The cook suspended her thoughts to examine the girl's work.

"We will need to instil more vigour into your egg-beating, lass," she said kindly, "but it'll do for now. Tell you what, you can make the servant's dinner, just a plain pottage and bread, it is January and after all those feasts at Christmas…well, we don't want to run short of anything before the spring comes. I'll finish the dinner for the family. I think it'll be far more than they will eat anyway so there should be ample leftovers for all of us to go along with the pottage."

"Yes, Goodwife," replied Jennet, obediently.

Later that afternoon, after dinner had been served and the pots had been scrubbed, Jennet took a walk in the grounds immediately surrounding Westby Hall. The dark clouds which had disappointed Jennet earlier in the day had relented and given way to a hint of winter sunlight, brightening the day and Jennet's mood with it. The improved weather and the early completion of her duties in the kitchen meant that Jennet had leapt at the opportunity for a walk when Goodwife Robinson had suggested it. In truth, for all the cook's pretensions that her young assistant may need to take some air, Jennet could sense that she would be happy to be left for an hour. Her daughter Anne had arrived in the kitchen to assist, as she often did in the afternoon, and Jennet sensed they preferred to be left alone together. Jennet knew that Goodwife Robinson, for all her kindly ways, found working with Jennet difficult. In return Jennet tried determinedly to be less reticent; however, it was in her nature and she had always found it difficult to evade her natural disposition.

Jennet had another reason for her eagerness to take a walk that afternoon. She knew that young Master Thomas, or Tom as she better knew him, was out on the estate and that there was every possibility of encountering him along the way. Tom had been her friend for as long as she could remember, indeed her whole life, and for Jennet, who did not feel naturally comfortable with most people, Tom was someone with whom she could feel at ease. Jennet was almost sixteen now, and with the prospect of many years of toil, marriage and probably child-bearing in front of her, Tom Lister was a reminder of childhood, of happy carefree hours spent hiding in the woods or catching small fish in the nearby river. Jennet reflected that those times were not so many years behind her, yet they had seemed to disappear so very quickly. This wasn't surprising really: Tom was the heir to his father's estate and as manhood loomed his formal training for the role he would assume one day had begun, leaving him with little time for recreation, certainly not with the village boys and girls anyway. Equally, as Jennet's years advanced, the skills which would carry her into womanhood had to be honed, and the practice of these skills, mostly at her mother's side, gradually took over most of her time. However, in a stroke of good fortune, since Jennet's arrival at Westby Hall about six months earlier, both she and Tom had renewed their childhood friendship. Although their relative social positions of master and maid now prohibited them from meeting at length, snatched meetings in the house and sometimes longer encounters on the estate were possible, and at least on Jennet's part, fully intended.

That afternoon Jennet took her usual route around Westby. Goodwife Robinson had said that she should not linger in the grounds in the immediate vicinity of the hall, since the Mistress had made it clear on more than one occasion that she did not appreciate looking out of her window to a view of her kitchen maid enjoying an hour's respite in the fresh air. Instead Jennet took the small track which led immediately from the door at the back of the kitchen and dairy, through the first set of trees and into a clearing. From there she roamed, darting between areas of field and foliage, enjoying the calm, gentle undulations of the surrounding countryside against the backdrop of Pendle Hill and the long westward valley beyond which lay Clitheroe and the outlying villages. January was a month of relative serenity at Westby: there was little activity on the estate except for absolutely necessary duties. Many of the beasts were slaughtered just after Martinmas leaving mostly sheep grazing peacefully on the low pastures, and the pigs, though present, often hid in their shelters to keep out of the cold. In the hall itself there was little entertaining to be done as most of the Listers' family, friends and associates kept to their own houses in the bleak winter weeks between Christmas and Candlemas, meaning that most days it was just Jennet and Goodwife Robinson in the kitchen cooking for the family and servants. However, Jennet realised, in a matter of weeks it would be spring, the season of lambing and planting and sowing and growing, and hopefully more benevolent weather, bringing with it Easter and visitors and banquets and more hands in the kitchen and regrettably, less time for walks.

Jennet's thoughts were interrupted by a figure approaching, just beyond the trees. Her face brightened as she realised it was Tom. Jennet had dared to hope that she might see him today and had begun to admit to herself just how much of a highlight her chance meetings with him were, how much she had come to depend upon them as a cheering interlude in her otherwise quite hard and monotonous days. She tried to force her legs not to run towards him but in the end she couldn't help it and once again in the presence of the young Master, Jennet completely forgot herself.

"Tom!" she shouted. "Are you on your way back to the house?"

Tom increased his pace to meet her at the edge of the small woodland area from which he had come.

"I thought it was you," Tom said, quickening his step as he walked towards her. "I had hoped I might see you today."

Jennet smiled, catching her breath and feeling embarrassed for running like a child. "You see me every day," she answered, without thinking.

Tom glanced down at his feet, feeling self-conscious. Jennet always had a way of making him feel like a silly boy again. He cleared his throat and looked up at her through his dark eyelashes.

"Well, yes, that's true. I meant I was hoping to see you out, alone, so that we can talk properly. It's not possible to talk at length in the house…" Tom's voice trailed off as he looked intently at Jennet. They both stood there dumbly for a moment, just looking at one another. In the end it was Jennet who broke the silence.

"I suppose we should be talking while we have the chance. As you say, it's difficult to talk in the house, we are both so busy and there are always others around. Goodwife Robinson certainly always has a watchful eye on me."

They both laughed at the thought of the old cook, then Jennet's face reddened as she reflected that her comment may have seemed insolent. She chastised herself for once again, being too comfortable with Tom. After all, he was Master-in-training of Westby now, not that boy by the river any more.

"I'm…sorry," she stammered. "It was rude of me to laugh about Goodwife Robinson."

"I laughed too," Tom protested.

"Yes, but you're…well, it's your house, you will one day be master of it and can speak as you please about anyone employed at Westby. I, on the other hand…"

"You can speak as you wish, in front of me," Tom interrupted her, speaking firmly.

Jennet smiled as Tom reached out a hand and patted her shoulder reassuringly. Jennet looked up at him. He had grown taller these past months, his shoulders had broadened and his beard was beginning to grow, dark like his hair. The only features of him which had remained unchanged were his eyes; bright blue, honest and intense. As Jennet looked at those eyes, Tom's hand reached to touch her cheek, though just as his fingers brushed delicately against her pale skin he snatched them back, as though thinking better of his actions. Tom cleared his throat again.

"May I walk you back to the hall?" he asked. "Goody Robinson will begin to wonder where you are."

"That would be nice," Jennet replied.

The pair walked silently for a few moments, seemingly trying to decipher the best words to spend on their last few minutes together. Finally, after clearing his throat several times, Tom spoke.

"Do you know I am to marry soon?" he asked.

Jennet nodded. The news came as no surprise to her. Tom had been betrothed to Jane Greenacres of Worston since he was a small boy and she was an infant. Tom was now approaching sixteen, and Jane Greenacres would be turning thirteen or fourteen, meaning that she was now of marriageable age. Jennet had always thought that the great families of the area had their children marry so young. She remembered the first time Tom had mentioned his betrothal, several years ago when they were still children. He had told her that he would probably be married before he was seventeen. Jennet had gone home that day and asked her mother about it, and her mother had remarked that it was normal, as the great families had to ensure that they had heirs to secure the family name, wealth and property for the next generation. When Jennet asked why people like her did not marry so young, her mother had told her that there was no need. In fact, she said, for people like them to marry young would mean to marry before they had established themselves. Men had to start to earn a secure and proper living and women had to learn the skills they needed to support a family. If they married too young, they married unprepared and risked poverty, made worse by the arrival of a baby every year or so. Jennet recalled the conversation clearly. She remembered that it was the first time it had struck her how different her life and Tom's life would be.

"When will you marry?" Jennet asked, returning her mind to the conversation with Tom.

"It is being discussed at the moment, between our fathers," Tom replied, "but it is likely to be in June or July."

Jennet nodded again, unsure how to reply. She doubted that the wedding would take place in June, as this was such a busy month for the local people who were occupied with sheep-shearing and haymaking, activities requiring a lot of time and community effort. Although these agricultural activities did not involve the Listers directly, Jennet believed that they would want the people of Gisburn to hold customary celebrations in the village whilst relatively free from other major duties. July, she felt, was the preferable month, albeit still very busy, being just before the harvest. Jennet did not express any of her thoughts to Tom; although he had told her to speak freely with him, she nonetheless felt it was insolent to convey an opinion to which he was likely to be indifferent anyway.

"I don't feel ready to marry," Tom blurted suddenly, "but I must, it is my duty. I am sure I will grow to love her; indeed I am fortunate that I have always known she will be my wife and have had the opportunity to get to know her a little. It would be easier if I could look upon her and feel love for her, but I do not. I find it hard to imagine that she should be my wife soon, that we should have children one day."

Tom looked down at Jennet, who was listening, silently and intently, to everything he said. Kind, quiet Jennet, who had always remained his devoted friend, even after the childhood adventures had given way to the stark contrasts between their lives. How beautiful she had grown over this past year; she too was nearing her sixteenth birthday and the delicate marks of womanhood were beginning to show on her. Her face, which had always been pretty in childhood, now bore features which, he longed to tell her, ladies at the royal court might be jealous of: a pale complexion, contrasted with big green eyes and, he knew from spying her once without her coif on, tumbling dark brown hair. As he looked at her now, Tom had the sudden urge to grab hold of Jennet, to hold her tight and to never let her go, not for Jane Greenacres, not for anyone. Instead, he took hold of her hand and clasped it tightly but gently for a few moments as they continued their walk back towards Westby.

"I am sorry, Jennet."

His apology was met by silence and a guarded smile from Jennet. She did not enquire as to what the apology was for. She imagined he was sorry for his outburst, so unbecoming of the future Master of Westby, and for exposing Jennet to it, dampening spirits on an otherwise happy meeting of two friends. She imagined that he might also be sorry for being so melancholy, realising whilst he was speaking that he was not the first young man to have to marry a girl chosen by his parents, and that it may turn out well, she may grow beautiful, and bear many sons, and he may grow to love her. What Jennet did not imagine, however, was that Tom Lister was truly sorry that he had not taken her in his arms and kissed her as they looked at one another on that beautiful winter's day, that he had let the opportunity slip away in a mist of hesitation, and that he may never have a similar moment with her again.

2

Westby Hall, Gisburn
Easter 1585

Jennet mopped her damp brow with the back of her hand as she bustled around the kitchen. The weather outside was unseasonably warm and in the kitchen, next to the fire, it was stifling. She was tired too; her day had started even earlier than normal, so early in fact that dawn hadn't even been on the horizon when Goodwife Robinson had woken her from her sleep, summoning her to begin her duties. Fatigue and heat were not a good combination and Jennet found herself in an irritable mood, venting her frustration on the bowls and spoons she was using. Goodwife Robinson, secretly pleased to find the girl less withdrawn that normal, did her best to lighten her spirits, but with little success.

"Cheer up, Jennet! It's only a day or two more and then the house will begin to return to normal, you'll see," Goodwife Robinson said gently.

Jennet shrugged. "I think this is harder than Christmas," she muttered. "I don't remember it being so hot in here at Christmas."

Goodwife Robinson chuckled. "Of course it wasn't, it was the middle of winter! As I said, it's only a couple more days. Goodness, when I was a girl the festivities lasted much longer! Alas, those were the old ways; we've less holy days now." Jennet was too cross to notice that the old cook's tone almost sounded like a lament. "So cheer up, and get on with your work. We've a lot to do and a great many guests to feed," she said sternly.

Jennet sighed. She knew that Goodwife Robinson was right, a fact which made her words all the more irritating. After the sombre piety of Holy Week, the Listers always held a grand feast on Easter Monday, a day traditionally reserved for festivity. Indeed, as a girl growing up in the village, Jennet couldn't recall a year when there wasn't some sort of celebration held in Gisburn. If the weather was favourable, like today, the Easter feast could even rival the summertime festivities. Jennet sighed again, wondering what she was missing in the village today, missing home for the briefest of moments before returning to her kitchen duties. As she worked, her mind continued to wander. Goodwife Robinson had said there would be a lot of guests today, which was undoubtedly true, and Jennet speculated to herself as to which of their family and friends would be in attendance. At least some of the extended Lister family would be there, as well as some of the Mistress's Houghton relatives and members of other notable families from the area. She wondered if Tom's bride-to be would be there. She hadn't yet set eyes on Jane Greenacres and she had to admit she was curious about her; like many of the other maids she wanted to see whether she was pretty and if her clothes were very fine. However, as she prepared the sweetmeats she had to admit to herself that there was another element to her curiosity, a sort of spite and dislike which made her wish the girl to be ugly and her dresses plain. Ever since Tom had told her about his impending marriage these feelings had crept over her, confusing and alarming her. Such emotions were sinful, she was quite sure of that, but they were also irrepressible. Try as she might, Jennet had come to realise that she struggled to bear the thought of a beautiful girl hanging on to Tom's arm, gazing lovingly into his eyes. She shook her head, trying to suppress her thoughts.

"We're getting there!" sang Goodwife Robinson. Jennet

scowled, the cook's cheeriness continuing to annoy her. "Now, don't let me catch you disappearing off to the banquet later, my girl. I know you like to see the young Master, but I daresay Jane Greenacres will be here today and no doubt both families will want them to spend time together. Besides, you know what the Mistress is like, if she catches you..."

Goodwife Robinson's voice trailed off, but Jennet understood her meaning perfectly. The Mistress of Westby was a stern, forbidding woman who did not take kindly to behaviour which she considered unbecoming of a servant. Jennet had been wary of the Mistress for as long as she could remember. She could recall quite clearly the look of disdain on her face as her precious Tom ran off to play with the local children, and how badly she scolded her boy when he came home with scraped or muddy knees. She was fiercely proud and protective of her son, and Jennet was fairly certain that if it had been her decision, Tom wouldn't have been allowed to play with the local children at all. Fortunately, his father had the final say on such matters and he was a far gentler, far more amenable sort of man. Jennet's father had always said how good the Master of Westby was, what a fair landlord he was, how kindly he treated his tenants. Neither of her parents, however, had ever had much to say about his wife. Since coming to work at Westby, Jennet had tried to give the Mistress a wide berth, endeavouring to be always obedient in her presence but never drawing too much attention to herself. She was always careful to ensure that her meetings with Tom took place away from her watchful eye, knowing that the Mistress would disapprove of her son continuing his friendship with a mere maid. Goodwife Robinson was right; she would be best advised to stay in the servants' quarters, well away from the festivities. She knew that, but she also knew that she would struggle to resist seeing Tom and perhaps sneaking a peek at his betrothed.

"Of course, Goodwife Robinson," she replied obligingly.

Jennet had intended to heed the Goodwife's warning and keep

away from the feast. Indeed, once all the food had been prepared and served she immediately set about her cleaning duties, scrubbing pots and tidying up with enthusiasm. She worked so hard that evening that Goodwife Robinson heaped praised upon her, filled with glee at the thought that they might finish their duties so quickly that they could retire early to bed. In truth, Jennet hoped to keep herself so busy that she wouldn't have the time to be tempted away. Her plan might have worked, had it not been for Tom. As she walked along one of the many corridors she felt someone grab hold of her hand, surprising her and almost causing her to drop the bucket she was carrying. Without saying a word, Tom led her along towards the great hall where the banquet was taking place, stopping at the top of a narrow set of stairs, looking through a doorway which gave them a full view of the room.

"I thought you'd want to see. You usually do," Tom said in a low voice, taking the bucket from her hand and setting it down on the floor.

"Tom! I've work to do. Goodwife Robinson will be wondering where I am," Jennet whispered softly in reply.

"You can take a moment, surely?" Tom asked. "I thought you liked to watch the dancing."

Jennet looked back into the hall. It was true; she loved to see the courtly dances, to admire the graceful movements of the ladies in their fine dresses. Often she would try to memorise the steps and later, when everyone else had gone to bed, she would twirl around with her eyes closed, pretending that she was the daughter of a gentleman, just returned from the Queen's court. As she danced, she would imagine herself in the middle of one of the Listers' feasts. She could feel all eyes upon her, the ladies watching enviously and the young gentlemen admiring her. In the midst of this spectacle was Tom, his gaze affectionate and intense...

"Are you looking for Jane?" asked Tom, his tone slightly mischievous.

"Is she not here?" replied Jennet simply.

"She was," said Tom with a wry smile. "However, she is a

delicate creature and too much food and wine and dancing makes her feel unwell. I was told by her mother that she has retired to her room for the evening."

"Do you miss her?" Jennet asked, realising as she spoke how foolish the question sounded. She wasn't even sure she wanted to know the answer. She didn't want Tom to tell her how lovely she was and how much he was looking forward to spending the evening dancing with her.

"Not really," Tom shrugged. "We've never had a proper conversation, you know. We're never left alone for long enough! And tonight, she doesn't stay to dance, but goes to her rooms instead and sends a message to me via her mother. She doesn't even bother to tell me herself," he finished.

Jennet looked at Tom quizzically. She couldn't tell if he was disappointed because he wanted to get to know Jane Greenacres better, or if the courtship simply irritated him because he found it farcical. She stayed silent, unsure what she could say that would soothe him. She tried to ignore the fact that his dissatisfaction pleased her, that secretly she was glad that he hadn't yet fallen madly in love with his bride-to-be. She didn't like that she felt this way; Tom was her friend, she should want him to be happy in the company of the young lady who would be his wife soon.

"I suppose I must let you go back to your duties," said Tom, changing the subject.

Jennet nodded and turned back towards the stairs. As she did so, Tom reached out and grabbed her hand, pulling her back slightly. "I wish we could dance together, you and I," he said simply. Jennet found herself locked into his gaze, unable to turn away. As she stood there and looked at him for what felt like an eternity, it dawned on her that she would like nothing more than to dance with him, to feel his touch as they twirled around the Listers' great hall. Her face grew hot as she was confronted momentarily with the strength of her desire, before she suppressed her feelings once again and gently removed her hand from his grasp.

"As you said, I have work to do," she replied softly, turning away immediately so that Tom wouldn't see that her cheeks were flushed and her hands were trembling. As she headed back down the stairs she heard another voice behind her and instinctively she froze, but she did not turn around. She knew the voice immediately; it was Tom's mother.

"Who are you talking to?" Jennet heard the Mistress ask her son, her tone typically stern and suspicious.

"It was just Jennet, mother," replied Tom, his tone guarded. "It was my fault, I asked her up here," he added defensively.

"Jennet, come here for a moment," called the Mistress, ignoring her son's words.

Jennet closed her eyes and bit her lip. Her heart was pounding so hard that she thought it might burst from her chest. Composing herself with a deep, considered breath, Jennet slowly turned around and walked back up the stairs. "Yes, Madame?" she asked, trying hard to keep her voice steady.

"What are you doing up here?" the Mistress demanded. "Do you not have enough work to do? Do I need to speak to Goodwife Robinson about keeping you busier?"

Jennet looked down at the floor, avoiding the Mistress's hard stare. "No, Madame," she replied.

"Well then, back downstairs and on with your duties," Tom's mother instructed her.

Jennet turned quickly and walked away. She clasped her hands together in front of her to stop them trembling. Behind her, she could hear the Mistress giving her son a few whispered words. Despite her fear of the Mistress, she couldn't help wonder what she was saying to Tom. She sounded angry; even though she kept her voice intentionally low, Jennet could still make out her harsh, chastising tone. What angered her more, she wondered; the fact that Tom was not with his betrothed, or the fact that he preferred to fraternise with the maids? Jennet bit her lip as she turned a corner and the noise of the feast became a distant hum. Tom spent time with one maid in particular, she realised. Just one maid and that maid had come to the attention of the Mistress now. She wrung her clammy hands together one more time as she reflected that she would have to be more careful from now on.

"I know your game, and it won't work," said a voice behind her. Jennet immediately spun around, alarmed. She had been so absorbed in her own thoughts that she hadn't heard anyone following behind her. Now she was confronted by the Mistress once more.

"I beg your pardon, Madame," Jennet replied, with a brief curtsey.

"You will remember that you are a maid here, Jennet," said Tom's mother, her tone typically forbidding and authoritative. "Whatever intentions you have towards my son, you will forget them. I know that he is kind to you, but do not mistake his kindness for any deeper affection. His only affection now must be for his bride, do you understand? Keep yourself busy with your duties, and keep your distance from my son," she instructed.

Jennet looked up and caught the Mistress's cold stare, wondering what had provoked this outburst. She had only gone upstairs to watch the dancing at Tom's behest. She would have understood Tom's mother chastising her for overstepping the mark in that sense, but no other. What did she mean by intentions? She didn't have intentions towards Tom; she knew that such ideas were futile, that Tom was destined to be a grand and powerful gentleman whilst she would always be a lowly maid. She knew that their friendship was barely permissible, never mind anything else. She knew all this, yet she also knew that when she thought about Tom her stomach fluttered a little and her face grew red. She knew that seeing him was the highlight of her day; indeed, sometimes she sought him out when she thought he might be alone, just so that she could spend time in his company. She didn't have intentions, but she had to admit to herself that she had feelings, stirrings which she always suppressed because she knew that there was no point loving a man she could not have.

"Yes, Madame," Jennet replied obediently.

3

Gisburn Village
10th June 1585

Jennet stretched her bare feet out on the soft green grass, digging her toes in firmly to fully enjoy the luxurious sensation. The sky was completely clear and wonderfully blue, causing the sun to shine with a relentless heat, unabated by the cover of occasional clouds. Jennet shifted uncomfortably, feeling the sweat trickling down her back and wishing that she could remove her bodice, even just for a few moments. As a child she would have stripped down to her shift and paddled in the river to obtain some relief from the summer heat, but alas she was no longer a child. Her sixteenth birthday had arrived in March, and if her mind had not noted its significance, her body had certainly responded. Her mother had commented that she barely needed a roll to accentuate the curvature at her waist which seemed to have appeared overnight. Although Jennet had brushed off her comments, remarking that she hardly had need of a roll anyway, being an impractical item of clothing to wear for all but the highest born ladies, she had to recognise that her mother was right, and like it or not, womanhood was now upon her. So, no more jumping in the river on hot days, she thought. She would have to just endure the heat in her bodice, as all the other women undoubtedly did.

"Jennet! Jennet, there you are lass, I've been looking for you," a gruff but kindly voice interrupted her thoughts. Jennet turned to see her father walking towards her, his cheeks rosy, a broad grin spread across his face.

"Father, you look like you're enjoying yourself," Jennet replied. Richard Balderston smiled at his daughter and gave a little dance in time to the music being played by the piper a short walk away, spilling some of the ale in his hand as he did so.

"Of course, 'tis one of my favourite days of the year. Music, dancing, wonderful food, good company, and sunshine, and not forgetting plenty of good ale," her father added, raising his cup.

The Whitsuntide feast was one of Jennet's favourite holidays also. Every year the villagers of Gisburn held a feast day, usually the Monday following Whit Sunday, but the day depended upon the favourability of the weather and the agreement of all employers. Gathering in the village, they enjoyed a grand feast to which every house contributed, and some entertainment, usually in the form of local flute and pipe players. It was an opportunity to enjoy the company of family, friends and neighbours while the good weather allowed for some unrestricted outdoor merry-making and was one of the major celebrations of the year, second only perhaps to the Christmas festivities. Over fifty years ago, there had been many more such events in the local social calendar, mostly feast days in honour of various saints, however with the coming of the new religion, as some still called it, many of these had been eroded away from tradition or even banned.

Jennet was too young to be able to remember the old ways, but even in her lifetime there were attempts to further curb local feasts and revels. Just twelve months ago in the neighbouring county of Lancashire, mere miles from Gisburn, Justices of the Peace had prohibited such events from taking place on a Sunday. At the time the news of this had been greeted by much muttering in Gisburn, with many feeling that although this new rule did not apply to them, it was nonetheless fortunate that their main summer feast traditionally took place on a Monday so it could not possibly be threatened if Yorkshire Justices decided to follow suit. The perceived threat to the existence of local feast days, along with their relative rarity, meant that they were cherished and embraced even more whole-heartedly by the local people. For many, Richard Balderston included, this meant that even more food and ale and laughter should be enjoyed than ever before.

"Come and dance with us," said Richard, offering his hand to his daughter. "Or have something to eat. Have you had enough to eat? There's still plenty of food."

Jennet rubbed her stomach, which was pressing up hard against her bodice due to the sheer amount of food she had already consumed that day; delicious, wonderful tasting food, but far more than she would normally eat.

"I couldn't eat another thing!" exclaimed Jennet. "My belly is too full to manage to dance, sorry." She shrugged apologetically.

"Alright, lass," replied her father, "go and talk to your mother, then. She's been complaining that she's hardly seen you today. You know she misses you since you went to work at the hall."

Jennet nodded in agreement. It was true that, although she still lived only a short walk from her family's home in the village, she saw much less of her mother than before. It was difficult, her days were long and her duties were often all-consuming, leaving her without the necessary time or energy to visit home. This separation from her family had affected her relationship with her mother the most and at times conversation was tense and strained. Jennet struggled to understand why. Her employment at Westby conformed to what was expected of a young Balderston woman, indeed women like her everywhere, and she was getting along well in her position, having shown herself to be helpful and capable, and a credit to her mother. In her naivety, she failed to appreciate that despite her mother's pride in her achievements, she felt a profound sense of the loss of her only daughter, knowing that she was taking her first steps along a path which would lead to marriage, her own home and eventually daughters of her own. The time they had spent together, side by side in their home completing their day's work could not be recaptured and Jennet did not truly appreciate the sadness that this caused for her mother.

Alison Balderston was sitting with a small group of other women from the village when Jennet dutifully marched over. Alison gave Jennet a broad smile, revealing as she did so a handful of delicate creases around her mouth and eyes, lines which betrayed a lifetime of both hard work and joy. Jennet shared many of her mother's features; pale skin which coloured only slightly during the summer months, and bright green eyes, which in the summer sunlight were set free to sparkle with the merriment and laughter of a day spent enjoying the company of family, friends and neighbours.

"Ah, my lass, have you had quite enough of your father's nonsense? I fear he's had too much ale."

Jennet laughed and sat down beside her mother, nodding and smiling a greeting to the other ladies as she did so.

"He's enjoying himself Mother, just the same as everyone else," Jennet replied.

"Ever the defender of her father," her mother replied, half addressing the other ladies with her remark. This roused some brief laughter and a few utterings about typical daughters, sticking up for their fathers. Jennet smiled in response. She couldn't deny it; as his only daughter, she usually took her father's side in family disagreements.

"Are you enjoying yourself today, Jennet?" her mother asked, changing the subject, "It's such a lovely day, it must be nice for you to be spending it outdoors instead of working in the Westby kitchens."

Jennet nodded. She had not talked to her mother much about her work at the great hall. She had mostly only talked about her training with Goodwife Robinson, recounting tales of making cheese or brewing ale the Westby way, or the first time she helped prepare a banquet for the family and how she was able to indulge a little on the leftover marzipans, candied fruits and a little bit of boiled meat afterwards. However, she had omitted any mention of the walks she had enjoyed out on the estate, especially during the winter months, and her snatched encounters with Tom Lister. She couldn't really explain why she hadn't told her; she didn't think her mother would be particularly disapproving of either activity, but for reasons she couldn't begin to understand herself, Jennet found herself feeling that these private moments, enjoying the peace and beauty of the Westby estate or the gentle touch of Tom Lister as he held her hand, should remain private.

"You're quiet this afternoon," said her mother, interrupting her thoughts, and examining her closely, "but you seem happy enough. Has your father introduced you to anyone today? He seemed keen earlier that you should meet someone, a young man he'd been talking to."

"Really, Mother? Do you know who?" she asked warily.

Alison shook her head slightly and made a dismissive motion with her hand.

"Oh your father hasn't really said much to me and I haven't been properly introduced to the lad although I think I caught sight of him earlier. He's from Giggleswick, apparently. Name of Preston, I think. Your father seems to have come to know his father and thought you may like to meet him. He's little older than you but not by many years."

Jennet's face betrayed her alarm. For all her mother's protestations that her only daughter should be in no hurry to marry, and certainly should not marry too young, her father was nevertheless always on the lookout for potential suitors. In one sense, Jennet felt she should be grateful; at least her parents obviously intended to consult her on the matter of choosing her husband and allow her time to get to know any suitors before making a final decision. Plenty of girls were not so fortunate, and were swiftly married to men they either barely knew or frankly detested. Jennet's mother and father's marriage had been a good match which was approved of by both their families, but they had also fallen in love by the time they made their vows in church

24

before God, and Jennet believed that both her parents wanted the same thing for their daughter. Nonetheless, she felt alarmed. The casual search for potential suitors was a reminder that she was now grown, and that she should soon be a wife and eventually a mother and shoulder all the responsibilities of keeping a home and nurturing a family. The thought of such responsibilities made her want to hide in the woods, like she was a child again.

"Oh, don't worry," Alison Balderston chuckled, recognising the look of horror on her daughter's face. "He's not married you off yet. You know your father; he's just considering your future. But it is the future, Jennet, it's not happening any time soon."

Jennet nodded again. Out of the corner of her eye, she spied the arrival of Tom Lister into the village. It was customary for a member or two of the Lister family to make an informal appearance at this village feast, usually after most of the food had been consumed but before the evening merry-making got under way and most of the village folk became the worse for wear. It was late in the afternoon now and the sun was falling lower in the sky, soon to give way to a beautiful sunset and the lighting of candles and torches in the street as the festivities continued for a little while longer. Jennet settled herself into her seat with a cup of ale whilst her mother and her friends chattered around her, absorbed in her own thoughts. She was glad that Tom had obviously been nominated to attend this year; she had seen very little of him through the spring and early summer, having busied herself with her duties as Mistress Lister had instructed, and Tom having spent much of his time with the Greenacres, preparing for his forthcoming nuptials in July. She wondered if she might manage to spend a few minutes in his company today, away from his mother's watchful eye, for as she saw him, she remembered how much she had missed him.

Later that evening, Jennet took the short walk from the village to her parent's cottage, on the edge of their farm. With the setting of the sun, the night had grown cool and Jennet had gone to fetch the shawl that she had flung off in the earlier summer heat. From there, she hadn't decided what to do. Her parents had welcomed her to stay at their cottage for the night; however, it meant rising early to walk back to Westby Hall to start work with Goodwife Robinson. Their day started at dawn, so Jennet would have to leave when it was still relatively dark to get back in time. Alternatively, she could walk back tonight but that would be in the pitch black and she knew her father would not be pleased at her walking in the dark unaccompanied, but at the same time neither he nor her brothers were in any fit condition to walk with her. Jennet sighed. She had had a lovely day, spending precious time with her family and enjoying the merriment that a feast day brings, but it was getting late and she was beginning to tire. She had just decided that she was too fatigued to march back over to Westby and had half-heartedly begun the search for a blanket, when there was a firm knock at the door. She chuckled, certain that it was one of her brothers or her father at the door, who in their drunken stupor had forgotten how to operate the handle.

"You're lucky I'm here to let you in!" she called. "I'm coming."

Jennet raced over to open the door, half-preparing to catch the person undoubtedly meandering drunkenly outside. However, to her surprise it was not one of her family, but Tom Lister standing there. Jennet blinked, almost disbelieving.

"Expecting someone else?" Tom asked mischievously, seeing her surprise.

"Er, well, yes I thought it was my father or perhaps Nicholas or William. Sorry, Tom, I wasn't expecting anyone else at this hour. I had just called home to get my shawl."

Tom looked over his shoulder nervously. He had good reason: the cottage was close to the village and there would be others passing by on the track at this time of the evening, heading home as the festivities drew to a close. A young Lister lingering on the Balderston doorstep talking to their unmarried daughter would undoubtedly provoke comment, even gossip.

"Yes, well that's why I called. Sorry to call on you so late, but I was about to head back to Westby and thought I might accompany you, if you were planning to go back tonight also?" Tom asked.

Jennet nodded in agreement. Of course she had just decided that she would stay, but it seemed sensible to go back tonight if Tom was offering to accompany her. It was fortunate that he had stayed later than members of his family normally did. She could smell the ale on his breath when he was speaking to her. She smiled. He must have been enjoying himself, having come without his father watching over him. Jennet was certain that Tom had arrived with a servant, but he appeared to be alone now.

"Can I… can I come in for a few moments?" Tom asked, looking over his shoulder again, "Just while you gather your things for the walk back. If I stand here much longer I'll be seen and we will be the talk of the village."

Jennet smiled and nodded again, moving aside to let Tom through the doorway. It seemed strange, seeing him there in her home, a grown man in his finery standing in her parents' simple cottage. Of course, he had visited before, but that was when they were children; he would barely remember it. It suddenly seemed strange to Jennet that she knew Tom's home so intimately yet he barely knew her home at all.

"Did you not have a man with you earlier?" Jennet asked.

"Yes, it was Percival, one of my father's men. Sent to keep an eye on me, I expect. I lost the fellow a while ago, he'd been singing and dancing but, er, it would seem that making merry got the better of him and I left him slumped next to the smithy's, sleeping. He'll be in for it when Father gets hold of him in the morning."

"Are you just going to leave him there?" Jennet asked, slightly aghast. Tom was correct; Percival would be in awful trouble when the Master found out.

"If it means I get to walk back to Westby alone with you, Jennet, then yes by all means," Tom chuckled, then fell silent as though immediately regretting the bold tone of his words. "I'm sorry, Jennet, I shouldn't have said that," he said after a few moments' silence, "I fear I have also had too much ale tonight. In truth the man is unconscious and between us we would never manage to carry him back to Westby. Indeed it would be more of a scene if we attempted it. I'm afraid we will have to leave him to his fate," Tom explained, with evident regret.

"Alright," Jennet agreed, "I will get my shawl and we will leave for Westby now, but I must let my mother know that I am not staying tonight and reassure her that I will be safe as I am travelling back with you."

Jennet turned to find her shawl and as she did so Tom placed a hand on her shoulder, stopping her abruptly and causing her to turn back to face him. Jennet looked up at him. The dim candlelight danced in his eyes as he gazed down at her intently, dropping his hand from her shoulder and reaching instead for her hand, caressing her fingers.

"You will always be safe with me, Jennet," Tom spoke softly, but said nothing more. He leaned down towards her face and gently touched her lips with his, once briefly, and a second time with a gentle conviction, moving his hand up into the small of her back to draw her closer to him. Jennet closed her eyes, allowing herself to be washed away into the moment, letting their kiss express everything she felt for Tom, that she had never dared admit even to herself. In the midst of her joy at freeing repressed emotions, however, came a feeling of doubt, even fear, causing her to break away from Tom's kiss.

"Tom, anyone could walk through that door at any moment!" Jennet exclaimed in a whisper. "Can you imagine if we were caught? You're soon to be married, to a woman of far gentler breeding than me. Think of the scandal this would cause. Think of what your mother would say!" Her tone was scolding.

For once, Tom was unfazed by the reminder of his reality. He looked unrelentingly into Jennet's eyes as he spoke. "I would only be sorry for any trouble I caused you, Jennet," he said. "I know I am to marry, God's death I have spent these past weeks in hers and her family's company preparing for the event and attending celebration after celebration in anticipation of our imminent nuptials. It is a good match, as it should be, after all we Listers excel at making those. I have accepted that Jane Greenacres will be my wife and the mother of my children. And she may be of gentler breeding than you, as you put it. However none of this changes the fact that you, Jennet Balderston, are my love. If I could choose, if it was my choice, I would choose you. You've always been my dearest friend and now you are the most beautiful, kind and delicate woman I could ever hope to know. I know that I can never have you, but it doesn't change the fact that I will always love you."

Jennet was taken aback by his admission. She had never heard Tom speak with such conviction. She had never even heard him curse; he was normally so softly spoken. Tonight there seemed to be fire in his words and his eyes, which burned with a desire for her. Jennet returned his gaze lovingly.

"I love you, Tom, but I don't know what to say. If we were to become lovers…" She hesitated, her words faltering. She had never spoken such words before, and she grappled with them, unsure how to frame them in the same poetic way that Tom had. She supposed these things came down to a difference of education: tutors taught well-bred boys how to speak eloquently, whilst mothers taught girls how to use the same set of kitchen ingredients with ingenuity. Until now, Jennet had never needed beautiful words.

Tom smiled, and touched her gently on the cheek. "Oh Jennet, no, I would never ask you to do that, my love. For one thing you would end up with child, and I care for you too much to do that to you. No, you must remain chaste and marry, one day. Marry a kind man who will treat you well."

Suddenly his beautiful words had given way to a compassionate practicality. Jennet felt saddened. Having both declared their love they now had to face the fact that nothing would change, that their realities would remain intact. In that moment, Jennet almost wished that it had all gone unspoken, that the kiss had not occurred. But then, to regret that kiss…no, she would cherish that kiss for the rest of her life. Jennet realised then what Tom already knew: what had happened between them was something to be grateful for, but that it could go no further, and they would have to be content with the memory of it. Tom, seeming to read her mind, articulated her next thought.

"Let's have our walk back to Westby, Jennet, under the stars and hand in hand, as any young lovers might. Let's have tonight before we must set our feelings aside and go on with our lives."

The walk back to Westby Hall that night was one of the most wonderful experiences of Jennet's life. It was one of those moments that she felt certain she would cherish forever. As soon as the two of them were out of sight of the village, Tom took hold of her hand, kissing it occasionally, and did not let it go until they reached the hall. They walked steadily, stopping a handful of times to embrace and enjoy the moment, relishing the comfort that, for tonight at least, they found in each other. As they approached Westby and were about to part, they were blissfully unaware that Tom's mother was looking out of an upstairs window, anxious to ensure her son's safe arrival home. They were unaware, too, that she bore witness to them as they held each other tenderly for the last time, that she saw their final kiss that night before heading to bed. They had been so lost in their moment that they had been unaware of the intruder into it, and they were wholly unprepared for the consequences that intrusion would bring.

4

Westby Hall, Gisburn
11th June 1585

"Well, what do you have to say for yourself?" Alice Lister asked. She had been pacing frantically about the room but with this question she came to a sudden, sharp standstill, casting her unforgiving gaze upon Jennet. Jennet gulped nervously.

"I'm very sorry Mistress," Jennet replied, voice shaking, eyes cast down.

The Mistress of Westby was not appeased by the apology. "Is that all you can say?" she asked, her voice filled with incredulity. "You're sorry? Have you any idea, even the slightest notion, of the gravity of your actions, girl? I warned you, didn't I? I warned you but you did not listen."

Jennet looked up, her eyes meeting her Mistress's gaze. She immediately wished she hadn't. The eyes which met with hers were narrowed, grey and cold, boring into her as though they might be trying to glimpse her innermost thoughts. Jennet remained silent, unable to fathom what it was that the Mistress wanted her to say, what explanation would satisfy those chilling slate eyes. She couldn't tell her how she felt when her son touched her hand, how she felt when he kissed her. She couldn't convey to her the happiness she had felt as she had fallen blissfully asleep the night before. She couldn't tell her how she had relived their walk back to Westby over and over again in her dreams. She couldn't simply tell her that she loved him. Love wasn't the sort of explanation which would do for a woman like Mistress Alice.

A maid came to the door and gave the Mistress a meaningful nod. "Ah, your mother is here. Good. This is most embarrassing for her, you know, and for your father. We have always held your family in such high regard," the Mistress said pointedly. "Send her up," she instructed the maid, who nodded obediently and closed the door behind her.

Jennet continued to stand there, silent, her heart thudding in her chest. In truth she didn't really fear Alice Lister anymore; her dismissal from her position at Westby had been a foregone conclusion as soon as her Mistress had seen her and Tom together. Harsh words were just that; words and nothing more. The anguish and disappointment of her mother, on the other hand, was something she dreaded. A tense silence hung in the air as Jennet waited for her mother's arrival and after a few moments, she could hear footsteps approaching outside the room. She drew a sharp breath as the door swung open.

"Ah, very good, you're here," said Mistress Alice, haughtily beckoning Alison Balderston inside the room with a patronising wave of her hand.

"Madame," replied Alison, curtseying briefly.

"I expect you know why you're here, do you not?" asked the Mistress.

Alison Balderston nodded gravely. "I understand my daughter has behaved very badly, and I am sorry to hear it, Madame."

"Badly!" exclaimed Mistress Alice. "Badly is an understatement, her behaviour is completely unbecoming of a young girl of this village. To seduce the son and heir of the Listers when he is betrothed to another is nothing short of immoral!"

Jennet looked at the floor again. She could feel her mother's eyes upon her: disbelieving, incredulous, disappointed. After a moment's pause she heard Alison take a deep breath, as though to steady her nerves over what she was about to say.

"Forgive me Madame, I think seduction is a strong word to use. Young Master Thomas and my Jennet have always been such close friends. Maybe they overstepped the mark and thought there was more to it than that. I'm sure Jennet won't make the same mistake again," she said, looking searchingly at her daughter for some sign of agreement. Jennet nodded cautiously in response, not daring to speak.

"Well, she won't have the chance!" scoffed Mistress Alice. "Whilst I am the Mistress of this house she is forbidden to see or speak to my son. She is dismissed from her position here, as I'm sure you'd expect, and she should return home with you today."

"Yes Madame," agreed Alison, curtseying obediently.

"And another thing," added Mistress Alice, "as far as I am concerned, your daughter has led my son astray. There can have been no fault on his part; he has been raised to be a gentleman and to behave accordingly. Thomas is about to be married for goodness sake. He knows what's at stake! Therefore I can only see that he must have had his good judgement momentarily blurred by this…this young harlot and her wiles!"

Jennet could sense her mother bristle. For all the wrong she may have done, Jennet knew that her mother would not take kindly to hearing her daughter insulted in such a way. If another mother in the village had spoken about Jennet like that, Alison would not have hesitated to set the full force of a venomous tongue upon them. But this wasn't another mother in the village; this was the matriarch of the Listers. This was someone to be obeyed, not challenged.

"Of course, Madame," replied Alison, with a grudging nod.

"You may leave," said Mistress Alice with another dismissive gesture of her hand.

Alison began to walk towards the door, Jennet following obediently behind. Jennet's heart pounded hard in her chest as she anticipated the short but undoubtedly agonising journey home. Her mother had been perfectly restrained and diplomatic in front of the Mistress, but once alone with her daughter she would not hold back. Jennet gulped hard, her throat dry, her stomach knotted with dread.

"One last thing Goodwife," said Mistress Alice, just as Jennet and her mother were about to step out of the room. "If there are any…unhappy consequences shall we say; the family will not recognise that Thomas played any part in it. There will be no involvement from us, no assistance of any sort. I hope you understand that," she said deliberately, labouring over the last point in particular.

Alison looked at Mistress Alice, mouth wide open in shock. For a moment she could neither move nor speak. In the end it was Jennet who nudged her gently, bidding her to leave.

"Come, Mother," she whispered.

The two women were about halfway down the main road leading from Westby Hall and back towards Gisburn village before Alison finally managed to speak. All the way down the stairs and out of the doors of Westby Alison had marched along in silence, Jennet following breathlessly behind. Outside the weather was beginning to change, the humidity of the previous few days finally giving way to a storm, and overhead dark clouds were beginning to gather. At first Alison had continued at a hurried and determined pace, forcing Jennet to almost run to keep up with her. Then without warning, she had stopped and turned to look at her daughter, her face flushed with exertion and anger.

"What were you thinking, Jennet?" she bellowed. "You've lost everything! Your position, your reputation, all gone! And for what? What did he promise you would happen? That this could go on after he was married, that no one need know?"

"He promised me nothing, Mother," replied Jennet, taken aback by the force of her mother's words and the conviction with which she held Thomas Lister responsible. Clearly Alison didn't believe for one moment that Jennet had led him anywhere that he hadn't wanted to go. "We didn't make any promises to one another. It was just a moment between us, a passing careless moment. I can't really explain it," she said, faltering over her words.

"A moment?" asked Alison. "I don't understand, Jennet. Mistress Alice seems to think that you've lain with her son! All that talk of unfortunate consequences, we both know she's worried that you're going to bear a Lister bastard. Why would she think that if it was no more than a moment between you?"

Jennet sighed. "I don't know why she thinks that. I can't explain what she thinks, but it's not true. I haven't lain with him. But I do love him, and he loves me. Perhaps that's why she's so angry, because Tom loves me and not that Jane Greenacres, the one he's supposed to love."

"Oh, lass," replied Alison, the motherly tenderness returning to her voice. "What do you know of love? Is that what Tom told you, that he loved you? Young men will say things like that for all sorts of reasons, powerful and wealthy young men especially. You've been very foolish, my lass, and I'm afraid it will cost you dearly."

Jennet stood silently for a moment, absorbing her mother's words. Although her mother and Mistress Alice had opposing opinions of what had happened between their children and who was responsible for it, they were agreed upon one thing: love had no place in it. Jennet wondered for a moment if her mother was right, if she was foolish and mistaken, if Tom's beautiful and affectionate words were completely without substance. But then, why would he have told her he loved her and then refused to lie with her, if his intention had been to dupe her? Jennet swallowed hard, recalling momentarily that it was she who had offered herself to him and not the other way around. Perhaps Mistress Alice was right. Perhaps she was a harlot after all.

"So you don't believe Mistress Alice's words, that I seduced Tom?" Jennet asked, seeking her mother's reassurance.

"Of course not! Like I said, you've been a fool. And I can't deny that I am also worried about you being with child, but I believe you when you say you thought you were in love. You have acted very badly, that much is true, but it's certainly not all your fault. But I'm afraid many others will blame you when word gets out, which it will. You have to be prepared for that, Jennet. You'll also have to prepare yourself for your father and brothers' reactions. They're men; they may not be as kind as I am," her mother cautioned.

Alison turned and continued walking up the lane. Jennet followed closely behind, brooding on her mother's words. She felt upset and confused, though unable to fathom what was distressing her most. Was it the thought of what her father was going to say? Certainly that filled her with dread. Or was it the fact that her mother seemed to think of her as a silly village girl, charmed by the local gentleman's son into thinking that she was in love with him? Jennet was undoubtedly hurt that her mother's opinion of her only daughter was that she was so weak and easily led. Or was it that she didn't seem to believe her when she said that she didn't lie with him? This wounded her greatly; not only was she a feeble girl in her mother's eyes, she was also deceitful. Next to this, she almost preferred Mistress Alice's opinion of her, for at least if she was a temptress she wouldn't be a victim or a liar.

"I do love him, Mother. And I didn't lie with him," she called, clenching her fists as a wave of sudden frustration washed over her. "I didn't lie with him!" she shouted this time.

But Alison Balderston didn't turn around. She didn't acknowledge her daughter's words at all. She simply continued to march up the lane as the first rumbles of thunder bellowed loudly overhead.

5

Gisburn Village
15th May 1587

"Come on lass, you're going to be late," coaxed Alison Balderston gently. She looked at her daughter fondly, who was fiddling awkwardly with her long dark hair. She knew Jennet had longed to wear a hat today, having seen some beautiful hats at the market in Colne, however Alison had cautioned against it. This was partly due to cost; a hat which would be worn probably only once was not a shrewd investment. She also felt that a tall hat was an unwise statement of grandeur, and whilst her daughter was not prohibited by law to wear such a hat, she felt that it would nonetheless provoke unwelcome comment from certain villagers when they caught sight of her in the church. She had advised Jennet to be content with a new petticoat and bodice, fashioned in a beautiful pale blue; and that otherwise her demeanour must remain humble and unassuming, which meant wearing her usual coif, or her hair loose. Alison had counselled her daughter to opt for the latter since, she had pointed out, it would be her last opportunity to do so; loose hair in public was prohibited for married women. Alison sighed, and examined her daughter closely. She looked beautiful, and Alison did have to admit that a tall hat would have finished her outfit nicely, but that she would have looked quite the grand lady in it. Yes, she thought, the hat would definitely have been a bad choice.

"I'm coming now, Mother," replied Jennet.

Jennet felt slightly awkward in this bodice, feeling unaccustomed to the fit of new and unfamiliar clothing. She was also incredibly nervous: she was used to attending church, of course, but she was not used to knowing that the eyes of every villager would be on her. This was her day, as her mother kept saying to her, a day she should remember all of her life. Jennet knew that, and of course it would be memorable, but nonetheless she was terrified.

Jennet bustled towards the front door of the cottage where her mother was waiting for her. For a moment then, there was silence. Jennet stood there and looked slightly dumbly, at her mother. Alison, in return, looked her daughter up and down one last time.

"Oh Jennet, you look beautiful," said Alison, so quietly she was almost whispering. "I wish your father was here to see you today."

Alison swiftly wiped a tear from her eye before it could roll down her cheek, and embraced her daughter.

"You'll be a wife by the end of today, lass," she said. "I hope and pray that we have chosen well enough for you. I hope that William will be a good and kind husband, just like your father was to me."

Fearing that she would cry, Jennet did not speak. Recently she had found that if she allowed herself to cry, sometimes the tears would not stop, but would continue unabated, a relentless stream of sorrow. It had been a difficult time for the Balderston family. Jennet's father had passed away at the beginning of the previous year, having injured himself whilst working on the farm and acquiring a wound on his abdomen which would not heal. Richard had initially brushed off his wife's concerns about the large, weeping sore on his stomach, maintaining that it would heal as previous wounds had. However, after a few days he became feverish and collapsed; his son Nicholas had found him lying unconscious in the pigs' pen, surrounded by the sows. Panic-stricken, Jennet's mother had sent for a woman who lived just outside the village and had a reputation for cunning knowledge. The woman had swiftly attended Richard and had treated the wound with a concoction of various herbs and vinegar; the sound of her father's cries of anguish when this potion was administered still rang in Jennet's ears. However, Richard's fever did not diminish, nor did the wound begin to improve. He lingered in a delirious state, somewhere between life and death, for a further two days and nights, before whispering weakly in his wife's ear of his love for her and his children, and drawing his last breath.

The death of Richard Balderston had occurred at a time when the tides of misfortune had already been flowing with their full force towards the Balderston family. As though her dismissal from Westby Hall had not been humiliating enough, talk of what had passed between Jennet and young Master Lister was soon all over the village, thanks to the loose tongues of the likes of Goody Robinson and her daughter Anne. For all the Goodwife's kindness towards Jennet during her time at Westby, she had been very quick to condemn her; to paint a picture of the young maid trying to seduce the gentleman's son on the eve of his marriage. No doubt the Mistress of Westby had supplied the brushes and canvas for such artistry, Jennet had thought bitterly.

Throughout the summer and winter which followed, Jennet resided in Gisburn with her parents, and was generally considered to be the pariah of the village; she was like the plague survivor, regarded with fear and suspicion in equal measure. None of the other local families would consider having her in their service, presumably fearful of the taint of scandal, and Jennet had no relations outside of the village who could provide a sanctuary. For those long months, she was trapped, miserable and alone but for her family, who treated her with condemnation and disappointment in equal measure. It did not seem to matter how many times Jennet had tried to explain what had passed between her and Tom, that they had been trying to put their feelings to rest

7

before his wedding, that she had only kissed him, that she had not lain with him; her family did not listen. Eventually, she stopped talking about it, or indeed about very much altogether, adopting a resigned silence as she resumed her work at her mother's side once more.

In January 1586, everything changed again. Jennet's father's death meant that the Balderston family had lost its head, and that his eldest son Nicholas would inherit the farm as the Balderstons in their good fortune had a lease which did not die or alter with the passing of each generation. However, Nicholas was barely twenty-one years of age and unmarried. This meant that although Nicholas legally inherited the Balderston's land holdings, in practice his mother and younger brother William would remain at his side to assist until he had a wife and children of his own to help him. Once Nicholas had established himself, William could leave as long as he had come of age, and their widowed mother was assured that she could remain there unless she chose to remarry. Nothing, however, was said about Jennet, and initially her position remained the same as before, assisting her mother and undertaking some outdoor work on the farm when it was required. However as winter turned to spring, then to summer, it became clear to her that her position there was not considered to be a permanent one. The notion first occurred to her in the kitchen, on one hot day not long before midsummer, when her mother broached the subject of marriage.

Jennet had immediately stopped kneading the bread and looked her mother straight in the eye. "What do you mean?" she had demanded, since the word marriage had not been mentioned to her since the previous year's Whitsun feast, prior to her ill-fated tryst with Master Lister.

"Nicholas has been trying to find you a husband for some time now. He feels we need to settle your position once and for all, now that your father's gone," Alison had confessed.

"What do you mean?" Jennet had repeated, pressing her mother for further information.

"You need to understand, lass, it's quite hard to find a good husband for a girl who's done…such as you've done," Alison had replied, hesitating over her words, "but it seems your brother has now found someone."

Jennet listened, her brow furrowed, as her mother explained that Nicholas had decided upon a good young man, albeit of slightly less means than they had hoped for, but again Jennet had to understand that such misfortunes were of her own making. The young man was William Preston of Giggleswick, the would-be suitor with whom she had narrowly missed making an acquaintance at that fateful Whitsun feast. Her father had thought of him very favourably at the time but, ever ambitious for his children, had decided not to settle on him as a potential husband for his daughter due to the lesser wealth of his family. However, Alison explained, with Richard's sudden death and Jennet's persistent unpopularity in the village, Nicholas felt it best that she marry and soon, to both settle her position and brush off the taint of scandal once and for all.

"You'll have time to get to know him," her mother had finished. "But you need to understand, Jennet, that you are expected to marry him. You've few options now, I'm afraid."

Jennet had met this news with resignation. In the months that had passed since her last encounter with Tom Lister, she had stumbled upon a new maturity; a level of understanding which placed reality in front of romantic notions, and made her realise exactly the position that both she and Tom had put her in that night. She had not come to regret what had happened exactly, although at times she felt a certain measure of anger towards Tom Lister and herself for being so foolish on their walk back to Westby. She even felt a little resentful towards Tom that he had been so seemingly unaffected by his own behaviour; his wedding had gone ahead as planned and he had escaped entirely blameless from the whole episode. Jennet reflected once again on how she should have appreciated how different life was for the two of them. He was a man, a wealthy man; of course he was not to blame.

With a bruised pride and a hardened perspective, Jennet met the courtship of William Preston with acceptance, albeit with a little cold indifference in the beginning. However to her surprise, she found him to be a pleasant and considerate man. At six years her senior he seemed more mature than most young men she knew, Tom Lister included, whilst his humble upbringing seemed to afford him a diligent and appreciative nature. He was undoubtedly handsome, with deep brown eyes and fair hair, his build muscular and his skin lightly tanned by a lifetime working outdoors. He treated Jennet with kindness and a tender, patient affection. He did not seem to expect passion, or declarations of undying love. Instead, he told her, he sought a wife who would be at his side in all things, who would be dependable, who would provide the well-kept home and the children that a wife should provide, and that he hoped love, like the crops they would tend together, would grow and flourish later. Indeed, the more time Jennet spent in his company, the more she developed a fond affection for him, and later that year, during Christmastide, she delighted her mother and brothers by informing them that she hoped to marry William in the first half of the following year.

And so, the fifteenth of May 1587 had arrived. As Jennet left her family's home with her mother and two brothers that beautiful, calm spring morning, she felt her life changing, grasping for its renewal, as though God had given her another chance at happiness and today she was taking it. She hoped with every fibre of her being that today would be her rebirth. Just as the barren trees of winter had abandoned their own hopeless decay and, tempted by the sun, had allowed deliciously green leaves to flourish, Jennet ventured to dream that she might bask in the light once more, having felt in the dark for so long. The short walk to the church was enjoyed in a haze of stomach knots and anticipation, and before Jennet knew it she had arrived at the door of St Mary's.

"Are you ready, sister?" asked Nicholas, touching her lightly and reassuringly on the shoulder.

"As I'll ever be," Jennet replied with a vigorous deep breath.

Jennet took her brother's arm, and together they walked into the church. Past the blur of friends and neighbours sitting in the pews, she could see William standing at the front, to one side of the priest, Reverend Gibson. He seemed typically calm, standing solidly, almost solemn were it not for the smile which hinted at the corners of his mouth when he saw his bride walking towards him. Jennet reached the front and stood by his side, before the priest, before God. Looking up at William, her betrothed, she suddenly recalled the first time she met him. She smiled as she remembered how hard he had tried to impress her, how he had seemed to sense her reluctance and had been determined to overcome it. She wondered then about why he had been so keen to court her, why he had tried so hard, why he had been willing to give up his life in Giggleswick and move to Gisburn to marry her. She realised that all this time she had been completely wrapped up in her own feelings and her own sense of duty about the marriage; she had never thought to ask him.

"Dearly beloved friends, we are gathered together here in the sight of God, and in the face of this congregation, to join together this man and this woman in holy matrimony, which is an honourable state, instituted of God in Paradise," began Reverend Gibson, interrupting Jennet's thoughts.

The knot in Jennet's stomach tightened as she heard that word: honourable. The memory of Tom Lister, normally relegated to a far corner of her mind, forced itself back into the fore once more. Suddenly Jennet felt herself to be anything but honourable, and with her cheeks reddening, she lowered her eyes away from William, whose gaze she had been holding. How could she stand in front of the priest and God today and make promises to this kind, gentle man, when on that night with Tom Lister she had so wantonly expressed her desire to lie with him? She had spent so much of the past couple of years insisting that she had not lain with him, that she had mostly neglected to admit to herself that she had indeed wanted to and it was only Tom's honourable behaviour which had prevented it. William had never asked her about what had happened with Tom Lister, but he must have heard the rumours, if not in Giggleswick, then when he had come to Gisburn to court her. Gisburn was a small village where gossip was a precious commodity; undoubtedly someone in the ale house would have had a loose enough tongue to refer to it after a few jugs of the local brew. It was as though it did not matter to him, Jennet thought, as though he might love her anyway, even if she had lain with another man, even if she had enjoyed it.

Suddenly an awful thought occurred to her: what if William believed that she had lain with Tom Lister, and had presumed that was why she had never spoken of it? What if William had construed her silence to be an admission of guilt? Indeed, she had kept silent on the matter through shame, but it was embarrassment at the thought of her own foolishness, rather than the guilt of committing the act, that had caused her to hold her tongue. Now, standing there, she felt crippled, cowardly, as though she should have explained herself before today, as though she had lied to him through her silence and therefore had committed yet another sin. On the other hand, Jennet thought, perhaps it was no real deceit, since on reflection wanting to lie with a man who was not her husband and actually doing it were tantamount to the same thing. Perhaps her immortal soul was in danger anyway. Therefore, if William believed that she had strayed from God's path that night, then technically he was correct.

"Will you have this woman to be your wedded wife, to live together after God's ordinance in the holy state of matrimony? Will you love her, comfort her, honour and keep her, in sickness and in health? And forsaking all others, keep only to her, as long as you both shall live?" Reverend Gibson asked William, interrupting Jennet's thoughts.

William, as though sensing Jennet's turmoil, took hold of her hand. He looked her in the eyes, reconnecting their gaze, and smiled slightly as he spoke.

"I will."

Jennet drew a shallow breath as Reverend Gibson turned to address her.

"Will you have this man to be your wedded husband, to live together after God's ordinance in the holy state of matrimony? Will you obey him and serve him, love him, honour and keep him, in sickness and in health? And forsaking all others, keep only to him, as long as you both shall live?"

Jennet could feel the congregation's eyes upon her. At least a few of them would be questioning if she was really going to go through with the wedding, wondering if they were going to enjoy the spectacle of her fleeing from the alter. Most would be feeling certain that she would remain there; in times gone by, a young woman like her, who had done what she had done, might have run to the sanctuary of an abbey and made her vows to God. However, with most of those now gone at the hands of King Henry, the only vows left for her to make were those sworn to a man. Jennet bit her lip. This time she did not look away from William, who was in any case looking at her expectantly, almost impatiently. There was no time for any more thought. No time to hesitate, no time to regret the things she had done. There was just this moment and those words which she must say so that her life might finally move on. Jennet gave William a slight smile, an attempt at reassurance for him and probably for herself and, with a sudden subtle hoarseness in her voice, she spoke.

"I will."

Part Two

1597 - 1600

6

The Road to Colne
March 1597

"We are going to have to walk a little quicker, Anna, I expected that we should arrive just after lunch. At this pace we will be fortunate to arrive before supper."

Anna Preston lifted her skirt from the ground to her ankles and scuttled hurriedly towards her companion.

"I struggle to keep up with you, Aunt," said the young girl apologetically. "You walk at such a strong pace, I think anyone might trail behind you."

Jennet smiled at Anna's comment. Her niece had an endearing habit of using compliments where apologies should be. She was right; Jennet could undoubtedly leave most companions trailing behind her, William included. Of course, Jennet thought, practice makes perfect. Since embarking on married life almost ten years ago, she had had sufficient opportunity to hone the skill of walking long distances at a pace; it was simply a matter of necessity. Sometimes, Jennet really longed for the use of a horse, especially on those days when her legs ached in protest and her back gave her trouble. However, as William reminded her when she occasionally complained, a horse was completely out of the question.

Jennet's thoughts turned to William. She was glad that her business today meant that she would be away from the cottage until dusk. They had argued the previous night, a terrific, vicious argument in which they had both said things, true and untrue, which would have been better left unsaid. The argument had begun in the usual way. William had meandered home from the alehouse with his brother, John, to be greeted by a complaint from Jennet about his spending their pittance of an income swilling ale. John, no doubt foreseeing trouble, had swiftly bid them both good night, and from there the argument had escalated. In anger, Jennet had called William a drunk, an accusation which she knew at the time was unfair as he spent far less time in the alehouse than many other men, his brother included. In response, William had defended his evening's pleasure by pointing out, justifiably as Jennet reflected now in hindsight, how hard he worked on their small farm, how he could only thank God for sending his brother to help lighten his burden as he had struggled for so long on his own. At the time, however, the mention of his struggle had made Jennet grow defensive. She had encountered her own difficulties; she had reminded him, caring for him and their home whilst bearing the burden of all those pregnancies which came to nothing.

The reminder of the babies they had lost caused William to fall silent and Jennet to weep. For the first eight years of their marriage Jennet had been with child at least once, and often twice a year; however, each baby had been born too early and had not lived. Sometimes the child had survived in her womb long enough to resemble a baby when born, with tiny, fragile fingers and toes. On those occasions Jennet had sorrowfully clung to the child, holding it sometimes in her two hands, willing it to live. Other times she had not even begun to loosen her bodice to accommodate her growing belly when the pregnancy had ended. She would bleed bright red, angry blood, so much blood that she would have to go to her bed and lie completely still, as though a lack of movement would prevent the baby from leaving her. But leave her it did, and although often she would never see the baby, she would know that it was gone.

That evening, confronted by the memory of the pain she had felt at the death of each and every child, Jennet had broken down. Those babies should have been our sons and daughters, she had cried out bitterly. They should have been ours to love, to nurture, to teach. She had looked to William then, for some comforting words, or for the solace which the familiarity of how he held her could bring; however, he offered neither. Instead, for the first time in their marriage, he appeared angry towards her. Standing there, fists clenched and jaw set hard, he simply muttered that perhaps this was God's punishment for what Jennet had done, perhaps God did not wish for her to know the happiness of having children and now, having taken every child from her, had seen fit to leave her completely barren. Jennet had simply stood there, dumbstruck, too shocked by his venom to respond and too weary to repeat the denial she had uttered countless times during their marriage. William had asked her many times over the years, ever since he had first heard the gossip in the alehouse and had marched home like a wounded soldier to confront her with it. Her answer had always been in the same: she had not lain with him. Her denial, she realised, was superfluous. William simply did not believe her.

"Why did you marry me, William? If you despise me, why did you leave Giggleswick and come to Gisburn and marry me?" she asked, her voice little more than a hoarse whine.

"Your brother," he answered simply, relaxing his jaw. He wore a sombre look on his face. "Your brother gave me a few conditions when agreeing that I could court you, and keeping you in Gisburn was one of them. It was your mother's wish, apparently. At the time I thought it nice that your mother wanted to keep you close by. Now I find it strange; surely your family would have been happy to send you away considering the circumstances! You can't account for a mother's love, I suppose. Of course, your brother did very well to keep those particular details from me at the time," he added, looking pointedly at her, his tone bitter.

"I still don't understand, William. Why did you agree to it?"

asked Jennet, her voice breaking.

"Why indeed! My father couldn't understand it, you know. He told me to choose a woman in Giggleswick and remain there. But one look at your pretty face and I just knew I would have to come back and keep seeing you, and as the months passed and I spent more time in your company…well, by the time we married I would have moved to the end of the earth for you, Jennet. I had hoped that you would come to feel the same way about me, but the fact that it has taken you ten years to ask why I moved here for you says it all, doesn't it? I see now what a fool I have been."

Remembering his words, Jennet shuddered.

"You've grown quiet, Aunt," said Anna. "Are you unwell?"

"No not at all, my child. I am quite well, even my back does not ail me too badly today. I have a lot on my mind is all," Jennet replied.

"Is it Uncle William?" Anna persisted with her line of questioning.

Although young, Anna was not one to let things lie. Jennet knew that the girl would have overheard every word of last night's argument and would not be satisfied unless some form of explanation was given. Most people would chastise this child for her insolence; however, Jennet loved the girl for her spirited and direct approach and was often guilty of telling her far too much. In some ways, Jennet wished she had been more like her as a girl. Perhaps if she'd asked more questions and been less accepting like Anna, she would not have fallen prey to her mistakes.

"Uncle William and I merely had a disagreement. It's nothing for you to worry about, Anna. However, I would be lying to you if I said that our cross words were not troubling my mind today."

Anna gave her aunt a sideways glance, as though to try and judge her mood before pursuing their conversation any further. She knew that relations between husband and wife were complicated and not always happy, but she also knew that people were not always willing to discuss these matters. Her mother had been dead for a few years now, but she could still clearly remember her own parents having similar discussions with raised voices, and equally she could remember her mother trying to reassure her that it was nothing the following day. Aunt Jennet, in fairness, was usually more honest. Sometimes, Anna reflected, it was almost as though she was too weary to lie.

"It's very sad that you and Uncle William don't have children. I would've liked cousins," Anna said sweetly, attempting in her own way to offer the comfort which her aunt had not received the previous evening. She continued to study her aunt's face, looking for her reactions, treading the path between offering solace and causing distress carefully.

"I have been sad about it for a very long time, Anna, but I have finally made my peace with it. It is not in God's plan for me, I understand that now. Anyway, I have you, my lass. I know you aren't an infant and I'm not your mother, but nevertheless you're a great comfort to me. You're the closest thing to a daughter that I'll ever know, and I thank God for you and your father coming to live and work with us."

Jennet shot Anna a look which Anna knew signalled that this was the end of the discussion. The young girl had been desperate to ask her aunt what Uncle William had meant when he said that God was punishing her, but having now read Jennet's face, she did not dare. Instead she walked the rest of the way to Colne, wondering what her aunt could possibly have done to offend the Almighty so badly that he might take her children away from her.

The pair arrived in Colne long after lunchtime and much later than Jennet had hoped. Jennet encouraged her niece to hurry, pointing out that they did not know how long it would take to find their destination and then they still had to walk back to Gisburn before dark. Hastily, Jennet and Anna made their way through the market place, which was bustling as usual. From there they headed towards Colne Water, near to which lived the woman Jennet sought, or so she had been told. The reason for their visit to Colne was for Jennet to make the acquaintance of a Katherine Hewit. Katherine

Hewit was the wife of a clothier, John Hewit, who was well-known locally for putting out carding, spinning and weaving work around Pendle and Craven. Tired of struggling to make ends meet on the farm and tired of arguing with her husband about the precariousness of their situation, Jennet had resolved to take in some of this work, especially now that she was armed with the spinning wheel which had arrived with Anna and John months earlier. It had belonged to Anna's mother; indeed it had been Anna's recollections of her mother at her wheel which had first given Jennet the idea.

The only difficulty was that Jennet did not yet possess the required skills. Her mother had taught her well in most things, but she had not seen fit to teach her how to handle wool and craft it into cloth since, Jennet presumed, she did not foresee that this was a skill that her daughter should ever need. Indeed, Jennet did not know if her mother had possessed these skills herself; nor would she ever know as Alison Balderston had died less than a year after her daughter had wed. The Balderstons had always had a large enough farm to support them completely and their only dealing with wool was to shear it from their sheep and to sell the raw fleeces at market, for profit. Those who carded, spun and wove wool, usually the wool of others, often did so because their crops and animals could not wholly support them. This had never been the situation of the Balderstons, but it was exactly the position that the Prestons found themselves in, and it was a position they had been in for some time. Therefore, the purpose in her seeking out Katherine Hewit was to enquire about having some work put out to her by her husband, but also about someone, perhaps even Katherine Hewit herself, teaching her the necessary skills first. In turn, she could pass those skills on to Anna, who as a small child had done a little carding at her mother's side but lost her mother to illness before she could teach her anything further. Together, they could work to earn some additional, desperately needed income.

Jennet and Anna found a row of small, modest cottages, not far from the water's edge, where she had been told that the Hewits lived. When she had made enquiries back in the village about clothiers who may be able to offer work she had only been given this name and a vague address, as such she was not exactly sure which house to call upon. For a moment Jennet hesitated, feeling suddenly flustered by the rush of the journey and bewildered by the sight of all these unfamiliar doors.

"Shall we ask someone here, Aunt?" Anna prompted.

Jennet nodded dumbly. Anna, sensing her aunt's hesitation, took Jennet gently by the hand and led her over to a middle-aged woman who was washing her linen by her front door.

"Good morrow, Goodwife," said Jennet politely. "I am looking for a Katherine Hewit, could you tell me, in which one of these cottages does she live?"

The woman looked up from her work, screwing up her eyes as she did so to study the woman and the girl standing before her. She then looked back down at the large tub she had been attending and continued scrubbing.

"One in the middle, third from the end," she answered, without looking back up.

"Thank you, and a good day to you," replied Jennet.

Jennet and Anna walked on to the cottage to which the woman had directed them. It was a humble looking dwelling and Jennet had to admit that she had expected something grander. Jennet felt suddenly discouraged; perhaps John Hewit was not as successful a clothier as she had been led to believe, perhaps he would not be able to offer any work. Well, she was here now, she thought, she might as well ask. Taking a deep breath, Jennet knocked firmly on the door. Almost immediately the door swung open and Jennet and Anna were greeted by a slightly flustered looking woman with bright, fiery red hair peeking from beneath her coif. On first sight, Jennet judged her to be a similar age to herself. She was a pretty young woman of very slight stature, with pale blue eyes and rosy cheeks; she had the complexion of someone who spent her life rushing around.

"Yes?" the woman asked, slightly abruptly.

Jennet was slightly taken aback by her tone.

"Good morrow to you, Goodwife, I am looking for a Katherine Hewit, does she live here?"

The young woman looked Jennet and Anna up and down before offering her answer.

"I am Katherine Hewit. I presume you are looking for work. If so it is my husband that you seek."

Katherine's tone continued to be abrupt. Jennet tried not to let it deter her; perhaps they had just caught her in the middle of her work, perhaps it was just inconvenient.

"If this is a bad time, Goodwife Hewit, we can return another time, when your husband is here, if you would prefer us to speak with him," Jennet said.

Katherine narrowed her eyes slightly at them both, as though trying to fathom something which was unclear to her about the two visitors on her doorstep.

"Do you live in Colne?" she asked. "I don't recall either of your faces."

"No, Goodwife, we've travelled here from Gisburn, we set off first thing this morning. My name is Jennet Preston, and this is my niece, Anna," Jennet replied.

"That is a fair distance!" Katherine exclaimed. "Where is your horse?"

The pair shook their heads simultaneously.

"You travelled on foot! In one morning! In all good conscience I could not send you away," Katherine said, her demeanour suddenly and completely altering. "Do come in and we can discuss this business further."

Katherine stood back to allow her visitors into her home. The pair entered into a modest but attractive cottage; although it was humble, inside it was pleasantly furnished and cosy. Jennet could tell that the wool and cloth trade was not treating the Hewits badly.

"Now then, can I offer either of you a small ale? You must be thirsty after your long walk," Katherine asked.

"No thank you," replied Jennet. "We don't wish to impose

ourselves on you for too long and the walk is not so long as you may imagine."

"Alright," said Katherine. "Down to business, then. What can I do for you?"

Jennet took a deep breath as though to prepare herself for a lengthy explanation.

"As you guessed when we were speaking outside, Goodwife Hewit, I am seeking some work, carding and spinning, as I am in possession of a spinning wheel." Jennet gestured towards Anna, who was shyly hanging back behind her. "Young Anna is willing to learn her trade from me also, so your husband could be assured of two very good and hard workers in us both."

"Hmm," mused Katherine, "I am sure that is the case. John doesn't always put work out to Gisburn as it is that little bit further away from Colne and he has always had plenty of willing workers nearer to the town. However, as it happens I know that John has a lot of work which needs to be done at the moment, so perhaps he will consider it, in this instance."

Jennet smiled. She almost got carried away with herself but caught herself just in time.

"There is just one thing I ought to mention, Goodwife Hewit," she said.

"Call me Katherine, please, and what is it?"

"I haven't yet got the skills I need to do this work; however, I am keen and a quick learner. Do you know of anyone who would be willing to teach me, if your husband wished to employ us?"

Katherine narrowed her eyes again. This seemed to be the expression she wore whenever she was thinking, which Jennet found to be unfortunate as it did spoil the friendly, open appearance of her pretty face.

"I may know of someone suitable," she replied, "should John wish to employ you both. He is not home at present, but I will speak to him later today and send word to you shortly. I trust we should find you easily enough in Gisburn?"

Jennet gave Katherine the directions to their cottage.

"If you do not hear from us within the fortnight, please presume that my husband has nothing to offer you," explained Katherine. "However, I will see what I can do."

Jennet nodded.

"I understand," she replied. "I am grateful for your time, Katherine. I bid you a good day."

Jennet and Anna made a quick exit from the cottage, conscious not to offend their potential employer by outstaying their welcome. Having found Katherine Hewit swiftly, they had some time left to spend at their leisure, and Jennet delighted Anna by taking her to explore the town's market since it was her first visit to Colne. By the time they both left town and headed along the road home, both were feeling slightly giddy, Anna with excitement and Jennet with a rare optimism. As hard as she tried to counsel herself not to have any expectations of her arrangement with Katherine Hewit coming to fruition, she could not help but feel an opportunity was within her grasp. As she watched Anna skip most of the way home in the fading light, she could not resist her urge to hope. Perhaps this would finally be a reprieve from poverty. Perhaps she would no longer have to worry about rents and bad harvests. Perhaps if William saw the effort she had made to improve their situation, he would become kind and tender towards her once again. If he was nicer, if he spent more time at home and less time in the alehouse, perhaps she could learn to love him as well.

Word came from Colne almost two weeks after their visit, just as Jennet was beginning to despair of the hope that she had clung to since that day. She had been out in the village when she saw a man on horseback whom she did not recognise. As she approached, she heard him asking after her whereabouts from passers-by and she saw one of the village women gesture behind her towards Jennet. Jennet's heart skipped a beat as she approached the rider.

"Are you looking for me?" asked Jennet.

"Are you Jennet Preston?" replied the man, without answering Jennet's question.

"Yes, I'm Jennet Preston," she answered.

"I bring word from the Hewits of Colne," said the man, handing her a piece of paper which contained a name and an address, "Here are the details of a woman they wish you to visit, she will teach you the skills you require. Your work will be delivered and collected monthly, as such its quantity shall be great and you should store it somewhere suitable. The first delivery will be in a fortnight's time, please ensure that you have learned the necessary skills by then."

Jennet nodded in response, and without another word, not even to bid her good day, the man left. Jennet glanced down at the paper. Her reading was slow and she would ask William to confirm the details that evening; however the handwriting was delicate and careful, and fairly easy to decipher. It was probably a woman's hand, thought Jennet, perhaps even that of Katherine Hewit herself. Slowly, Jennet read out the name of the woman who was to be her teacher.

"Elizabeth Device."

7

Malkin Tower, Blacko Hillside, Forest of Pendle
April 1597

Jennet wiped her brow with the back of her hand. The day was growing warm, indeed unseasonably warm for the time of year and Jennet had been walking all morning. She had set out early, still feeling enthused after the promise of her trip to Colne came to fruition in the guise of her visitor on horseback just a couple of days ago. Indeed, even William, having previously shared his misgivings about this venture, doubting that his wife had the necessary time or talent for the undertaking, seemed cheered by the promise of work. Now, he told her that very morning, she must make haste to equip herself not only with basic skills, but with the ability to do good quality work so that the Hewits might continue to employ her services. On this, Jennet needed no encouragement and, feeling determined, she had left her young niece to serve the men their breakfast and bid them all good day.

The walk had been a pleasant one, the calm spring weather affording Jennet the chance to enjoy the beautiful, gentle countryside which had been the backdrop to her walks for as long as she could remember. As she departed from the familiar comfort of the road to Colne, which had been her route for most of the way, and on to the moorland, she gradually felt her journey become more difficult, a continual uphill struggle which had made the backs of her legs ache with the strain. However, glancing up now and blinking away the sweat which had trickled, uninvited, into her eyes, Jennet could see a small cottage nestled into the hillside and dared to hope that she had finally reached her destination. As she neared the cottage, Jennet felt giddy with a curious combination of excitement and desperation. If this was her destination then that would be the day's first success, but if it was not, she genuinely did not know where else to search. She had travelled from Gisburn to Colne many times but had rarely ventured from the road she knew into the Pendle countryside. Indeed, she reflected, this cottage was barely any distance from the road at all and she must have walked passed it many times, yet she had never previously noticed its existence. Despite living near to Pendle all of her life, she realised that she barely knew its geography. If this was not the right cottage, she just hoped that someone would be at home there so that they might be able to send her in the right direction.

Slightly out of breath with both nerves and physical exertion, Jennet found herself at the front door. Breathing heavily, Jennet took a moment to absorb her surroundings, and she began to doubt that she was in the right place. She sought a place called Malkin Tower, yet the house before her did not look like a tower at all. Instead it was a cottage, one of a reasonable size, she thought, but one which looked like it needed a little care. There was, however, no doubt that it was occupied: from outside Jennet could hear the shrieks of children within. She bristled slightly, unable to resist contrasting the delightful sounds of the little ones playing with the aching quietness of her own home. Shrugging off the thought, Jennet knocked loudly on the door, so that she might be heard over the din. After a few moments, the door swung open.

"Can, can I...uh, who are you?" stammered the woman who answered.

At first glance Jennet estimated that she was of a similar age to herself, and deduced that, if this was the right address, she was probably Elizabeth Device.

"My name is Jennet Preston. I am looking for Elizabeth Device," Jennet answered.

To her shame, she realised that she was staring at the woman in front of her. She could not help it, for if this was Elizabeth Device, she had one of the most curious faces that Jennet had ever encountered. Everything about her appeared to be normal; fine, delicate lips, a straight nose, prominent cheekbones defined by a life of hard work and, Jennet ventured, a less than sufficient diet. Everything was normal, Jennet thought, until your gaze reached the eyes. Whilst one eye sat in the expected position, the other appeared to sit lower down on her face and seemed to be incapable of focussing correctly, preferring instead to cast its vision downward, as though conscious and ashamed of its own awkwardness.

"I, I, I am Elizabeth Device," replied the woman, continuing to stammer.

Jennet realised that she probably sensed, indeed anticipated, people's reaction to the sight of her face, and the stammering, nervous way in which she presented herself probably owed itself to that knowledge. Jennet suddenly felt pity for the woman: before years of pregnancy, marriage and hard work had begun to take their toll on her, Jennet had often been complimented on her pleasant looks, and as she had grown into womanhood and the early years of her marriage, she had taken a pride in her appearance. She reflected that the poor creature standing before her had probably never felt attractive on a single day in her life.

"That is good news!" Jennet enthused, trying her best to set Elizabeth at ease. "I have come to the right place. My name is Jennet Preston, of Gisburn. I was given your name by Katherine Hewit. I am to take in some spinning and carding work from her husband, John, and she said you would be able to teach me the skills I need to carry out this work."

This time it was Elizabeth's turn to look her visitor up and down.

"You mean, you can't spin or card?" she asked, incredulously.

Jennet was taken aback by Elizabeth's sudden directness.

"Well, no, it's not a skill my mother ever taught me and I have never sought wool work until now. Not in making cloth, anyway. We have a few sheep so of course I help with the shearing but then we sell the wool…" Jennet trailed off, realising that her lengthy explanation was not necessary.

Elizabeth looked at her visitor squarely with her one good eye.

"Hard times?" she asked.

Jennet nodded, trying not to cast her eyes downward as she did so.

"You'd best come in then," said Elizabeth kindly. "I suppose now is as good a time as any to teach you. I hope you don't mind working with a lot of noise about you, though. I've three children and my mother at home with me."

Before Jennet could answer, Elizabeth led her inside. The interior of the cottage, much like the exterior, was in great need of a bit of care, but it was undoubtedly spacious, which was fortunate considering it housed so many souls. Its size, however, really was its only redeeming feature and Jennet couldn't help wonder how Elizabeth and her family came to be living in a place such as this. It was in a state of utter disrepair in parts and its character and size would suggest it might have housed animals rather than people at one time. It really was a very curious building. Conscious not to seem rude or distracted by visibly examining her host's home, Jennet's attention turned to the three children who, seemingly oblivious to the arrival of a guest, continued to run around manically. Immediately, Elizabeth called them to order.

"James, Alison, Henry! Come and meet our visitor. This is Jennet Preston. She's come to spend the afternoon working with me."

The three children obediently sidled over to Jennet to welcome her. The eldest, whom from Elizabeth's address she assumed must be James, she guessed to be around seven years of age. Alison, the daughter, looked to be about five; and Henry, the youngest, was an adorable little boy of no more than two.

"Don't let the angel faces fool you," Elizabeth chuckled fondly. "Devils, the lot of them. How many are you blessed with?"

"Sorry?" asked Jennet.

"How many children do you have?" asked Elizabeth.

"Oh, erm, I don't have any children. William, my husband and I, we were not blessed," Jennet replied, unable to disguise the sadness in her voice.

It was not a question she was used to being asked as people back in Gisburn knew her circumstances well enough to avoid the topic of children altogether. Elizabeth looked at her sympathetically and to Jennet's surprise, placed a comforting hand upon her shoulder.

"Oh, poor lass," she said to Jennet. "Come, we will get to work and you can tell me all about it. My mother is here too. She's been unwell and is sleeping at the moment. Only the Lord knows how she manages to sleep with all this noise, but she does. I'm sure she will be through to meet you later though. She is very good at giving advice. You never know, she may be able to help you."

Jennet doubted it, but was nonetheless comforted by the lending of a supportive and friendly ear and smiled gratefully at her new acquaintance.

The two women worked and talked all afternoon, with such a familiarity that they might have been lifelong friends, meeting after many years. Elizabeth chatted freely about her family and her work, about how she had always lived at Malkin Tower with her mother, only leaving briefly after she married John Device seven years earlier. John's income wasn't enough for them to maintain their smallholding, Elizabeth told her, and their struggle became intolerable once children began to arrive. So they had returned to Malkin with their young family, an arrangement that suited everyone, especially as her mother was aging and needing more and more care every year, not that she would ever admit it. Now they lived and worked here together, John undertaking whatever labouring work he could find and Elizabeth making a small income from woollen work put out to her by numerous merchants and clothiers, not just the Hewits. When Jennet made the mistake of assuming that Elizabeth's mother would surely now be too elderly to undertake any sort of employment, Elizabeth laughed mischievously in response.

"Ah!" she exclaimed through her chuckle. "Don't let Mother hear you say that! I forget that you are not from around these parts. Let's just say that Mother has long had her ways and means of making an income. I'll let her tell you about it though."

"Now I am curious!" Jennet declared in response.

"Anyway," said Elizabeth, changing the subject. "I've been boring you with the details of our lives for far too long. Tell me about yourself. Don't take this the wrong way, but you look like a lass with a story to tell."

"Oh?" asked Jennet evasively. She was so used to everyone in Gisburn knowing her story that she did not quite know where to begin to tell it. She glanced at Elizabeth, who continued to look at her, expectantly. Jennet drew a deep breath.

"Well, I don't quite know where to begin really. I've always lived in Gisburn, my name before marriage was Balderston. I worked briefly at Westby Hall for the Listers before marrying William, who is from Giggleswick," Jennet explained. She breathed a slow sigh. That hadn't been such a difficult story to tell after all.

Elizabeth put down the wool she had been working with and looked at Jennet, smiling with intrigue. She clasped her hands together and leaned towards her guest.

"Westby Hall! The Listers! That must have been exciting!" she exclaimed.

"Well it could be, at times," continued Jennet, "I worked in the kitchen so helped prepare many a grand banquet. The Listers knew how to feast."

"I am sure they did," replied Elizabeth. "So you left once you were set upon marrying William?"

Jennet nodded. She was keen to avoid any further discussion of her time in the Lister household. She was accustomed to the whole village of Gisburn knowing about her shame, but she did not see any reason to spread that knowledge any further afield, even if it meant telling a small lie.

"So how did you meet William?" Elizabeth asked. "You said he's from Giggleswick."

"Our fathers knew one another," replied Jennet. "We were introduced by them."

This part was at least, a little closer to the truth, but to reveal exactly how her marriage had been arranged would be to reveal what had happened with Tom Lister, so again Jennet found herself avoiding going into detail.

Their conversation was interrupted by the cries of the youngest child and Elizabeth briefly left Jennet working so that she could attend to him. When she returned, she was keen to continue the discussion where they had left it, and immediately and boldly approached the subject of children. If there was one topic that Jennet was less keen to discuss than the Listers, it was her childlessness.

"I have made my peace with it," she told Elizabeth, flatly. "We have our niece, Anna, living with us now and she is a great comfort to me. She has lost her own mother so I try to be the best mother I can for her."

Elizabeth nodded, clearly sensing that this was a very raw subject for her visitor. Before she could say anything else a shaky but loud voice came from the other side of the room.

"Be a little more sensitive, Bess," the voice scolded. "Can't you see she finds your questions distressing?"

Jennet and Elizabeth looked up to see an elderly figure standing sternly in the doorway. Jennet took this to be Elizabeth's mother. She was very aged and walked unsteadily, as though she could benefit from the aid of a stick. Her face was set heavy with lines and her wiry grey hair sprang wildly about her coif. Despite her frailty, however, she had an air of authority about her. She was the sort of woman that you stopped and listened to.

"I'm sorry," her mother continued, addressing Jennet. "She means no harm, she's just nosey."

Elizabeth reddened at her mother's words. This did not discourage her mother, however, who continued regardless of her daughter's embarrassment. It was immediately clear to Jennet that Elizabeth's mother was the dominant person in their relationship, indeed since her arrival into the room Elizabeth had visibly shrunk into the background.

"I am Elizabeth's mother, also called Elizabeth," the old woman continued. "Elizabeth Southern. But I am known around these parts as Old Demdike."

At that moment Jennet would have been curious about Elizabeth's surname Southern, having already been told that her married name was Ingham, were it not for the pronouncement of this most unusual, and Jennet felt, slightly offensive-sounding, nickname.

"Old Demdike?" Jennet repeated, still incredulous at the name.

"Aye, that's me. Or at least, it has been the name by which I have been known for many years," Demdike replied, chuckling. "You sound surprised! I suppose it is a bit of an odd name. Or perhaps it isn't odd at all, considering what I do. Now, I don't know what my daughter has told you about me as you have talked this afternoon. I have only been overhearing your conversation for these past few minutes, before that I was sleeping. I have been unwell, you see. Anyway, I don't know what she has told you so I'll start at the beginning, if you would like me to. You two seem to have been exchanging stories this afternoon. Would you like to hear mine?"

Jennet nodded, eagerly. Elizabeth looked slightly exasperated, as though she was about to hear a tale she had heard one hundred times and did not care to hear once more.

"My husband passed away in 1573, after little more than ten years of marriage. He left me with two children, our dear Elizabeth and her older brother, Christopher, who was not my husband's child. I had been married to Thomas Ingham by my family; he was the best they could do for me given I had spoiled myself by bearing another man's child before marriage. Thomas was not an unkind man but he was foolish, especially with money, and he died leaving us with no income, and no home. My family, taking pity on me and the children, provided Malkin Tower as a place for us to live. However, I still needed to have an income so that I could pay the rent. I had always known that I had certain gifts, certain talents that local people would pay money for, and I had already done a little work here and there in this regard while Thomas had been alive. So, I began to use my skills locally and got paid for my trouble, barely enough to cover the rent, but we managed. We still manage," Demdike paused, taking time to consider her words, as though she must explain herself carefully.

"What are these talents that you speak of?" Jennet probed.

"Folk around here come to me if they need help, lass, and I provide whatever assistance I can offer," replied Demdike, shooting Jennet a pointed look.

She clearly was not willing to elaborate further and offered enough clues that Jennet should be able to decipher her meaning: she was a cunning woman. Obviously she was regarded as quite a powerful one, thought Jennet, judging by the nickname afforded to her locally. She knew little about the practices of wise women, as some called them, and having seen her father die despite the best efforts of one, she had come to believe that their power must be limited. However, standing in front of Old Demdike as she was now, Jennet had to admit that there was no denying the belief this woman had in her own abilities; she had said little about what she could do but it was quite clear she had every confidence that she held some sort of power.

"A charm," interjected Elizabeth, as though reading Jennet's thoughts. Jennet had almost forgotten that Elizabeth was in the room.

"The main way she assists people, it's a healing charm she uses, one passed down through the generations of her family," Elizabeth continued.

Old Demdike raised her hand in protest.

"Bess, you really don't need to go into all the details, I think your friend understood my meaning." Demdike turned to address Jennet, who realised she was nodding passively. "She's never been keen to learn from me. She could learn, she is my daughter after all, but she never seems comfortable with it. She's happier working with her wool."

Elizabeth nodded her head vigorously.

"At least you cannot hang for spinning some wool, mother," Elizabeth said sharply.

Jennet was taken aback by her tone; she did not think Elizabeth would have the nerve to address Demdike in this way.

"I'm not a witch, lass" replied Demdike, barely whispering the word. "I undo the work of a witch; I never do her work for her."

"I'm sure Edmund Hartley thought so, too," snapped Elizabeth. "And yet he dangled from the gallows when Master Starkey judged his actions to be doing harm rather than the good he intended. It is a dangerous time to be plying that trade, mother, and I haven't the stomach for it."

The mention of Edmund Hartley's hanging was clearly intended to dampen her mother's zeal; however, it did much the opposite. Demdike appeared illuminated by the mention of his name.

"Hartley! I'm glad you brought him up, lass. I've been thinking about Hartley this very afternoon, between my dreams, and I've settled upon finding his circle. You may not wish to learn my ways, daughter, but you can find it in yourself to help me," announced Demdike, turning again to Jennet.

"I don't see how, all by myself, Mother. It will be dark and your sight is poor as it is. How should I manage if you fall, or if we are caught? It sounds too dangerous," Elizabeth replied.

A slow smile spread across Old Demdike's face. "Perhaps this young lass here will help you," she said, looking at Jennet. "You've helped Jennet learn to spin, perhaps now she can help you. They do say one good turn deserves another, after all. Tell me, Jennet Preston, how much stomach do you think you have, this very evening, for an adventure?"

Jennet smiled at Demdike. She barely knew the old woman and her daughter, and only knew about Edmund Hartley what she had heard locally in rumour; the terrifying tales of bewitchment, invocation of spirits, and his demise at the gallows. Stories had been circulating irrepressibly around Gisburn just as they had no doubt been all over Pendle. Elizabeth was correct, it was a dangerous time to practice the cunning arts, and any venture relating to Edmund Hartley would be fraught with risk. Despite this, Jennet resolved immediately to go with the two women. Demdike was right; she was in Elizabeth's debt, but her enthusiasm to go was about more than repaying a favour. Sitting there in that huge, draughty and unfamiliar building, it occurred to Jennet that she hadn't been offered an adventure since childhood. This realisation immediately conjured up irresistible images of happy days spent playing in the woods or down by the river, hiding in makeshift dens created in the overgrown foliage. She smiled, not caring for a moment that this proposed adventure was not a game fuelled by childish imaginings, but a very real, very dangerous undertaking.

"Yes, I'll come," she answered, a smile spread across her face.

8

Southern Pendle Forest, Near Huntroyde Hall
April 1597

"Are you sure we should be looking for this?" Jennet asked. Her earlier excitement had been replaced by nerves, and she kept glancing over her shoulder anxiously. The evening seemed unusually dark for the time of year, even by the standards of the Pendle countryside where day could often become night with remarkable rapidity. The weather was also beginning to turn, and Jennet noted the force with which the wind was toying with the tall trees overhead, teasing apart the delicate branches so that they appeared to swirl against the backdrop of the fading light. Although much of what was known as Pendle Forest had long ceased to be covered with the thick foliage to which it owed its name, this particular area did contain some small areas of woodland, and it was one of these little woods that Jennet and her two companions now sought.

"Mother is determined to find his circle," replied Elizabeth. "Anyway, we've come too far to turn back now. Look, over there you can see the light from Huntroyde. We must be close."

Jennet nodded. Elizabeth was right: ever since Edmund Hartley's execution a month ago, the talk of the forest had been filled with tales of the bewitching and the magical, and through these tales Elizabeth's mother had heard about a magical circle used by Edmund to ward off those who would do the devil's work. Old Demdike had not been able to curb her curiosity and according to Elizabeth she had talked of little else these past weeks. With good reason, Jennet had thought, when Demdike had enthusiastically recounted the full tale to her during their journey. The recent events at Huntroyde Hall were nothing short of fascinating.

Two years earlier, a cunning man of high repute, Edmund Hartley, had been brought to Huntroyde to cure the two Starkie children, John and Anne, of the bewitchment which had taken hold of them in the form of seizures. After administering certain charms and remedies, Edmund appeared to have been successful, and the children were cured until about six months ago when their symptoms returned. In making more strenuous attempts to cure the children permanently, Edmund had created a circle so powerful that he could use it to command spirits to help him identify and defeat the witch who was cursing the children. The circle had ultimately proved to be his undoing, as he involved his employer, Master Nicholas Starkie, in the ritual and in the end, when Starkie decided that it was Edmund who was bewitching his children, he brought the story of the circle as evidence against him. Invocation of the spirits was, of course, punishable by death and Edmund was sent to the gallows. However, none of this had seemed to deter Old Demdike's enthusiasm and she was determined to find the circle. Jennet was not certain of the exact purpose of her quest, although she suspected that the aged cunning woman hoped that, through mere contact with this magical artefact, she might emulate a practice which had previously been beyond her powers.

"Ah!" exclaimed a voice. "Here it is!"

Jennet peered in front of her, forcing her eyes to focus in the dim light. In the dusk she could just see a circle carved in the dirt and not much more. She could see Demdike slowly and deliberately bend down and trace her fingers over the ground. The old lady's eyesight really was poor and Jennet reflected that it was nothing short of miraculous that she had managed to locate the circle this evening, which really showed her determination to find it.

"A circle made up of four parts, just as I thought." Demdike spoke affirmatively.

"Should you touch the circle, Mother?" asked Elizabeth. Jennet could sense her growing reservations about their expedition.

"Perhaps not lass, but its magic is spent, I am sure of that."

The conversation was interrupted by the sudden and fierce howling of the wind and the three women shivered with the realisation of the growing cold.

"Let's return home," said Elizabeth. "I feel a chill in the air, and we don't want to get ill. Besides, I left John with the children and he will be wondering where I am by now. Have you seen all you need to see, Mother?"

In the dark Jennet sensed the old lady nod in agreement and the women turned to follow their path back home. As they did so, they heard the sharp and urgent sound of twigs breaking underfoot. Fearing their discovery on Starkie land, Jennet tried to stifle a gasp as she turned to see who was there. To her surprise, she could not decipher any human shadows in front of her. Instead, in front of the circle, where they had been standing moments earlier, were two eyes, glowing green and staring intently at her. By now the light had almost faded from existence, but Jennet could just about make out four legs and a creature which was just about the size of a dog. She breathed a sigh of relief.

"It's just a dog," Jennet informed the others. "It's nothing to worry about."

"A black dog," replied Demdike.

The three women returned to Malkin Tower late that evening, much later than Jennet had anticipated; in her ignorance of Pendle's exact geography she had not realised just how far away Huntroyde Hall would be from her new friends' home. At this late hour, it was impossible to return to Gisburn tonight, in the dark and unaccompanied. Her companions realised this and upon arriving back at Malkin, they offered her some blankets so that she might stay the night. The three children and John, Elizabeth's husband, were sleeping and for the first time Jennet was able to appreciate the peace and calm of this house, alone and isolated as it was on the Blacko hillside.

Jennet was tired and weary from another long walk, yet also elated, fuelled by the adrenaline of their venture. Her two companions had talked of nothing but the strange black dog they encountered at Edmund Hartley's circle all the way home. It had just looked like an ordinary dog to Jennet, but Old Demdike seemed quite fixated upon it, as though it held some significance to the remains of the ritual she had examined, as though it had held the key to what had happened to Edmund Hartley. The more Jennet thought about it, the more it unnerved her, and the less inclined she felt to ask about it, even now in the safety of Malkin Tower.

"Won't your husband worry?" asked Elizabeth, interrupting Jennet's thoughts and clearly concerned for her new friend.

"Probably," replied Jennet. "But he would be more concerned if he discovered I walked home alone, in the dark. If you don't mind the best thing for me to do is to stay here for tonight."

"Of course we don't mind," replied Elizabeth, kindly.

Both women glanced at Old Demdike, who was muttering to herself about the evening's events.

"What is it, Mother?" asked Elizabeth.

The old woman appeared to be wild with her ideas. Jennet was momentarily concerned by her incessant mumbling, as though she was suffering a sort of madness. Hearing her daughter address her, Old Demdike looked up and remembering they had company, she composed herself.

"The sight of that black dog is troubling my mind," she replied, with a hint of weariness. Clearly the afternoon's events were beginning to tell on her physical and mental state.

"But surely, it was just a black dog? An animal from the nearby estate perhaps and it had simply lost its way and found itself in the woods?" asked Jennet.

Demdike looked at Jennet and released a sharp intake of breath, appearing to physically deflate as she did so.

"It'll be difficult for you to understand, Jennet, I know. But you have to believe me when I tell you that it was not a mere black dog that startled us all tonight." Old Demdike lowered her voice to a whisper. "Some say that the Starkie children are troubled still, even now that Edmund Hartley lies cold in the ground and despite the efforts of the two preachers who have been brought to Huntroyde to cast out their demons. I have heard that they are menaced by animal spirits and mainly by a black dog."

Jennet gasped. "So it is true, then? Edmund Hartley was a witch? He brought the devil to Huntroyde to torment the children after being employed to help them?"

"Many folk around these parts think so, no doubt the Starkies do too," replied Demdike. "I have my own theory: the black dog is one of the animal spirits that Edmund Hartley invoked to counter the magic of the witch who was attacking the Starkie children. However, because this spirit was attached to Edmund Hartley, because Hartley was his master and Hartley is now dead, the spirit remains here still, haunting the lives of those responsible for his master's death."

Jennet was incredulous. "And we saw it tonight?"

Demdike laughed. "Fear not, Jennet. The spirit has no business with us, you can sleep soundly." The old woman yawned. "Speaking of which, I am exhausted and you must be too. We should all get some rest."

Demdike turned to head towards her bed then quickly turned back to Jennet as though she had forgotten something.

"Oh, Jennet?" she said.

"Yes?" replied Jennet, half-yawning herself.

"I have something to help you with your troubles," said Demdike, giving Jennet a meaningful stare.

The old woman handed Jennet a piece of cloth, inside which something was wrapped. Jennet gasped as she opened the piece of cloth, for inside was a small object, modelled in clay and shaped like a man's penis.

"What am I to do with this?" Jennet asked, barely able to whisper.

"Place it under your pillow and sleep with it there every night. Once you are with child, leave it under your pillow until after the child is born. I gathered from your words to my daughter earlier that you have suffered the loss of many children. This will help you, as long as you don't remove it until after you are safely delivered from child-bed," Demdike advised in a very matter-of-fact manner, as though she might be a physician offering a remedy to a patient.

Jennet nodded in response. It was the strangest-looking item and indeed the strangest idea that she had ever heard. She could only imagine what William would say when he saw it. She couldn't imagine what he would say if it actually worked.

"Thank you, this is very kind of you," she replied, with genuine gratitude.

"It's no trouble, Jennet," Demdike said kindly. "You came with us tonight, hardly knowing either of us, and facing considerable danger, yet you came nonetheless. I doubt my daughter would ever have agreed to come with me if it hadn't been for you. This is my way of thanking you."

Demdike glanced at Elizabeth, who had been listening quietly and who smiled in agreement. Jennet nodded again. Without a further word between them, the three women retired to their beds, exhausted by the day's events. That night, Jennet dreamt of the child she wanted, the child she had dreamt of many times before, the daughter with the brown curls in her hair, the freckles on her nose, a nose which wrinkled when she laughed. This time, however, the dream seemed different: they were running through the grounds of Westby Hall, laughing, and the girl was so vivid that Jennet could almost touch her. When she awoke, instead of sobbing as she normally did, Jennet smiled. This time she felt sure that the girl would be born, and that she would live.

9

The Prestons' Farm, near Gisburn Village
September 1597

Jennet stood up from her spinning wheel, arched her back, and smiled. It had been another satisfying day of work, but as the afternoon drew to a close, Jennet and Anna were beginning to lose the best of the daylight, signalling the end to their working day. Besides, there was still the dinner to prepare, plain though it would be. Jennet knew that since she had started taking in work from the Hewits, the fayre prepared in her kitchen had suffered a little. To her surprise, William had not complained. Jennet suspected that like her, he had come to appreciate that in order to prosper in some things you had to allow others to slide.

Indeed, the Prestons really had prospered of late. Since the spring, work had come thick and fast from the Hewits in Colne, delivered like clockwork every few weeks. Having learned the skills she needed from Elizabeth Device, Jennet had taught Anna to card the wool and together they settled into a daily work routine. Through the summer they had benefitted from an abundance of work, especially after shearing in June, and they had made the most of the long, light days, often working from breakfast until dinner time. The Hewits, or at least those sent by them to deliver the wool, had warned that work would slow a little over the winter, with less wool being delivered and shorter days in which to card and spin. Nevertheless, Jennet could not help feeling immensely satisfied with her efforts and looked forward to a winter where she would worry less about how they would eat than she did the winter before. In fact her enterprise had gone so well this year that she was on the cusp of convincing William to allow her to purchase a horse for her personal use, taking the pressure off her poor legs and back and allowing her to visit friends with greater ease, particularly those new friends she had made in Blacko.

Jennet smiled at the thought of Elizabeth Device and her mother, Old Demdike. Since that day spent learning to card and spin and that strange and eventful night trawling the woods near Huntroyde, Jennet had become firm friends with the family. She made time to visit them usually weekly, or at least whenever she afforded herself a break from her spinning and left Anna to take charge of William and John's meals. Over the past few months she had spent many a happy afternoon at Malkin Tower, enjoying the noise of the children, the friendly chatter of female company and the fascinating, sometimes odd recollections of Old Demdike, who was never shy about sharing a story or two from her past. Indeed, Jennet had reflected on more than one occasion that this was the first time that she considered herself to have true friends since childhood; having been something of an outcast in Gisburn for much of her adult life, she had forgotten what friendship was like and how much she could relish it.

William was not quite so keen and Jennet reflected that in some ways, this was understandable. After all, the first time he became acquainted with the name Elizabeth Southern was when he was presented with the phallic object gifted to his wife by the old woman. His reaction was more or less one which Jennet had expected: utter horror and reproach for the disgusting thing, as he called it. Even after Jennet explained what it was for and how it could help, it took a fortnight before he relented and allowed her to place the object in their bed. It had remained there ever since, for all the good it had done. Jennet sighed, remembering the disappointment she felt that, so far, the gift from Demdike had not had the desired effect. Initially, it had certainly seemed to make William more amorous, almost rekindling the early months of their marriage; however, as it became apparent that the magical object had yielded no results, his ardour had turned to mistrust, of both the thing itself and its giver. He complained regularly that his wife spent so much time in the company of women he had never met, cunning women no less, and was not appeased even when, for the umpteenth time, Jennet explained to him that it was difficult for them to travel to Gisburn, given Demdike's age and Elizabeth's young dependents. In truth, neither fact seemed to be an obstacle to these two women getting around the area, as their excursion to Huntroyde had demonstrated. It was Jennet's reluctance to invite them to visit her home which had really prevented William from making their acquaintance. It wasn't that she was ashamed of her family; indeed she knew that they would find them all courteous and charming. However, if they were to come to Gisburn, they might hear of the Lister episode which plagued her reputation locally still. Jennet could barely admit her own pride to herself and certainly could not admit it to William so instead she made excuses, but in truth she could not stand to think of her new friends thinking ill of her.

This was not the only piece of information Jennet had kept from her husband over the past few months: she had not told William about her expedition to find Edmund Hartley's circle at all. She had arrived home the morning after that strange day to a worried, fretting husband who, she judged, was best appeased by the simple explanation that she had spent longer learning from Elizabeth than expected and the two women had kindly offered her dinner and a bed for the night. As the weeks then passed by and William began to express his concerns about his wife's new friends, Jennet felt increasingly justified in keeping this information from him; not only would he be furious that she had lied to him, he would be seriously worried about her getting involved in their cunning work. He might even try to prevent Jennet from seeing her friends. Although he was usually a gentle man, Jennet had learned that when provoked he could be just as obstinate and even unkind as most people were capable of being. But then, Jennet reflected, she was being unkind, deceiving family and friends to protect her pride. Certainly over the past few months she had bowed her head a little lower in Church, feeling certain that God was watching and disapproving. Perhaps that was why, despite Demdike's magic, she had still not conceived a child, perhaps it was further punishment for her dishonesty.

"What are you thinking about, Aunt?" asked Anna, and Jennet realised that she had been gazing out of her window for some time.

"Oh, not much lass, just taking a few moments to gather my thoughts," replied Jennet, before swiftly changing the subject. "Now come, let's get us all a meal prepared. The men will be home soon and hungry, as I'm sure you are."

Anna nodded in response. The pair headed towards the kitchen just as the front door opened. Jennet swung round in surprise, realising she must have lost track of time. William and John could not have finished early on the farm, it might be past harvest time but there was still plenty to do before the winter.

"William?" she called out. "Is that you, home already?"

"Yes," answered a familiar voice, moving towards her. "We're a little early today, but not much before our usual hour. I presume from your voice that dinner is not yet ready?"

William Preston peered around the doorway and gave Jennet a mischievous smile to let her know he was teasing.

"Yes… sorry. Anna and I must have lost track of time," replied Jennet apologetically, turning back to the fireplace.

"It doesn't matter," said William.

He walked over to his wife and, wrapping his arms around her waist, gave her an affectionate kiss, burying his nose into the nape of her neck. Jennet stopped what she was doing and turned back towards him to return his embrace. He had been very attentive lately, and although their attempts to conceive a child had subsided somewhat, William had not ceased to show his wife a lot of affection. Jennet reflected on how improved things were between them compared with last spring before she began working for the Hewits, when they were arguing about money and saying awful things to each other.

"I have our final accounts for this past year and all looks very well indeed," said William, talking into the place on her neck where his nose was buried and sending shivers down Jennet's spine as he did so.

"Really?" Jennet replied.

"Yes. The harvest was one of the best we've had since we have had the farm, and with the income earned from the work you've done for the Hewits…well, let's just say that even after we've paid the rent, we need not worry this winter. We may even look to get you a horse in the spring, if that's still what you want."

Jennet clapped her hands and jumped with delight. "Really?" she said again. She was lost for words; she knew their fortunes had improved considerably, but nonetheless she was taken aback by such good news. She was not used to having her prayers answered, and how her poor legs and back had prayed for a horse these past years.

"Thank you, William. You don't know what this means to me," Jennet said, embracing her husband again.

"You don't have to thank me, Jennet. You're as responsible as I am for the success we've enjoyed this year. I know how hard you and Anna have worked. You deserve a horse. It is the very least you deserve," William smiled at Jennet. "Just don't use it to spend too much time visiting those friends of yours in Blacko, or I may change my mind and sell it."

William's smile was wicked but his voice was cautionary and Jennet knew that where her friends were concerned, she would always be treading a fine line with her husband.

"Anyway," he continued, "I think all this is cause to celebrate. That's partly the reason for our slightly earlier arrival home. After dinner, would you like to come to the alehouse with me? John has agreed to stay here with Anna tonight and keep her company, not that it will be long before she begins to join us there; our niece is growing up quickly. I know you haven't always enjoyed the alehouse, but I hoped we could spend a nice evening together. What do you think?"

Jennet hesitated. William was right, she hadn't ever really liked the alehouse and since John and Anna had lived with them, she had been quite content to use her niece as an excuse to stay behind while the men enjoyed themselves. It was a place of gossip and sometimes scandal, two things which Jennet was always keen to avoid. She was probably just paranoid, but she was certain that the other villagers were whispering about her whenever she went there, harking back to old gossip about her and Tom Lister. However, William's face this evening looked so hopeful and eager that she could not refuse him.

"Why not?" she replied cheerfully. "Come, let's eat something before we go," she added, turning back to finish preparing their meal and thinking as she did so about how she could make herself invisible enough to others so that she might enjoy her evening.

It had been quite a long time since Jennet had set foot in the alehouse. She observed that it was largely unchanged; the same old wooden tables, benches and stools still in use, the same familiar smell of stale ale lingering in the air. If Jennet closed her eyes, she could still see her parents enjoying an afternoon's merriment in here; she could still hear her father's laughter echoing in her ears. No doubt she would see her brothers in here tonight, which would be the first time for a while. Since she had married and their mother had died, her brothers had gone on to take wives themselves and had bothered little with their sister, a fact which Jennet tried not to become bitter about.

William led Jennet to a small table in the corner of the room, where they sat quietly, sipping their ale. Jennet tried to ignore the faces looking over at her, giving her sideways glances. She tried to convince herself that it was just surprise, because she was hardly ever seen in here and nothing more. She tried hard to concentrate on her conversation with William, who was keenly chatting over farming matters as though she was merely the substitute for John's company this evening, with the same conversation taking place regardless. A few more ales passed each of their lips whilst the alehouse grew busier and busier and the glances became more numerous. In the end, fuelled by a bit of drink, she could not resist mentioning the stares to William who was supping and chattering, oblivious.

"Folk are looking at me, William," she said.

"Are they?" asked William, slightly dumbly. "Well, perhaps it is just because they are not used to seeing you in here, you admit yourself that you have not been for a long time. Or," he paused, allowing his eyelids to droop slightly, "they are wondering who the beautiful woman is that William Preston is spending the evening with tonight."

William grabbed Jennet's hand and held it tightly in his grasp. Jennet tried to smile and feel reassured, but William could sense that she was not convinced.

"What? Jennet," he asked, sounding exasperated. "What do you think they are talking about? No one from the village ever sees you, so you can't possibly provoke any gossip! Why are you so worried? Please, let's enjoy our evening. If you see anyone you would like to speak to then, please, go ahead! You hardly speak to anyone from the village these days. You seem to prefer your friends further afield."

Jennet bristled at the jibe; she knew that when William had drunk quite a lot of ale, he could become quite brutal with his words. She did not wish to argue and decided to ignore the comment.

"You're right, I am sorry. As you say, they are perhaps just surprised to see me here," Jennet replied, trying her best to be conciliatory.

However, William was not quite prepared to let the matter lie.

"Is it Lister? Is that what you think they're whispering about?"

he asked, slightly mockingly.

"No," replied Jennet, although it was clear to them both that she was lying.

"It is. It is!" William continued. "You think they still gossip about you and Master Lister, after all these years! Even in a small village like Gisburn, Jennet, topics of conversation change quickly. Come on, you and Tom Lister have not seen each other in years, so even if you did lie with him, that is very old news indeed."

Jennet bowed her head and looked to the floor. William had always thought that she had lain with Tom Lister, she knew that. For years he had chosen to throw the accusation at her, usually fuelled by ale and with venom. Jennet looked up at her husband and looked him squarely in the eye.

"I have told you a thousand times since we married, William. I did not lie with Tom Lister. Something happened between us, a kiss and some affection, but it was one evening and never again. When I married you I was still reeling from the scandal around it and too ashamed to speak of it. I only wish I had told you, perhaps if I had you wouldn't think so badly of me now," said Jennet defiantly.

"It is not that which makes me feel angry, Jennet," replied William. "I believe you're telling me the truth when you say you didn't lie with him. I am angry because I know that you wish you had lain with him." William put up his hand to stop Jennet's protest. "You do wish it, even if you cannot admit it to yourself. I feel angry because I love you, Jennet, in fact I love you more each year we are married. And I believe you have a great affection for me, too. But you must know, as I know, that you will never love me like you love Tom Lister. You will always love Tom Lister, and it is your love for him which has blighted our marriage."

Jennet looked at her husband, stunned by his words. She could not object, for in her heart she knew that she was hanging on to a love for a man who had long since left her life, but was very much still present in her consciousness. As they walked home together that night, hand in hand yet reeling from the emotional chasm realised between them, Jennet felt stung by the truth in her husband's words, and at a loss as to how to close down that part of her heart dedicated still to Tom Lister, once and for all.

10

The Prestons' Farm, near Gisburn Village
June 1598

The day was warm, a sticky, uncomfortable heat which made Jennet shift restlessly on her stool. In the end, she had to stand and pace the floor for a while, trying to relieve her discomfort. It was quite impossible, she thought, to work peacefully in these temperatures anyway, even without being in her current, albeit happy condition. Jennet smiled and placed a loving hand on her belly, which was large with child. She had discovered the news shortly after Christmas time. Having felt unwell and disinclined to eat for most of the festive season, she had visited Elizabeth and Old Demdike in early January and unburdened herself of the symptoms which were worrying her, fearing that she was sick. Instead of sharing her concern, both women had straight away offered their happy diagnosis. At first Jennet had been shocked and disbelieving; she had been unable to get with child for so long, she had no longer believed it was possible. In denial, she had not spoken a word of her condition to her family, but as her stomach began to swell in the early spring it became impossible to disguise and she had to admit it, to them and to herself.

William had been delighted. Despite all their previous losses, he could not caution himself to contain his excitement. It had been so many years since she had last been with child, he had said, that he had doubted it would ever happen again. Jennet, on the other hand, could feel nothing but sheer terror. However, as she grew bigger and spring turned to summer, she began to realise that this was the longest she had ever held on to a child, and she began to hope. Perhaps, just maybe, the gift from Demdike, still sitting undisturbed in their bed, was finally working and would safely deliver the child they both longed for.

"Surely it won't be much longer now, Aunt," said Anna reassuringly, sympathising with Jennet's obvious discomfort.

"A few more weeks yet, I think Anna. Elizabeth and Demdike seem to think the baby will have arrived by Midsummer's day. I hope they are right because this heat and this huge belly are beginning to tire me. It is just impossible to sleep, and it is difficult to keep up with all this work," Jennet said, gesticulating at the wool filling the room.

Anna smiled, although she was clearly not sure what else to say to ease her aunt's suffering.

"I'm sorry lass, I shouldn't complain. If I am safely delivered of this child then I am a lucky woman indeed. A bit of suffering along the way is a small price to pay," said Jennet.

Their conversation was interrupted by the door opening. It was William, calling home for his lunch. For most of their married life he had spent all day out working, usually taking a lunch with him, but for these past few weeks he had made a habit of calling home midway through the day. It was as though, as the baby's arrival grew nearer, a wave of protectiveness had come over him and he felt compelled to check on her.

"How are you feeling?" he asked Jennet with obvious concern.

"The same as I was this morning when you left," Jennet snapped with slight irritation. "Hot and tired."

William chose to ignore his wife's tone and affectionately patted her stomach.

"How is the baby?" he asked.

Jennet shrugged.

"How should I know? Hot too, probably, she's not moving much today. I suppose that is a blessing in itself as at least I'm relieved of the constant kicking. The baby is so large now, the kicks are becoming sore," Jennet complained.

William smiled. "Still convinced this one's a girl?" he replied, ignoring his wife's complaints.

"I told you, I have seen her in my dreams. I feel certain we will have a daughter," Jennet replied, still feeling short-tempered. William didn't take her intuition about the child's sex seriously. More superstition, he had said when Jennet had first told him about her dreams, it's about as likely to mean something as that…thing sitting under your pillow is to make a child.

"Yes… well, not long to go now, my love," William replied, kissing her lightly on the cheek. He had clearly decided to avoid discussing Jennet's dreams today.

"So everyone keeps saying," Jennet quipped crossly. "It is easy for a man to say, knowing that he will never have to endure all this."

That final remark seemed enough to silence William. He headed towards the kitchen to find some bread and cheese, not daring to ask if his wife had prepared anything for him to eat. As Jennet watched him walk away, she regretted her harsh tone. She knew he was only trying to be kind, that he was as excited and as nervous as she was about the impending arrival. Given everything that had happened to them in their marriage and all their failed attempts to have a child, his concern was perfectly understandable. It was just that she was so hot, and worried, and happy, and impatient; it was hard not to take her emotions out on others.

Jennet's thoughts were interrupted by a knock at the door.

"Goodness me," she remarked to Anna resolving to be more cheerful. "This baby has not yet arrived and already I have visitors?"

Jennet opened the door to find Elizabeth Device there, looking frantic. Stunned to see her friend arrived, unexpected, on her doorstep, Jennet was dumbstruck. Before she could recover her speech, Elizabeth breathlessly burst forth with her plea for help.

"I am so sorry to trouble you like this, Jennet," she began, gasping for breath and trying to compose herself. "I didn't know who else to turn to. It is Mother, she's gone mad, at least, she is raving about all sorts of things. I don't know what to do. I panicked and came straight over here to find you. What should I do?"

Jennet continued to stand there, astonished and unable to absorb what she was being told. After a moment she recovered herself enough to move from the doorway and invite her friend inside.

"Where have you left your mother?" Jennet asked. "And where have you left your children?" she added, suddenly feeling as panic-stricken as her friend.

"Don't worry about the children, John is at home with them," she replied. "I've left Mother there too, told her not to move until I get back. Honestly Jennet you wouldn't recognise her, it is as though her senses have just...well, gone! She speaks only about a dog, a small brown dog called Tibb, who came into our home and tried to, well, do horrible things... I don't really understand what she's rambling on about, but I'm so worried, and so afraid."

Elizabeth paused, still struggling to compose herself. Hearing all the commotion, William reappeared from the kitchen.

"Who is this?" he asked his wife, although Jennet expected that he already realised who their visitor must be.

"This is Elizabeth Device," she replied. "She has called because she is concerned for her elderly mother and has come to see if I can offer any help."

Jennet tried her best to behave casually about the matter, however William was not fooled.

"Your mother sounds very sick and I am sorry for it," he addressed Elizabeth directly. "But you can see the condition of my wife, surely you cannot expect her to visit your mother today? She cannot make the journey, on foot or foal. What if she were to catch your mother's sickness?"

Elizabeth opened her mouth to speak, but thought better of it, pressing her lips together as though to prevent ill-chosen words from slipping out. She looked helplessly at Jennet, her eyes pleading with her. Jennet looked back at her, equally at a loss as to what to do.

"I can go with Aunt Jennet, Uncle," said Anna from the corner of the room. "I will see her safely to her horse, and walk beside it so that it does not gallop."

"That is a kind offer, Anna," replied William. "But the fact remains that this woman's mother is sick, and your aunt is with child. Whatever sickens her could endanger them both."

Jennet suddenly felt exasperated by her husband's stubbornness.

"Oh, William!" she exclaimed. "Whatever it is, it sounds like it's in her mind and not her body. I don't think that it is something the child or I can catch."

Elizabeth nodded in agreement. "It's true," she said, "she isn't sick in a way that's catching. If she was, I wouldn't ask Jennet to come."

William looked at the three women and, feeling outnumbered, let out a resigned sigh.

"Alright," he said. "Anna, I want that horse to travel slow and steady. A woman so heavy with child should not be on a horse at all, but I fear your aunt would not make the journey on foot now. I trust you to see her there and back safely."

Anna nodded sombrely, understanding the gravity of the responsibility resting upon her shoulders. Jennet reflected that the child was barely a child anymore; in moments such as these she could see Anna visibly growing into her womanhood, just as Jennet had at the same age. Jennet focussed her mind: right now there was no more time for dwelling on sentimental thoughts, Old Demdike was ill and Jennet had to try to help. Without any delay, the three women left the cottage and made their way along the dry, dusty road to Blacko.

They arrived at Malkin Tower in the middle of the afternoon. Tethering their horse to a nearby tree, Jennet and Anna were greeted by three excitable children, apparently running their poor father ragged and seemingly oblivious to whatever was ailing their grandmother. Inside, Jennet found Old Demdike sitting in her chair, still as a statue, muttering to herself; short, nonsensical utterances which stuttered forth from her lips uncontrollably. As Jennet softly approached the old woman, taking care not to startle her, she could see that her face was distorted; her mouth and eye appeared to droop on the left hand side. Gently, Jennet placed an arm around her shoulder.

"Demdike?" she began. "Elizabeth? Your daughter says you are unwell, can you tell me what ails you?"

The old woman seemed oblivious to Jennet's presence and continued her murmuring.

"Old Mother Demdike, what ails you?" Jennet tried again, a little more insistently.

This time, Demdike appeared to respond. She turned her head slightly and looked at Jennet.

"Tibb," was all she said, before looking away again.

"Who is Tibb, Demdike?" probed Jennet.

"Tibb's a dog now, a dog…he came…he suckled at me…" Demdike trailed off, and fell silent.

Jennet noticed that the old woman's speech sounded different, her words slurring sloppily from her mouth as though she had no control over their articulation. She did not really understand the meaning of what Demdike was trying to convey to her, but she felt moved to try to reassure the old woman, who was clearly confused and distressed.

"It's alright, nothing can hurt you now," replied Jennet, realising as she did so that she had no idea if this was true or not.

Jennet turned towards Elizabeth, who was hovering, agitated and concerned.

"Has she eaten anything?" Jennet asked her friend.

"Not since yesterday morning, when it happened," Elizabeth replied. "I have tried to get her to take a little ale, and she has taken some, but she will take no food from me."

"Keep trying to get her to drink, Elizabeth," Jennet advised. "We can only hope that in time she will begin to eat again. Whatever has happened, she has obviously had a terrifying experience which has driven her out of her wits. I think only time will tell if she is going to improve. Until then you must keep her rested and pray for her recovery. Unless you have money for a physician I don't see what else we can do."

Elizabeth nodded, sighing despairingly. "We have no money for a physician. Mother wouldn't see one anyway, she doesn't hold with their healing ways. She probably has a remedy for this malady of hers but alas, it is locked away inside her, along with the truth of what happened to her yesterday morning. Oh how I wish I had learned more from her, then I could be some help!" Elizabeth lamented.

"You are helping, you are here and caring for her. You cannot do more." Jennet tried to reassure her friend.

"Thank you, Jennet," Elizabeth replied. "I knew you would know what to do."

Jennet smiled. She did not wish to share with her friend that her sole knowledge of caring for the sick came from attending to her dying parents. She hoped that this wasn't a fate facing Elizabeth now, but given the old woman's age and current condition, she was not at all confident that she would survive this.

"Anna," said Jennet, turning to her niece. "You will stay here for the next few days, to help Elizabeth attend to her mother."

"But…" Anna began to protest.

Jennet put up her hand firmly. "Elizabeth has three young children to care for, as well as her mother. Her husband needs to be at out at work. I think right now, Elizabeth needs an extra pair of hands more than I do. You are a good girl, I know that you will make yourself useful." Jennet tried not to sound patronising. "I will arrange for your uncle to collect you in a few days' time."

Anna nodded in agreement, but still looked concerned.

"What will Uncle William say?" she asked. "He asked me to look after you."

"Leave your uncle to me," Jennet replied. "I had better head back to Gisburn, I think I will be in enough trouble already, without travelling back in the evening." Jennet winked at her niece mischievously.

"Don't rush back, Aunt," Anna cautioned. "Remember what Uncle William said, the horse must not gallop when you're on it."

"I know lass, thank you. You are a good and sensible girl, I know you will be a great help and comfort to Elizabeth here," Jennet replied, embracing her niece affectionately.

With a few more words of reassurance to them both, Jennet left Malkin Tower and, after mounting her horse with some difficulty, she steadily began to make her way back to Gisburn.

The evening had just begun to draw in as Jennet saw Westby Hall in the distance, indicating that her journey was nearly at an end. Thankfully the day's heat had begun to abate, and the cool evening air provided some blessed relief. She had abided by her niece's reminder and had ensured that her horse had trotted all the way home; a frustratingly slow but necessary speed. In truth, Jennet could not have brought herself to travel any faster, however impatient she felt to get home and rest. Not long after leaving Malkin Tower she had begun to feel unwell; she was nauseous and had an ache in her belly which was growing worse. At first, Jennet had assumed that it was a reaction to the heat and the day's stressful events, not to mention all the travelling she had done. She knew if she was honest with herself, that she had acted fairly recklessly today, and now, in some considerable discomfort, she was beginning to chastise herself for it. With each movement of the horse the niggling ache had grown into a stabbing pain, ripping through her stomach and making her retch with the agony. Jennet knew that she could travel no further.

With great difficulty, Jennet dismounted from her horse to rest awhile on the ground. She hoped that sitting still would help enough that she could continue her journey home, only a short distance away now; however, it did not. The pain grew worse still and Jennet, all alone out there on the fringes of Westby, began to panic. Perhaps this was it, she thought, perhaps the baby was trying to come now, excited by all the events of the day into making a slightly early entrance into the world. How could the child come now, she fretted; out here, with no shelter? How could she deliver the child alone, without anyone to help her? Feverish with the pain and worry, Jennet tried to call out for help, but the only answer which came was the desolate sound of her own echo. Jennet sunk further into the ground, suddenly feeling a wet sensation, as though she was sitting in a warm brook. She reached down to touch the waters, feeling certain now that this was the baby letting her know she was on her way. I will meet my daughter soon, she thought. She wiped the sweat from her brow with the back of her hand, realising as she did so that the water she had touched was not clear like she expected, but an angry, bloody red which had stained her whole hand. Realising now that something was seriously wrong, Jennet looked down in horror at the river of blood which was all about her, drowning the parched grass she had been sitting on.

"Oh, my child! God, don't take my child!" Jennet cried out in desperation and despair.

The sight of all that blood was too much for her to bear and, groaning in agony one last time, Jennet closed her eyes and faded away.

11

Westby Hall, Gisburn
July 1598

Jennet's eyes flickered open. She looked around her, feeling disorientated, eyeing the room in which she was lying in a mist of confusion, realising she had no idea where she was. The bed in which she was lying was comfortable, indeed perhaps the most comfortable bed she had ever lain in, and it was situated in the middle of a pleasantly furnished room. Jennet wondered if she was dreaming; all she could recall were dreams, she seemed to have had a lot of them of late and this was perhaps just another. For as long as she could remember she had been travelling in a strange land, filled with spirits and conjurors, cunning folk and strange talking dogs. At the centre of it all, guiding her, had been her child, the daughter with the brown curls and freckles on her cheeks. The girl, she realised now, she had not yet met; waking just now confirmed that it had all been a dream. Jennet gasped, her memories of what had happened flooding back to her. The small noise she made with that sharp intake of breath provoked a startled sound from someone else in the room, and Jennet realised then that she wasn't alone.

A woman appeared at the bedside. She was a similar age to

Jennet, smartly dressed in clothing befitting a woman in service in a good household, clothing like that which Jennet could recall wearing a long time ago. She had a slightly pinched, mean looking face with a mouth that naturally curled downwards. She looked familiar to Jennet, but at that moment Jennet couldn't possibly think where she could know her from. The woman peered clinically at Jennet, as though checking for signs of life.

"You're awake!" she exclaimed. "I must fetch the Master at once!"

The woman ran out of the room, leaving Jennet alone to muse on her confusion. How did she end up here? Where was she? The last thing she remembered was being in pain and being heavy with child. Jennet reached down and touched her belly, wincing as she did so because it felt swollen and tender, but not large like she remembered it had been. Jennet listened desperately for the sound of a crying infant, but all she could hear was the frantic chatter of voices from beyond the room. Before Jennet could ponder any further, the door swung open. The woman who had peered at Jennet moments earlier had returned, this time with a man following her.

"Jennet? Jennet! Oh, thank God!" the man said, approaching the bed.

From her horizontal position, Jennet tried to study the man as best she could. He had a kind face and a well-groomed beard which, like his dark hair, was beginning to turn grey. When he looked straight at her, smiling, Jennet observed that he had bright blue eyes, eyes like someone she used to know, eyes like…

"Jennet? Do you not know me?" asked the man, clearing his throat. "Do you not know where you are?"

Jennet tried to reply but her throat was so dry, she could only croak a response.

"Anne, fetch Jennet something to drink," the man instructed the woman, who was still peering from the edge of the bed. With the resigned sigh of someone being deprived by duty of a delicious piece of gossip, the woman left the room.

"Anne is as cheerful as she ever was," said the man, grinning mischievously at Jennet. "Although I doubt you remember her either, if you can't remember me," he added, his voice growing sombre.

The woman returned with some ale and, helping Jennet to sit slightly in bed, gave her a cup which Jennet drank from thirstily. Handing the empty cup back to her, Jennet looked at them both silently, waiting for one of them to speak.

"Jennet, do you remember anything?" asked the man, gently.

"Tom? Is it you? My child," Jennet croaked, still struggling to speak. "Where is she?"

Tom and Anne looked at one another, as though trying to decide which one of them should speak first. In the end, Tom sighed and took hold of Jennet's hand.

"You had a son," he replied, "but he was born too soon, he was too small and he did not live. When we brought you here you were very sick, you were bleeding and in a lot of pain. Our physician did all he could to save your child but once born, he never took his first breath. I am truly, deeply sorry."

Jennet began to sob; dry, silent tears, as though her body had not the will or the energy to make the liquid or the noise to accompany them. She did not speak again all afternoon, she only sat in that bed and wept for the child whose birth she had slept through, the son she had not been able to hold. After a while Anne left her, but Tom remained, silently holding her hand all afternoon and into the evening, trying to be of some comfort in her hours of grief until eventually, exhausted, Jennet once again fell asleep.

When Jennet woke again, it was dark, so dark that she could barely make out any objects in the room, and she could not tell whether or not she was alone. Disorientated and panicked, she felt around the bed for something, anything.

"Hello?" she called out, hoping someone was there.

"Jennet? Are you awake?" said a familiar voice. "It's me, William. Hold on a moment and I will light a candle."

William scrambled around in the dark until, moments later, there was a dim light at the bedside. "There we are," he said. "That's better. I've been here since the evening, when they sent for me, but you were sleeping again by the time I arrived. I must have fallen asleep myself. They said you had woken up earlier today. I cannot tell you how relieved I am, my darling. We had all prepared ourselves for, well…never mind that now, you are awake."

"William, am I really at Westby Hall?" Jennet asked, still confused.

"Yes," William replied gently. "You are at Westby Hall. Did you really not recognise Master Thomas Lister? He said when you woke you did not seem to know him, seemed quite upset about it too." Even in the dim candlelight, Jennet could see William was trying not to smile about it.

"How long have I been asleep?" Jennet asked wearily.

"A little over a week," William replied. "The physician said you were so weakened from the birth, your body so badly drained of its humours, he told us to prepare ourselves for the worst. It is nothing short of a miracle that you have come back to me."

William gently stroked Jennet's forehead, and for a few moments the pair just looked at each other, in silence, as though appreciating a moment that they might have never had.

"Tom told me that the child did not live," said Jennet finally.

"Yes," replied William, drawing a shallow intake of breath. "He told me he had broken the news to you. He shouldn't have told you Jennet, not so soon after you woke, it's no wonder you fell asleep again. The shock must have been terrible."

"I asked him," Jennet replied, slightly defensively. "Tom Lister could never lie to me. And I fell asleep again because I wept until I was exhausted."

"Well you must weep, as I have wept, as we have both wept for all the others we have lost, Jennet," replied William. "You must rest as well. I want you home as soon as possible."

"Am I not coming home tomorrow?" asked Jennet, surprised. She had assumed that now that she was awake, she must not outstay her welcome any further.

"No," he replied with a resigned sigh. "Tomorrow the Lister's physician will visit you, but Master Thomas thinks he will recommend you remain at Westby Hall until you have recovered a little more. You are still very injured, as I'm sure you know. I wish you could come home sooner, Jennet. I don't like you being here, in this house, so close to him," he added, trying to choose his words carefully.

Jennet winced at the reminder of her sore belly, which was too painful still to move beyond a gentle shuffle. She could just about manage to sit, propped up as she had earlier, but walking was completely inconceivable. There was no possibility of her going home yet, no matter how much William wished it.

"How did I end up here?" Jennet asked, still trying to piece together everything that had happened.

"Did he not tell you?" asked William. "Master Thomas found you, unconscious and bleeding out there in the fields. He brought you here. He saved your life, Jennet."

The physician visited the following morning and, as predicted, recommended complete bed rest for Jennet for at least a couple of weeks. Jennet tried to protest, weakly, fearing that she was becoming a burden to the Listers; however, the physician was firm on the matter. She should not move from the bed, he said, and should only return home once she had recovered her strength.

"Two weeks!" William exclaimed once the physician had left. "I thought a week perhaps, but two? It's too much Jennet, it's too long."

For a while William paced up and down the room, mulling over the physician's words and making Jennet feel dizzy as she watched him helplessly from her bed. The thought of such a long stay at Westby had clearly agitated him, and Jennet knew that he would find the next fortnight excruciating, knowing that she was recuperating in such close proximity to the man she had fallen so hopelessly in love with as a girl. Right now, however, Jennet could not find the strength to care. She could think only about her own suffering; her painful belly, her dead child. After a while William left, telling her that he must attend to the farm for several hours, duty finally overcoming his paranoia. He promised that he would return in the evening to sit awhile with her. He would bring Anna, he said, to cheer her and because the child was driving her father and uncle mad asking to see her aunt. The housemaid, Anne, who had sat with Jennet for so many of her sleeping hours had now been relieved of her watch-woman duties and only returned briefly to bring her food and drink, and to help her use the bedpan, keeping strictly to her duties and refusing to engage in conversation. Now that she was a little more alert, Jennet realised that the familiar, peering woman must be Anne Robinson, who had been a girl like herself the last time they had met. The gossiping daughter of the old cook, Jennet thought bitterly, it was no wonder she was so churlish towards her.

For the hours in between Anne's surly visits, Jennet lay alone, despairing of her incapacity and wallowing in her grief. She blamed herself bitterly for the loss of the child. Despite Tom's assurances that the child had been too small, Jennet knew that the child had been almost fully grown, he should have lived. Jennet convinced herself that it did not survive because of her actions that day; the baby had arrived traumatically, drowned in blood and it was because of her. She had only been trying to help Elizabeth and her mother, she thought, how could an act of selflessness cost so much? She must be cursed; cursed by God to be punished eternally for the sins she had committed and any attempts at penance for those sins, any acts of kindness, would not be rewarded. Tears streamed down Jennet's flushed cheeks as she realised that there would never be any redemption for her.

"Jennet? Are you awake?" said a voice from outside the door, interrupting Jennet's thoughts.

"Yes," she replied. "Who's there?"

"It's me, it's Tom. I know Anne isn't with you, I know this isn't proper, but may I come in?" asked Tom.

"Yes, please come in," she replied, glad of the company to force her to suspend her self-pity.

Tom Lister walked in and Jennet drew a heavy breath. She was propped up in bed, looking and feeling terrible, her face a tear-stained and streaky mess, her belly barren and painful. Through all her suffering she could not ignore Tom Lister's utter beauty; his smile, his beard, his eyes, the chiselled refinement of age worn wonderfully on his kind face. William was right, she thought; she had spent so many years forcing Tom Lister to the back of her mind, trying to atone for her sins, trying to love her husband, to do her work, to have a family, and yet, he was always there. She had not seen him for years, but looking at him now, despite all her pain and grief, she felt the same affection, the same attraction, that she felt that night, a mere giddy girl on the way back to Westby Hall.

"How are you feeling?" Tom asked, clearly concerned. He perched himself on the chair next to the bed.

"Weary," Jennet replied, "but I will try to recover quickly and return home. I am so grateful for your kindness. William told me that it was you who saved me. He believes I would have died in that field if it hadn't been for you. But now that I am awake I must leave you as soon as possible, you have been so generous but I cannot burden myself on you and your family any longer than I must."

Tom shook his head in response. "I have paid the physician for your care until you are absolutely fit and well and ready to return home. You must not worry about being a burden, I would not see you home until you have completely recovered your strength," he insisted.

"Oh! The physician! I had not even considered his payment," Jennet exclaimed.

Tom put up his hand in response. "Do not worry about the physician. He has been paid, and will continue to be paid by me. You owe me nothing, Jennet. On the other hand, I owe you an enormous debt. I think we both know that. I hope that my recent actions will go some way towards making amends to you," Tom said, looking at Jennet meaningfully.

"Tom…" Jennet replied weakly, her voice trailing when she realised that she did not know what to say to him. She was that girl again, lost for words.

"Jennet, I was more responsible than you for what passed between us all those years ago. I came to your house, I made the advances. Yet you are the one who has suffered for it, in so many ways have you suffered. When I found you, lying in that field, I believe God was telling me that it was time to repair the damage between us," Tom said.

Jennet nodded, muted by his frankness. He spoke to her with such conviction. The Master of his estate, Tom Lister was a stuttering boy no longer. Taking her hand in the same tender way that she so fondly remembered, Tom looked into her eyes, his gaze bright blue and intense. He spoke with little more than a whisper.

"I have missed you all these years, Jennet. I just want you to know that. I have a good wife and wonderful children, but I wish you could have been at my side. Do not worry, I would not try to woo you all over again, we are both older and wiser, not to mention married! But, if you have ever felt sad about us over these past years, please know that I too have felt bereft of what we were not able to have."

He leaned over the bed and gently kissed Jennet, his beard bristling against her cheek, sending shivers down her spine.

"If you ever need anything, Jennet, you have only to ask. I will leave you to rest now."

Tom left the room, leaving Jennet feeling slightly stunned, lingering over his words. Once again, Tom had made her feel contrived: on the one hand, she was comforted that he had pined for her as she had for him, but on the other hand it was painful to acknowledge that this fact changed nothing. They both might be older and wiser but, Jennet reflected, neither of them had managed to reconcile themselves with the irretrievable loss of one another, they both just lived with the feeling of emptiness. After a short while she fell asleep, a deep peaceful slumber to rest her weary body and soul. When William and Anna arrived later that evening Jennet was still sleeping; dreaming about sunny childhood days down by the river with her friend Tom, days when life was not so complicated and painful. She heard both of her visitors speak to her but refused to wake, even when Anna tried to coax her with news from Blacko concerning Old Demdike. She stayed still, eyes closed, preferring to indulge herself in her fantasies of happier times, wanting to hide from the aching truth of her reality.

12

Malkin Tower, Blacko Hillside, Forest of Pendle
December 1598

The afternoon outside was cold but indoors, with so many people crammed into the Devices' home, Jennet felt cosy and warm. Cradling her cup of ale, Jennet watched as the children ran around wildly and the adults chattered, bursting into periodic laughter. It was quite a gathering that Demdike and the Devices had put together. For the first time in their friendship, Jennet appreciated that despite living on the apparent fringes of the local community, seemingly isolated on the Blacko slopes, the family actually had a considerable social circle. They also knew how to hold a good feast; the ale was good, the table was laden with delicious food, and Jennet had spent the day in great company, some familiar faces and some new. Amongst the plethora of guests at Malkin was Katherine Hewit, the clothier's wife, with Alice Gray, also from Colne, and Old Demdike's son Christopher Holgate with his wife and children.

Jennet's attention turned to Old Demdike, who was buzzing around the cottage like a queen bee, clearly enjoying herself and indulging her maternal affections for her son and Holgate grandchildren, of whom she saw little. Jennet reflected on how recovered the old woman looked, smiling and colour rising in her cheeks; incomparable with the pale, wallowing shadow she had been in the summer, cowering from the spectre of madness. By contrast, tonight she was enlivened, revelling in the festivities as though she might be a woman twenty years younger. Jennet smiled. These were the moments in life which she knew she should treasure; the carefree moments, free from hard work and sickness which she should cling to in life's more painful times.

"Are you alright, Jennet?" said a voice, interrupting her thoughts.

It was Elizabeth. Like Old Demdike, she too looked the picture of health, her eyes sparkling in the dancing candlelight, her usual shy demeanour suspended by plentiful ale and the company of good friends and family.

"Yes, just enjoying watching everyone, your mother especially. I was just thinking how well she looks tonight and how much she seems to be enjoying herself."

"Yes, it's hard to believe how ill she was a few months ago," replied Elizabeth, echoing her friend's thoughts. "She loves a feast, of course. She always rises to the occasion."

"It is a wonderful evening," Jennet said. "There's so much food and ale!"

"Well, yes," replied Elizabeth. "Our friends and neighbours are very kind. They often give Mother gifts at Christmastime. To thank her, I suppose."

Jennet nodded. She had been curious as to how the family had afforded all this food and drink; of course, gifts in kind were a logical explanation.

"Your William looks like he is making merry, just like my John. They've both had a belly full of ale," remarked Elizabeth, pausing then to consider her words. After a moment she spoke again.

"I am so glad he agreed to come tonight, Jennet. I know it has been difficult these past months, since…well, you know how sorry I am for what happened."

"Why should you be sorry?" replied Jennet.

"I feel it was my fault, what happened," confessed Elizabeth. "You must know that. I came to your door that day and asked you to come to Malkin when you were obviously in no fit state to do so. I am sure William holds me responsible and he would be right. I was terrified after it happened, firstly that you would die, and then when you didn't, that I wouldn't see you again because your husband would forbid it."

"My husband may blame you, Elizabeth, I can't pretend that he doesn't," she replied, biting her lip briefly at the memory of some of the dreadful things William had said about Elizabeth after Jennet had returned home. She shuddered, trying to suppress her thoughts. "William is not an unkind man," she continued. "He would not forbid me to see you."

Elizabeth looked at Jennet quizzically, as though trying to fathom the logic of what her friend was saying. Jennet, realising her friend did not understand her meaning, tried to press her point further.

"William knows that I feel sad, a lot of the time. The loss of our last child has been almost more than I could bear. When I awoke at Westby Hall, at first I wished that I hadn't, I wished I could sleep forever because living seemed too painful. However, as time has gone on I have learnt to live with my sadness, but only because I find solace in certain things; in my spinning, in Anna's company, in your company. Without you I would only be sadder and William is not cruel, he would not wish me to hurt any more than I already do," said Jennet. She recalled how she had broken down one afternoon as William had denounced her friendship with Elizabeth for the umpteenth time and how from then on, he had been forced to soften and accept it. She shuddered again, this time at the memory of how low her spirits had been.

Elizabeth nodded and smiled, reaching out and grabbing her friend's hand supportively. She frowned then, as though something still troubled her.

"Elizabeth?" Jennet asked. "What is it?"

"I understand that I am a comfort to you, Jennet, as you are always to me. But I don't understand how. After what happened, surely you must blame me? Am I not a reminder of what happened, whenever you look upon me?" Elizabeth asked, as though finally lifting a weight from her shoulders which had been troubling her.

"No, Elizabeth, I do not blame you. I cannot blame you. You came to me as a friend, for help. You were desperate, your mother was ill. I would have done the same thing in your position and as your friend I came to your aid, as any good friend should. I didn't lose the child because of you," Jennet bit her lip again, fighting back tears. "I lost the child because of me. It was my fault."

"Oh Jennet," exclaimed Elizabeth, putting a comforting arm around her friend's shoulder. "How could it possibly be your fault?"

"I am being punished by God," replied Jennet, with a slight sob.

Elizabeth sighed, and guided her friend away to a quieter corner of the cottage, away from prying ears.

"I always knew there was a story, Jennet," she said. "Now, will you tell me all about it, because I think you need to tell someone."

Before Jennet could stop herself, the whole sorry tale poured forth from her lips: how Tom Lister had wooed her that night, how she had allowed herself to be swept away with it all and in her foolishness, how she had been shamed and become the talk of the village. Despite her marriage to William, arranged to salvage what remained of her virtue, she explained, she had been something of an outcast in Gisburn ever since, lonely and unable to bear children, a fitting punishment from God, surely. Elizabeth listened silently to the whole story, her face bearing little expression other than intent concentration. Only when Jennet had finished, did Elizabeth move to speak.

"I don't think you did anything all that terrible," she said quite plainly, although clearly not without careful consideration of her words.

Jennet was incredulous, muted by her surprise. She stared in disbelief at her friend as she continued.

"I know women who have done far worse things with men before marriage, who have borne little or no apparent punishment from God. My mother for one! Christopher and I do not share the same father, as well you know, and she was not married when she bore him. Yet Christopher was born, alive and well, and Mother did not suffer any pains from God for it. You didn't even lie with Master Lister, Jennet, you shared a brief romance is all. Your virtue was intact when you married William. It is wrong that anyone should have made you to feel such shame for what? A kiss? A kiss and no more."

Jennet could not believe her ears. At first she wanted to argue but then, as she thought about it, she began to realise that Elizabeth was right. Everyone had made her feel ashamed of herself; her mother and father while they lived, her brothers, even William, especially William. She had carried this shame about with her for years, feeling its punitive weight upon her back, and now, for the first time, someone had raised it slightly from her and tried to put her grave sins in some sort of perspective.

"Jennet," Elizabeth continued, "I think if anyone is punishing you, it is yourself. Now, if you told my mother your story, she might say that you were cursed, but by a witch, not God. This is always possible, we cannot rule it out. If you upset the local folk as you say you did, someone may have had a curse put upon you. This would explain the loss of so many children and I will speak to Mother for you about a remedy for this. I think that you do not help yourself, you need to let go of Tom Lister, let go of the guilt you feel about what happened, and focus all your efforts on William and having a child together, before it really is too late."

Jennet nodded. She wasn't sure about a witch's curse, this was something she had never really considered; however, she trusted Demdike's judgement on these matters and if there was something she could do to help her, then so be it. Elizabeth was right about one thing, though: she had punished herself for all of her married life and perhaps it was time to stop.

"It's quite romantic, though, isn't it?" said Elizabeth suddenly, with a mischievous grin.

"What is?" asked Jennet.

"Master Lister coming on horseback to save your life, sweeping you up and taking you back to Westby. Then paying for the physician and seeing you nursed back to health," giggled Elizabeth.

"Yes, I suppose it is," replied Jennet, resolving to say nothing about Tom's bedside confessions. Elizabeth was a dear friend, but if Jennet was ever going to move beyond the spectre of Tom Lister, she knew she had to forget that the conversation between them ever took place.

The feast began to dwindle towards its end that evening, and as night came many of the guests made their way home from Malkin Tower. Jennet had decided to stay the night at Elizabeth's home and travel back to Gisburn the following day. Elizabeth would surely need the help, she had told William, since her mother was elderly, her husband was drunk, the children were so young and the cottage, frankly, was in a state of chaos following its occupation by so many people. William had agreed and had left a little while earlier, taking Anna and his brother with him. Since then Jennet had set about tidying up the cottage, leaving Elizabeth to attend to the children while both her husband and mother snored loudly in their chairs. By the time the children had settled and the cottage had returned to some semblance of normality, it was very late indeed.

"I am tired now," sighed Jennet, slumping into a chair.

"It's very late," remarked Elizabeth, sitting down beside her. "Thank you for all your help this evening, Jennet."

"You're a good lass. You've had a hard time of it, harder than you should," interjected Old Demdike, sleepily opening one eye at a time. "Elizabeth told me all about your troubles earlier. I am glad you told her. We always knew you had a story, but now that we know what it is, perhaps we can help you."

"Mother thinks you may have been cursed," said Elizabeth, "if you really upset people in the village, not to mention the Listers, as much as you believe you did."

"Hmm," mused Jennet, half in agreement.

For the first time, she thought seriously about who might have felt so wounded by her offence as to inflict such a grave punishment upon her. Certainly, Tom Lister's mother had been greatly angered by what had happened; however, she was a highly unlikely candidate. Everyone in the village and beyond knew that Alice Lister was a devout follower of the old faith; this was so well known that she had been reported to the authorities for it and had been forced to pay fines. A woman so filled with religious conviction to continue to follow the Pope despite all the risks associated with her choice surely wouldn't become involved with witchcraft, whatever her quarrel. Beyond Alice Lister, though, Jennet struggled to identify one face in the disapproving crowd in Gisburn who could have done this to her. After the gossip spread from Westby Hall, Jennet's condemnation was near-universal. Jennet gasped. The gossip, mostly spread by Mrs Robinson and her daughter Anne, the same Anne who treated her with such contempt during her recent stay at the great hall. Jennet's mind conjured the image of Anne's spiteful, putrid face, her sneering mouth, her peering eyes, oozing with contempt even after all these years. If Jennet could imagine anyone in Gisburn bearing her such malice as to curse her, it would be Anne Robinson.

"It doesn't really matter who arranged for the curse to be placed upon you, although it would be helpful to know the name of the witch who did their bidding. But after all these years it's unlikely that we should find out the answer and there are too many witches roaming about these parts to even take a guess," said Demdike. "What matters now is how we deal with the curse. This is where I can help you, lass."

Old Demdike heaved her weary old bones out of the chair in which she was sitting and walked over to the corner of the room. When she returned, she was clutching a small bottle. It was an oddly shaped object, with a bulbous bottom and a straight funnel to its top. Old Demdike handed the bottle to Jennet, rattling its contents slightly as she did so.

"The bottle already contains a handful of pins. I need you to add a strand or two of your hair, and some of your water. If you're able to use the pot just now then that would be helpful, if not we can do this in the morning," said Demdike.

"I can do so now," replied Jennet, leaving the room.

She returned a few moments later with the pot, feeling glad that John was still snoring loudly, oblivious to their conversation. On the other hand, she thought, since this was the trade which Old Demdike plied, John was likely accustomed to hearing discussions of urine and all manner of other bodily secretions used for Demdike's remedies.

Demdike took the pot and emptied some of its contents into the bottle. Jennet plucked a couple of strands of her hair and handed them to Demdike, who added them to the concoction. Demdike then sealed the bottle, held it solemnly before her, and uttered what Jennet could only assume was a charm, or some sort of protection spell.

"Three biters hast thou bitten. The heart, the eye, the tongue," said Demdike. "Three bitter shall be thy boot. Father, Son and Holy Ghost in God's name. Five Pater Nosters, five Aves and a creed, in worship of the five wounds of our Lord."

Demdike made the sign of the cross across her chest, a symbolic act which made Jennet wince slightly, as it was so rarely seen nowadays and was frowned upon by many. She then carefully handed the bottle to Jennet.

"This is a witch bottle, Jennet. It will afford you protection against the witch's curse, as well as hopefully bringing some harm to the witch herself. You must bury it somewhere around your house, preferably within the walls themselves, if not there then the ground will do. Once you do this, you will be protected for as long as the bottle remains there," Demdike advised.

Jennet nodded in agreement. She was still in some disbelief that she could be under a witch's spell; she had spent so long believing that her hardships were the result of divine punishment that it was hard to think about her misfortune any other way. However, she did not doubt Demdike's skill and ability as a cunning woman and therefore resolved to trust her judgement. If Demdike thought she was cursed, then she probably was.

"Thank you, Mother Demdike," said Jennet. "Is it true what you say, that there are many witches around these parts?"

"Oh yes," replied Demdike. "Just look what happened to the Starkey children, driven mad by a witch's curse. Edmund Hartley suffered the pains for it, as you know, but the real witch is probably still out there, along with many others."

Jennet was wide-eyed, incredulous. "Have you ever encountered a witch in the flesh, in the course of your work?" she asked.

Demdike and Elizabeth looked at one another, nodding in agreement as they did so.

"Chattox," Demdike replied. "I must tell you about Chattox."

Tired though they were, the three women sat up late into the night as Demdike and Elizabeth both relayed stories to Jennet about the witch Chattox; confusing, long-winded stories involving people Jennet had never heard of, complicated family connections and even more complex quarrels between them. Chattox, Demdike explained, was the name given to a local woman named Anne Whittle, a woman from West Close with whom Demdike had once been close friends. Before she was widowed, Demdike too had lived at West Close, just below the village of Higham, and for a long time Demdike had regarded Chattox as a sort of apprentice, teaching the woman many of her skills. The pair had grown apart somewhat after Demdike and her children left the West Close area for Blacko after the death of her husband, although Demdike still regarded her affectionately and visited her from time to time.

A few years ago, Demdike began to hear unpleasant tales about Chattox and her daughter Anne Redfearn. Despite being a married woman, Anne was rumoured to have had some sort of dalliance with one of their neighbours, a man called Robert Nutter. Elizabeth interjected that she had heard that the relationship had soured and Anne, feeling like the woman scorned, had instructed her mother to place a curse upon the young man. The result was that, by the following Candlemas, Robert Nutter was dead, and his father, Christopher, followed him to the grave just months later. Demdike was appalled by the reports of her old friend using her skills for such ill purposes; moreover the Nutters were Demdike's relatives through marriage so the attack on them felt personal. In a rage, she had gone to West Close to confront Chattox but found no remorse from either herself or her daughter, who both admitted their crimes but defended them; Anne claimed that Robert Nutter had forced himself upon her and that the curse was placed in revenge for his attack upon her virtue. In anger, Chattox and her daughter began hurling insults at poor Demdike, who had fled from West Close and never spoken to either of them since. To this day, however, she still heard tales of their misdeeds in that part of Pendle; the residents of West Close apparently treading on egg shells in their dealings with Chattox and her family, daring not to offend them for fear of meeting the same end as the Nutters.

"Did you not consider going to the Sheriff?" Jennet asked, when Demdike eventually paused for thought.

"Lass, I taught Anne Whittle all she knows. If she was sent to the gallows for witchcraft, then surely I would follow her. Who is to say that I too have not been using my skills for ill? I ply a dangerous trade. There are those who regard cunning work and witchcraft as one and the same; someone like Chattox proves that it is just as easy to use these skills for ill as it is to do good," Demdike replied.

Jennet nodded in agreement. Demdike's reasoning was sensible, but then someone could not survive as long as she had, doing the work she had been undertaking, by being irrational and hot-headed. Nonetheless, it was nothing short of amazing that, if this witch Chattox was so notorious, no one had ever thought to make a complaint to the Sheriff. Perhaps, Jennet thought, this was testament to the extent to which people feared her; her power was considered to be beyond the Sheriff's reckoning, above the law even. Jennet, her thoughts running away from her, began to wonder if Chattox's abilities had surpassed even those of her former mentor.

"Do you think Chattox could have been responsible for your illness, Mother Demdike?" Jennet asked.

Demdike chuckled at the idea, clearly unperturbed. "Oh goodness, no. That wasn't Chattox, it was Tibb," replied Demdike.

"Who is Tibb, mother?" asked Elizabeth, jumping in before Jennet could ask the question. Jennet had a feeling that this was a question Elizabeth had wanted to ask her mother for some time.

"Tibb is…hard to explain," replied Demdike. "He comes sometimes, and shows me things. He is like a spirit, except that I don't know where he came from because I have never invoked the spirits like Edmund Hartley did with his circle. The first time I met him he appeared as a man, a handsome young man at that, at a stone pit near Goldshey. At that first meeting we talked a little and he said he may be able to help me from time to time, at the time I didn't really grasp his meaning. When I saw him again on that Sunday morning, when he appeared to me as a dog, I will admit he did frighten me; he was aggressive and he showed me things which I didn't really wish to see."

"Why did he take the form of a dog?" Jennet asked.

Demdike shrugged in response. "Spirits seem to like the animal form. Like the one we saw that night at Edmund Hartley's circle, do you remember him? The little black dog, staying close to the circle, looking for the master who invoked him. But that's what's strange about Tibb, I never called him to me, yet he comes and shows me things, sometimes terrible things," Demdike said, with a shudder.

"What did he show you, Mother?" asked Elizabeth. "It must have been dreadful, to make you so ill for so many weeks. It was almost two months before you fully recovered from it."

Demdike looked at Elizabeth, then Jennet, eyeing them both sombrely.

"Death," she replied. "He showed me death."

13

St Mary's Church, Newchurch-in-Pendle
May 1599

Jennet lowered her gaze as the small casket was placed gently in the ground. It was a grey day in late spring, so dull in fact that only the milder air betrayed to them that it wasn't winter. A fitting day for a funeral, she thought. Standing next to William, his arm placed comfortingly around her shoulder, she could hear the soft, mournful sobs of her friend Elizabeth, her shoulders shuddering in tandem with her tears. Jennet could not begin to understand the depths of her grief; even though she had lost many babies and still mourned for them every day, she could not even begin to imagine how it must feel to bear a child, to nurture him, to watch him grow and flourish, and then to lose him. Jennet wished she could reach out to her friend and do something for her, to beg God to bring her child back to her, but as she watched the first fistfuls of dirt being flung on top of the coffin, she knew that wishing was futile. Little Henry was dead and gone and nothing could rouse him now; nothing could take away his mother's pain.

Henry's sickness had begun benignly enough. He coughed a lot and seemed a little weary, but Demdike and Elizabeth hadn't worried at first. Childhood illness is common, Demdike had said, with a little rest and a few well-chosen remedies it will pass. However, as the days wore on the child only grew sicker; he became feverish and listless, slipping in and out of consciousness and disinterested in either food or drink. By the time a week had passed and his condition had not improved, Elizabeth and Demdike both began to fear the worst, and though Demdike persevered with her remedies it became clear that she could not help him. Then, two nights ago, as his mother slept by his side, holding his small hand in hers, little Henry had finally slipped away, his hot little body exhausted by the effort of breathing, his will to live finally defeated by illness.

"Come," whispered William. "There's nothing more we can do now."

Jennet turned to leave with her husband. He was right, there was nothing they could do, and as much as she loved Elizabeth and wanted to help her, she knew that she must leave her with her family, to begin to deal together with their grief.

"Jennet, are you leaving?" said a voice behind her.

It was John Device, Elizabeth's husband, the placid older man who, despite his wife's closeness with Jennet, had always assumed an air of quiet distance and had never had much to say to her.

"Yes," replied Jennet, softly. "We thought we should leave you all in peace. We will go back to Gisburn this afternoon."

"Peace! Elizabeth shall have no peace, I know that. The poor child is barely cold and is she already tortured by his death, trying to find a way to blame herself," said John, his tone both desperate and mournful. "She needs her friend, Jennet," he continued, uncharacteristically venturing to place a hand on her arm. "Please come back to Malkin Tower and be at her side. I can't comfort her like you can. She needs you, even if in her grief she will not admit it."

Jennet looked to William, who was standing beside her, helplessly. She could see in his eyes that he could not understand what his wife would be able to do, but he knew that he could hardly prevent her from going to Malkin Tower, even if he wished to. William had learnt some time ago that nothing could come between Jennet and Elizabeth, not even him. After a moment's consideration, he simply shrugged.

"Go if you must, Jennet," he said with a sigh. "I will return to Gisburn, I have work to do."

His tone was coarse, but Jennet chose to ignore him. She could not understand how, given the circumstances, he could possibly object to John Device's plea for help. Bidding William goodbye and without giving any indication of when she intended to return to Gisburn, Jennet took her horse and headed for Malkin Tower.

The atmosphere at Malkin Tower was quiet and sombre. Of course this was to be expected, Jennet thought, but nonetheless it was in stark contrast to the usual busy, happy home that she had come to know and love. Even the children, Alison and James, were uncharacteristically calm and quiet, evidently trying to come to terms with the loss of their little brother. James sat next to his father, their jaws both set hard as though trying to prevent tears. Little Alison, meanwhile, clung to her grandmother's lap, sobbing periodically into Old Demdike's chest. Demdike was quiet, drifting in and out of consciousness as she so often did in the afternoons, whilst trying to comfort the child. Jennet sat with Elizabeth, who was still and silent, staring into an apparent abyss in front of her. She seemed to be in shock, Jennet thought, as though she could not quite believe that she had just been to church and buried her child. Jennet thought about all the emotions she had drifted through each time she had lost a baby; shock and disbelief, denial and sorrow. She looked at her friend and felt helpless, wishing she could take her pain away. Perhaps William had been right; it was useless her being here, she could not help.

"Elizabeth," she said gently. "Can I get you anything? A drink, perhaps?"

Elizabeth looked at Jennet, and simply shook her head. They continued to sit there, in silence, for what seemed like an eternity. Jennet didn't know whether to stay or leave, she was at a loss as to what to do for the best. Perhaps, despite John's insistence that she come, she was actually being a hindrance to Elizabeth, perhaps her friend really did just need to be with her family, to come to terms with her grief in private. With this thought in her mind, Jennet was just about to stand up and excuse herself to return to Gisburn, when Elizabeth flew out of her seat and fled towards the door.

"I'm sorry, I can't just sit here anymore!" she exclaimed, tears streaming down her face.

Elizabeth turned and ran out of the cottage. Jennet, John and Demdike all looked at one another in surprise. John began to rise from his seat to go after his wife.

"No," said Demdike firmly, bidding him to sit back down. The old woman gestured towards Jennet. "You go after her, lass," she said.

If Jennet had not been so concerned for her friend, she would have wondered about why Demdike had asked her to go and not John, and why John had been so complicit with the old matriarch and had done as she asked, without any objection. In this world, men so rarely did as women asked, but then Demdike's family was hardly typical. As it was, Jennet had no time to reflect on these matters; she had to find Elizabeth, whose state of mind was clearly frail. Jennet headed out of the door of the cottage to find her friend. The day outside was bleak, the spring rain drizzling down lightly but thoroughly, quickly soaking her clothing. The sky above was grey and pallid, making the usually picturesque Blacko landscape appear appropriately miserable. Jennet squinted, trying to prevent water from rolling into her eyes, and walked around the cottage, looking for Elizabeth.

"Elizabeth!" she called out, her voice echoing across the hillside but not receiving a reply.

Jennet stood quietly, listening. She didn't think Elizabeth could have gone far. Dotted around the outside of Malkin Tower there were several small, semi-derelict buildings, perhaps used once to house animals. The rain was growing heavier and Jennet ventured that her friend may have sought some shelter within one of them.

She headed for the first, and largest building; a pile of stone in such a state of decay that it barely had a roof upon it. Jennet slipped in through a gap in the masonry where there had likely once been a door. Inside, it was damp and cold. Jennet shivered.

"Elizabeth?" she asked, softly.

"Over here," called a voice in reply.

Elizabeth's voice came from a dark corner, behind a large pile of stone and timber. In the dim light, Jennet clambered carefully over to her friend who sat, shivering and sobbing. Jennet sat down beside Elizabeth and placed an arm around her shoulder.

"Oh, Elizabeth, you will catch your death of cold out here," said Jennet. "Come back inside, I will stay with you, I will stay as long as you need me to."

"My dear Jennet, you're so kind," replied Elizabeth, grabbing hold of her friend's hand tightly. "But I can't bear to go back there. How can I go in there and carry on, when my little Henry is dead?"

"Elizabeth, you have two other children who you must care for, you must carry on for them. I can't imagine how much pain you must be feeling right now, but James and Alison love you and they are mourning for their little brother too. They need you. You must know that."

Elizabeth nodded in agreement, wiping her eyes and nose with the back of her hand; a futile act, since as soon as she dried her eyes, more tears welled within them, spilling down on to her cheeks. Jennet hugged her friend tighter.

"You mustn't blame yourself," Jennet continued. "Henry's death was not your fault. He was ill, and he was young, and too often young children succumb to sickness. You did everything you could for him, Elizabeth."

Elizabeth stopped sobbing and looked at Jennet squarely. "I don't blame myself," she replied. "I blame John. It's his fault that Henry is dead."

"John? What, your husband?" Jennet asked, confused. "What did John do?"

Elizabeth flashed Jennet a sour smile. It was the first time that

Jennet had ever seen such a look pass across her friend's face, and it alarmed her. It was more than grief, Jennet thought, Elizabeth was angry, bitter even, her face twisted with poisonous thoughts.

"It turns out that John has been paying that witch Chattox for protection! Almost ten years we have been married, and in all that time he has been giving that woman oatmeal every year in payment for…well, goodness knows what, really! I mean, after he married me, what did he think that woman could offer him that my mother couldn't? I am so angry, Jennet. I feel foolish, and betrayed. Mother is right; you can't trust men to do right by you! I was a fool to marry him," Elizabeth said, spitting her words.

Jennet was both aghast and confused by what she was hearing. How did this arrangement come to pass in the first place and what was it really for? It made no sense. As Elizabeth pointed out, his mother in law was probably the most powerful cunning woman in Pendle, whilst Chattox was her mere former apprentice. Surely any man with sense would have employed the protection of family for free rather than paying for the services of another? And how did any of this relate to the death of poor, unfortunate little Henry?

"I don't understand," replied Jennet, unable to articulate the rush of questions swirling around her head.

"Nor do I," quipped Elizabeth, with another embittered chuckle. "He says when he first lived near West Close, before he married me, he was harassed by Bessie Whittle, Chattox's other daughter, a notorious thief with a vile temper. She's quite the thing, you know, like no other woman you've ever seen. Anyway, he claims he paid Chattox the oatmeal in return for her warning off Bessie and the arrangement has stood ever since, continuing even after we left our smallholding to live here."

"Ah, I see," said Jennet. "That does make sense now. He's not paying for cunning work; he's paying her to keep her daughter away from you all."

"Does it make sense, though?" asked Elizabeth. "Why continue to pay her after marrying me, and after moving to Malkin? Surely the threat of my mother, not to mention being at a greater distance away from them all, would have been enough to justify ceasing payment? But no, he continued to pay her like the coward he is. Or, his whole explanation is complete fabrication, maybe he's been lying with Anne Redfearne all this time and the oatmeal was a bribe, to buy her silence. She's certainly the sort for it, to take her pleasure and payment."

"Elizabeth!" Jennet exclaimed. "You can't surely believe that! John loves you!"

"Aye," she replied coarsely, pointing at her face. "He loves his squinting Lizzy. That's what they call me, you know, round these parts. I thought no man could love me because of my face and perhaps, after all, I was right."

Elizabeth buried her head in her hands, her back heaving with great, heavy sobs. Jennet hugged her closer, shushing her as though she was a child.

"Come now, this talk will do you no good," Jennet said. "You are my beautiful friend, whatever men may say, and I hate to see you beside yourself like this." Jennet paused for a moment, considering her words. "Forgive me, I understand how angry you are with John and rightly so, but I still don't understand what all this has to do with your poor Henry."

"Because he stopped paying her! I found out about his arrangement and forced him to stop paying Chattox right away. He did so and now my Henry is dead. Chattox must have cursed us all in vengeance and my little Henry has paid the price. He has paid for his father's deceit and cowardice and now I cannot even look at John, let alone share his bed," Elizabeth replied, the tears tumbling down her cheeks once again.

Jennet held her friend tightly, letting her sob woefully into her chest. It all made sense now, Jennet thought. It was little wonder that John had wanted her to come today to offer comfort to Elizabeth which he, plainly, could not give. It was also why he had not challenged Demdike in the slightest when she had ordered him to sit back down and had sent Jennet after Elizabeth in his stead. Despite the enormous wrong that he had obviously done to his wife, Jennet could not help but feel pity for John Device; whatever his actions he did not intend for his son to die, and he must have been feeling his loss just as keenly. She did not convey these thoughts to Elizabeth, of course, because her measured sympathy would do her friend no good. Instead she just sat there, comforting her in that damp shack for what felt like hours. Eventually, when it was growing dark and colder, and Jennet longed for a warm blanket and a cup of ale, she moved to speak.

"Elizabeth, I know you say you cannot face it, but you must come back inside. It is growing dark and the children will want you. Come, let's go and see them now."

Elizabeth nodded with resignation and Jennet helped her to stand. Seeming as frail physically as she was emotionally, it took a moment for Elizabeth to steady herself on her feet. As they reached the gap in the stonework which served as an exit, Elizabeth paused for a final time to speak to her friend.

"You're right, Jennet, I know I must carry on. I will care for my mother and raise the two children I have left, just as I did before. But I will not speak to, nor lie next to John Device, ever again. My husband is dead to me. Should he ever ask you how I feel about him, you may tell him what I said."

Jennet shuddered at her friend's words: John was dead to her. Death. There seemed to be far too much death surrounding the Device family, it was as though it was following them around. Firstly, Tibb had visited Demdike merely a year ago, plaguing her with visions of death, about which she was still unable to speak. Now, young Henry was dead and Elizabeth was consigning her marriage to the grave. Too much death and perhaps, thought Jennet, if Chattox really was behind all of this, there was still more to come.

14

Malkin Tower, Blacko Hillside, Forest of Pendle
October 1600

Jennet mopped Elizabeth's brow with a cool cloth, trying to calm her and keep her comfortable as she moaned in response to her pain. She watched as Elizabeth's face became distorted by her discomfort then relaxed again as the pain passed. She tried to time her words of encouragement between the pains, when she felt her friend was more lucid. Jennet found it hard to hide her fascination; despite having passed her thirtieth year, Jennet had never seen a woman in child-bed before. She had been the last child her own mother had borne, and her only personal experience was the loss of a multitude of premature infants. Acutely aware of her inexperience, Jennet frantically tended to Elizabeth's hot brow and cheeks until, clearly irritated, the groaning woman swept her hand away.

"Don't mind her," said Demdike, trying to reassure her. "The child will not be far away now if she's starting to feel that way."

"Good," replied Jennet. "She seems to have been suffering the pains for a long time now."

"Oh, lass," chuckled Demdike. "You should have seen her when she was having James; it seemed to go on for days. This one has been quite quick, she has been lucky so far."

Jennet looked down at Elizabeth, whose eyes were shut as though she was trying to sleep in between the waves of pain sweeping over her. In that moment of calm, Jennet said a quick prayer to herself, begging God for the safe delivery of the baby. It had been a difficult time for Elizabeth since Henry's death over a year ago and Jennet feared she would not survive the loss of this child. For months after Henry's death Elizabeth had seemed lost to her grief, fluctuating between tears of sorrow and a despairing silence. She barely spoke to anyone, and true to her word she steadfastly ignored her husband John, regarding him only with angry, silent glances.

However, as the summer had turned to autumn, then winter, the mist which had come over her seemed to clear a little, and Elizabeth's mood became less mournful and she began to seem more like her old self again. Having fretted about her friend for months, Jennet had breathed a heavy sigh of relief that the worst of her grief seemed to have passed. Her concern, however, was not suspended for long. One cold day in January, not long after Christmas, Jennet had made the journey over to Malkin to see her friend. It was rare for her to visit in the depths of winter; however, since Henry's death her visits had been more frequent and often unannounced, and the absence of snow that particular winter meant that the journey was no great hardship on horseback.

In any event, Elizabeth had clearly not been expecting her friend to visit that day. As Jennet tethered her horse to her usual tree and headed for the front door, she could hear odd, muffled noises coming from one of the derelict outbuildings, in fact the very same building in which Jennet and Elizabeth had spent so many hours on the day of Henry's funeral. Fearing that the Devices had intruders, Jennet tiptoed over to the building to see who was in there. Peering around the corner, Jennet could see two figures up against one of the crumbling walls. As Jennet forced her eyes to focus better in the dim light, she saw that one of the figures was in fact Elizabeth, her skirts lifted high, her head thrown back whilst the other figure, presumably a man judging by his build and the apparent situation, pushed himself upon her, grunting. Jennet gasped as she realised that this man was not John Device; although the light was poor she could tell that he was much taller, and in any case she seriously doubted Elizabeth's ageing husband's capacity to have his way with her, standing up against a wall like this. Poor John had been ailing and was likely inside Malkin Tower, blissfully unaware of the infidelity taking place so nearby.

"Jennet!" Elizabeth exclaimed, before Jennet had time to decide whether she was going to make her presence known or creep away, unseen. Elizabeth pushed the man away from her and, frantically pulling her skirts down, ran towards her friend.

"Jennet! Oh Jennet I am sorry you saw that. I have wanted to tell you so many times recently about all this, but I knew what you would say. I feared you would judge me," said Elizabeth, her shame evident.

"Only God can judge you," replied Jennet, regretting her harsh words the moment she uttered them.

"God! The God who gave me a coward for a husband, the God who stood by while my poor Henry was bewitched to death. Forgive me Jennet, but I don't feel very close to God right now," Elizabeth quipped defensively.

"No, of course you don't," replied Jennet apologetically. "I am sorry; I should not have said that. I don't judge you, Elizabeth, but I worry for you. I know you have endured a lot these past months, but are you sure about what you're doing?"

Jennet eyed the man who was still hovering beside the wall, looking uncomfortable. Clearing his throat, he stepped forward. In the better light, Jennet was able to scrutinise him. He was indeed very tall, with dark hair and dark brown eyes. Jennet judged him to be no more than thirty years old and he was very handsome. She could certainly see why, on appearance alone, grief-stricken Elizabeth had allowed herself to become smitten with this man. The question was, Jennet pondered, what exactly did he want from Elizabeth, other than his pleasure of course?

"Richard Sellers," he said, extending his hand to Jennet.

Jennet did not accept his gesture, returning instead to speak to Elizabeth.

"So, when did all this begin?" she demanded to know.

"Before Christmas," Elizabeth replied, hanging her head a little as she spoke, as though she was a child being reprimanded for stealing bread. "I have known Richard for a long time. We are neighbours; he farms just east of here, at White Moor. He knows all about my troubles and offered me some comfort. Things just developed from there, really."

"Are you married?" Jennet asked the man, addressing him abruptly.

Richard shook his head in response, prompting a sneer from Jennet.

"It's easy for the unmarried man to take his pleasure with another man's wife, is it not?" Jennet asked him, not expecting a response to her question.

"Jennet, I know what I am doing," Elizabeth insisted. "I no longer love John. I cannot love John. He is well aware that I have begun a, well, whatever you want to call it, with Richard, I haven't hidden it from him and yet he doesn't try to fight for me; he is too weak and too cowardly. He has also given up on our marriage, and I often wonder if he will just leave Malkin Tower for good."

Jennet was aghast at what she was hearing. "What does your mother say?" she asked.

"Not much. She doesn't approve, I don't think, but she is hardly in a position to judge. She has done some things in her time, believe me. I think that at the moment, she is just glad to see me happy again. Which I am, Jennet; I am happy. This makes me happy."

At that moment, Jennet had wanted to scream at Elizabeth. It was lustful and sinful to find such pleasure in the flesh, let alone the flesh of a man other than your husband. No good could come of it, only God's wrath and surely eternal damnation; anyone who attended church, even if only occasionally, would know that. She knew, however, that it was pointless to say these things to Elizabeth, as they did not seem to matter to her in the same way they mattered to Jennet. That much had been clear ever since that night a few years ago at Christmas, when Elizabeth had brushed off Jennet's years of guilt over her behaviour with Tom Lister as a mere triviality. Instead, Jennet had only cautioned her to be careful and reminded her how likely it was that her behaviour would result in a child.

Sure enough, Jennet had been right and as springtime arrived once again and the first anniversary of Henry's death loomed, Elizabeth had discovered that she was indeed with child. At the same time she also found herself without a husband who, as predicted, did leave Malkin Tower, but perhaps not in the way that Elizabeth had expected. Poor John Device finally succumbed to his various ailments and died, quietly and without complaint, just as he had lived his life. Jennet reflected that his funeral had been an odd affair; upon his death Elizabeth had seemed almost relieved, stating that it was likely the work of Chattox and therefore, with John's demise, she hoped their misfortunes had finally come to an end. Yet, by the time the funeral came around she seemed almost to have had a change of heart and transformed into the grief-stricken widow at his graveside. To see her, Jennet thought, you would have taken her for the devoted wife, not one who had not spoken to her husband for almost a year.

Perhaps, Jennet thought, with John's passing Elizabeth had discovered some guilt of her own; indeed, after his death she swiftly put aside Richard Sellers. In fairness to Richard, when he had found out that Elizabeth was with child he had endeavoured to behave honourably, recognising the child as his own and promising that the child would not be left wanting on his account. Elizabeth had told Jennet afterwards that she had thanked him for his kindness, and would accept whatever he was willing to give towards raising the child; however, she had made it clear that she wasn't looking for another husband. She never explained why and Jennet didn't ask, presuming it was either due to guilt or simply a realisation that she didn't actually love him. In any case, as spring became summer and Elizabeth's belly began to bloom like the flowers in the sun, the focus and excitement of everyone at Malkin Tower was the anticipated arrival of a new child.

That night, the child was finally on its way. In the flickering candlelight, Jennet saw Elizabeth screw up her face tightly, a grunting noise passing from her pursed lips as she responded to some uncontrollable urge within herself.

"That's it, that's it," said her mother, lifting Elizabeth's skirts out of the way, anticipating the baby's arrival into the world. "Jennet, can you help please? My eyes are not what they were," she whispered.

Elizabeth grunted again, this time more loudly, her usually pale face growing flushed with the effort. Then, all at once she relaxed her entire self and, without a moment's hesitation, Old Demdike carefully scooped up a crying infant from beneath her, gently wrapping the child in a shawl and handing the baby to Jennet.

"It's a girl," Jennet announced, her voice a stunned whisper, before handing the baby to her exhausted mother.

Elizabeth looked down lovingly at her new child. Jennet stayed beside her, watching these first few precious moments passing between mother and daughter. She felt so happy she could weep; after everything that had happened to Elizabeth, she deserved some joy. Jennet silently thanked God for bringing the child safely to them, despite the baby being conceived in sin. Perhaps he was a forgiving God after all.

"She is so beautiful, Elizabeth," whispered Jennet.

Elizabeth nodded in agreement, a wave of pain passing over her face as she did so.

"Elizabeth?" said Jennet, panicking slightly, feeling sure that the pain should all be over by now.

"Don't worry about her, Jennet, it's an after pain is all, brings out all the rest of what the body no longer needs," Old Demdike informed her, scooping up something large and bloodied and taking it away with her. "I think that's all of it now," she said, returning to check with the aid of a closely held candle to compensate for her failing eyesight.

"I'm going to call her Jennet," said Elizabeth, relaxing again and putting the baby to her breast.

"Oh, Elizabeth…" began Jennet, her words failing her.

"I am naming her after my dearest friend," continued Elizabeth. "I just hope that one day you may have the joy of bearing a daughter."

Jennet fell silent. Throughout these past months of Elizabeth's pregnancy, watching her belly become larger as the baby grew, and move as the baby kicked, and throughout these hours of her labouring to bring the child into the world, Jennet had tried to focus entirely on her friend, trying to resist thinking about her own empty womb, her own heavy heart. Now, Elizabeth's words, kind and well-intended though they were, brought all those emotions to the fore. Jennet shed a solitary tear.

"Oh Jennet, I am sorry, I didn't mean to upset you," said Elizabeth, apologetically.

"No, I'm sorry," replied Jennet, wiping her eyes. "There's no need for me to be shedding tears. I am so very happy for you Elizabeth. I had hoped that I may carry a child that will live but since the last time, and despite your mother's remedy…well, nothing has happened. I think I have to accept that the time for children has passed for me."

"My remedies can only do so much," interjected Demdike. "Babies will only occur if you lie with your husband, Jennet."

Jennet was grateful that the dim candlelight would not betray the slight reddening of her cheeks. Old Demdike was so wily and perceptive, and of course, she was right. Jennet struggled to admit it even to herself, but despite her longing for a child, she found it increasingly difficult to want to lie with William. It was ironic really; since she lost the last child William had been kind and attentive, he had tolerated her friendships and had borne her frequent trips to Malkin Tower without complaint. Yet, despite all his efforts Jennet felt distant from him; she had always known that their marriage had been arranged for the convenience of her family, that he had been her best option at the time; however, she had always endeavoured to feel affection for him, and to make the best of it. Now, after all these years, it was as though the effort of trying to love him fatigued her. He had been right, that time he had had a little too much ale and had accused her of loving Tom Lister more than him. It was true; she had tried to deny it all these years but seeing Tom Lister at Westby after losing the baby, feeling her heart skip a beat at the sight of his deep blue eyes and the gentle touch of his hand, had only served to remind her what it was to feel passionately about someone. She loved William like a friend, or a brother, but she did not desire him.

"It is difficult, when you don't love them, or you fall out of love with them," said Elizabeth, empathetically. "I did love John once and he had been my choice, but then after Henry's death I fell so sharply out of love with him that I couldn't bear him to come near me. Not that he tried," she added.

"William does try," replied Jennet, feeling inexplicably defensive of her husband. "He's a good man, it's just that…" her voice trailed off, at a loss as to how to explain her feelings to her friends.

"Master Thomas Lister," said Demdike, trying to give voice to Jennet's thoughts. "It's just that there's Tom Lister. Oh yes, I know all about him!" she added, in response to Jennet's look of surprise. "Your sweetheart from years ago, is he not? But you can't forget him."

Jennet shook her head, unsure even as she did so whether the gesture was in denial or agreement with what Demdike was saying.

"Forget him, Jennet," urged Elizabeth. "William is a good man, and if you try you can be happy with him."

Jennet met Elizabeth's plea with silence, unsure how to answer her. Demdike, sensing the end of this particular conversation, sought to change the subject.

"It is late, my dear," she said, addressing Elizabeth. "But I think you should eat, you haven't eaten since before the pains started and you will need your strength. I will go and see what I can find for you. Some bread, perhaps."

"There isn't much," said Elizabeth. "We are a little short on food since that rotten daughter of Chattox broke in and stole from us," she continued, addressing Jennet.

"What?" asked Jennet, aghast.

"Oh yes, just yesterday and not long before my pains started. Mother and I were out a little while with the children, Mother thought that the air and a walk would help the baby along as I was getting fed up waiting. As we came back we heard a noise coming from inside the cottage, and as we opened the door at the front and went inside we saw Bessie Whittle clamber out of a window, clutching a bag of oatmeal and some of my linen. Honestly, Jennet, you had never seen the like of her; wild, feral creature she is, dresses almost like a man and wears her hair all loose and tangled. I still can't quite get over the shock of it! No doubt it was the frightening sight of Bessie Whittle, and not the walk, which brought this little one into the world," Elizabeth finished, glancing down lovingly at the tiny girl now asleep in her arms.

"I thought, with John now in his grave, they might have the compassion to leave you all in peace," replied Jennet, thinking aloud.

"Compassion! From Chattox's lot! Never!" exclaimed Elizabeth, glancing at her sleeping infant again. "Mother thinks she broke in to collect the rest of John's debt, and hopes that will be an end to it," she continued, lowering her voice.

"I hope that will be an end to it," repeated Demdike, returning with some bread. "I do not want a war between us. Feuds between families in the forest are common enough, and bad enough, but war between two women of our abilities is frankly dangerous."

"What do you mean?" asked Jennet.

"Oh lass, as I told you once before, there are those who regard cunning work and witchcraft as one and the same thing. By my reckoning, Chattox has already turned to using her abilities for ill. If a feud between us comes to the attention of people in the forest, it could spell danger for us all. If we draw attention to ourselves we risk being accused of far more than just brawling and stealing," Demdike finished, giving Jennet a pointed look.

"Surely, Mother Demdike, you are more powerful than Chattox, she was your apprentice, and she is no threat to you?" Jennet asked.

"Well, yes," answered Demdike, chuckling a little. "But if I were to overcome her with my abilities, all it would mean is that I would be the first to the gallows. Don't you see? It's a dangerous game. I haven't lived so long in this way by disagreeing with others. I use my remedies to help, to heal, to earn our keep. Keep which we need even more than ever, now that John has gone and we have another mouth to feed," Demdike added, giving Elizabeth a meaningful glance.

Jennet studied Demdike's face and realised that she looked worried, her brow furrowed and her eyes dark with fear. She recalled Tibb, and how he visited Demdike and made her mad with visions of death. Perhaps, Jennet reflected, Demdike feared that Tibb hadn't just meant the deaths of Henry and John, but the deaths of them all. Tonight had been all about bringing new life, but the looming prospect of more trouble from Chattox cast the hope she had felt from her mind. Jennet shuddered, and looked down at the little baby, her namesake, sleeping peacefully in Elizabeth's arms; a small flicker of innocence, Jennet thought, born into a dark world.

Part Three

1606 - 1607

15

The Prestons' Farm, near Gisburn Village
May 1606

"Oh lass, you look beautiful!" Jennet gasped.

Anna smiled at her aunt and gave a twirl in response. "Do you really think so?" she cooed. "I do like these," she added, tenderly touching the flowers which Jennet had delicately placed through her long hair, which she had left loose.

Jennet looked at her niece affectionately. After so many years, she thought of her as a daughter; she had lived with them since she was little more than a child, a small, skinny thing with an infectious spirit, an unassailable curiosity and a kind heart. Now she was fully grown, almost in her twenty-fourth year, and she was getting married today. She had become engaged to a local boy a little while ago, a young man of her own choosing and of good prospects. Jennet recalled the first time Anna mentioned the young man, how her cheeks reddened and how Jennet remembered thinking that it was the first time she had ever seen Anna act coy. A little probing was all that was needed to extract the truth from her, that she liked this boy after meeting him several times in the village, that he wanted to court her and did Jennet think that her father and Uncle William would be in agreement? Jennet asked to meet the boy in question before agreeing to anything, but in truth she trusted her niece's judgement; she was wily, astute and determined. She was everything that Jennet had not been at her age.

The young man, Thomas Singleton, did not disappoint, being handsome, friendly and apparently very tender towards Anna, and the match was swiftly approved. The two Preston brothers welcomed a marriage for her; indeed, Jennet reflected, they both seemed slightly relieved. The question of Anna's marriage had arisen frequently over the past few years, ever since her father had first raised the subject one evening during dinner. Jennet could recall the conversation clearly; John was a quiet, reserved man and his frank discussion of his daughter's future had caught Jennet by surprise.

"We will have to think about a husband for you, Anna," he said gruffly, his mouth still half-full with food. His sudden statement caused everyone to look up and stop eating.

"Sorry?" asked Anna, her eyes wide.

"You'll need a husband," John repeated.

"John! You're worrying the girl," Jennet interjected with a chuckle, trying to keep the conversation light.

"She'll end up an old maid if she doesn't find a man soon," John persisted. He looked at Jennet squarely for a moment, then glanced at William for support.

"John's right," William said hesitantly. Clearly he hadn't wanted to be brought into the conversation. "The longer she waits, the harder it'll be to find someone suitable."

"You both speak so coldly about it!" Jennet exclaimed. "This is marriage you are talking about, not trading goods at a market. Anna's happiness should be the most important thing. She should be allowed to choose, however long it takes."

The men exchanged that familiar, here-she-goes-again glance that always made Jennet feel irritated. "Anna, how do you feel about marriage?" she asked her niece, determined not to be discouraged by the men's apparent resistance to her emotional appeal.

"I suppose I might like it," replied Anna reluctantly. "I would like to choose though. I don't want to marry, well, anyone just for the sake of being married."

"Nor should you!" said Jennet. "You should find someone you really like, someone who makes you very happy. You should marry for love," she added.

"Oh?" remarked William, looking up again from his food. "Can love not occur in an arranged marriage, Jennet?"

Jennet bit her lip, realising immediately that her remarks had offended William. "Of course it can," she replied, taking hold of his hand in an attempt to reassure him. "I'm just saying that we should trust Anna's judgement. She's a sensible girl, isn't she? If she'd like to choose, then I think we should all trust her to find a good husband."

Jennet had won the argument that evening, and both William and John had conceded that Anna should be allowed time to make her own choice. However, as a few summers passed and no young men were brought home and introduced, her father began to worry that his daughter would run out of time and be condemned to spinsterhood. Jennet, ever Anna's defender, had found the notion ridiculous and had said so. Secretly, however, Jennet had been relieved at the lack of suitors. Anna had been a source of female company and comfort for so many years; it was hard for her to imagine their cottage without her presence.

Now, the day had come for her to marry and leave Jennet for good. Jennet knew that in one sense her sentimentality was silly; Anna was staying in the village as her husband-to-be had secured a smallholding on the Lister estate, just a few moments' walk away. She would still be able to see her often and when the time came, enjoy all the grandchildren who she prayed would arrive. At the same time, she knew she would feel completely lost without the help and support she had come to rely on at home. She would be the only woman now in a house of men and she wouldn't be as readily able to disappear on journeys to Blacko, leaving Anna to attend to the work in the house. She knew these regrets were selfish and silently prayed for forgiveness for them; however, she could not help but feel a little bitter at the irony that Anna's departure would in turn make her feel that bit more trapped.

"Aunt, are you ready to go?" asked Anna, clearly impatient to leave and enjoy her day and not willing to tolerate Jennet's dithering any longer.

"Oh, yes, of course. If you're ready, I'm ready," replied Jennet. "The men are waiting somewhere outside. Let's go, shall we?"

Together, the four of them headed towards St Mary's, just as Jennet herself had done almost twenty years ago. The day was still and beautiful, the heat radiating from the late morning sun. Jennet noticed how Anna seemed almost to glow in the sunlight, her pale skin and clothing all lit up, making it seem as though her sheer joy was exuding from her. The bride walked with her father, arm in arm, almost skipping along, her delight and excitement evident. There were no nerves, and no hesitation, only the anticipation of enjoying her wedding day and all the happy years to follow afterwards. This must be what it's like to marry for love, thought Jennet.

A little while later, Anna and her new husband emerged from the church and all but danced into the alehouse where, as planned, a feast was to be served to celebrate their wedding day. Jennet had not been keen on holding a celebration there. Whilst she knew that Anna loved any excuse to dance and enjoy herself, she also knew that her father, uncle and some of the company they kept had a propensity for drunkenness which she wished to avoid. However, Anna could not be swayed on the matter and, once John and William got wind of the idea, Jennet knew that she was fighting a losing battle.

"Aunt, this is such a wonderful day! The sun is shining, there is plenty of food, lots of ale and I am married!" declared Anna, twirling around excitedly. "Please try to look a little more cheerful."

"I'm sorry, lass. You know how wary I am of the alehouse. But you're right, it's your day and I will put a smile on my face for you," replied Jennet, flashing her niece a forced grin.

Anna wasn't convinced. "Oh Aunt Jennet," she said despairingly. "I do worry about you, you know. You talk to so few people, apart from your friends in Blacko, of course. What will you do now that I'm no longer at home?"

Jennet shrugged in response. Anna was blunt as ever, but she was also right. She couldn't call round all the time; she would have her own cottage and probably a child or two before long. For the first time in a very long time, Jennet was acutely aware of how lonely she was going to feel.

"Speaking of Blacko, where are your friends? I thought they were coming along this afternoon?" Anna asked.

"Elizabeth was hoping to, I don't think her mother will make it as someone will need to look after the children. James and Alison are growing up fast, but Jennet is still only small. Anyway, in truth I'm not convinced even Elizabeth will come along. It's difficult for them, it's always difficult..." Jennet allowed her voice to trail off, not wanting to get into the specifics of her friends' troubles.

Anna nodded knowingly. "I know they're your friends rather than mine, Aunt, but I often wonder about them. Two women living out there, quite isolated really, no man at home to bring in an income, and all those children to feed. How do they survive?"

Jennet shook her head. She had never said much to Anna about Demdike's work. All those years ago, when Demdike had given her the witch bottle, Jennet had sneaked it into the cottage and hidden it within the wall, behind a loose stone, and had said nothing about it to Anna. Anna was the sort of girl who wanted to know about everything. She had endless questions and Jennet worried that Anna would ask questions that she wouldn't be able to answer as, in truth, Jennet still wasn't sure she believed in the power of these things. After all, she couldn't be sure if the witch bottle had worked; she hadn't lost any more babies, it was true, but she had never got with child again either. She also feared that Anna would tell her father or uncle about it and they would have certainly been dismissive, William in particular. Jennet recalled his reaction to the penis-shaped object. He had found that laughable, but she suspected he would find the notion of a witch bottle to be no laughing matter.

"They do odd work for local employers," she replied, sounding intentionally vague. "And Elizabeth spins, as you know. When their earnings from this are all gone, to be quite honest with you, they beg."

Anna gasped in response. "Begging?" she asked. "Well surely that will land them in some trouble?"

"What choice do they have?" Jennet answered her, slightly defensively. She didn't exactly approve of them begging but she knew they had little alternative; they had to eat.

"I suppose," replied Anna, slightly glibly. "As you mentioned spinning…" she continued, changing the subject but pausing as though to gather her thoughts. Jennet sensed that a delicate subject was on the approach. "What will you do now that you don't have me to card? I worry about that too, Aunt, you can't get through enough work by yourself to still make your arrangement with the Hewits pay, surely? Have you thought about what you will do?"

Jennet laughed. "Anna, you worry too much! I will be fine, I will sort something out. Now, enough of your fretting and enjoy the rest of your day!"

Anna nodded and took her leave, finding some of her young friends from the village who were dancing over on the other side of the room. Jennet sighed. In truth, she didn't know how she would manage without Anna. It wasn't just the sheer amount of work she would have to face alone that worried her either. The thought of sitting at home all day without her, spinning and carding from dawn till dusk, waiting for William and John to come home for dinner and eat before heading to the alehouse for the evening, frankly churned the bile in the pit of her stomach. Jennet looked at the cup of ale in her hand, conscious that she had been holding it for a long while and had barely taken a sip. Ale had never held much temptation for her, other than to quench a thirst; however, suddenly it looked delicious. Jennet raised her jug to her lips and, like a man, gulped down the contents in several large mouthfuls.

She wiped her mouth with the back of her hand. She would have another, then another, and more. She would drink until she was in a stupor, until she had drowned her misery in the bottom of her cup.

Unsteady on her feet, Jennet could feel the walls of the room spin and move, as though they could fall in on her at any moment. She fiddled clumsily with her collar, feeling hot and suffocated. The alehouse was still full and everyone around her was talking, singing, laughing and dancing; it was clear that the celebrations were going to go on well into the night. Jennet moved awkwardly amongst them all, looking for William. She couldn't bear the heat in the room any longer. She needed some air. She needed to go home. She looked about her frantically, trying to force her eyes to remain focused and stop making her feel as though she was spinning. Oh, how she disliked the ill-effects of too much drink! Where was William? She couldn't see him amongst the crowds. She was certain he couldn't have left; he would never leave a feast early. Finally, she spotted him, slumped in a corner, fast asleep. His brother John was beside him, in much the same manner. Jennet sighed. She wouldn't have an escort home tonight, then. Turning her back on the two men, both slumbering like babes, Jennet meandered towards the door.

The air outside was cool, still and refreshing. Jennet closed her eyes and took a deep breath, feeling better for a moment. Then, opening her eyes in horror, she felt her stomach heave and she rushed around the side of the stone building, emptying its contents all over the ground. All of tonight's merriment purged away, like sin, Jennet thought. She felt better now, cleansed somehow, but weakened by the emptiness of her stomach. She moved herself away from the large wet area she had created on the ground, as though to disassociate herself with it, and closing her eyes again, slumped down against another wall, enjoying the forgiving night air on her face. She was quite sure she could sleep there, right there, all night. Her cottage suddenly seemed far away to her and the prospect of walking home alone, in the dark, proved daunting. No, she had a shawl around her shoulders in case it grew cold; she would sleep there tonight. Jennet allowed herself to drift, her mind wandering over the day's events as it headed towards peaceful slumber. What a beautiful bride Anna had been, how radiant and happy she had looked. When Jennet had left the alehouse, Anna had still been dancing, this time with her new husband, her arms wrapped around his neck, her eyes staring deep into his. How in love she had looked...

"You, down there! Are you alright?" said a voice. Jennet was instantly brought back from the brink of sleep by this abrupt tone and the clatter of hooves.

"Yes, yes, I'm quite well," she replied, staggering to her feet. Peering in the dark, she could not see who it was and she suddenly felt worried, out here all alone. Gisburn was a small and safe community, but there was the occasional outsider who came into the village and caused trouble, the marauding sort of person who liked to roam the country and see what he could take from others. What if this man meant her harm?

The man disembarked from his horse and approached her. Jennet backed right up against the wall again, as though it might be able to swallow her up and protect her.

"Jennet, Jennet Preston? Is that you?" said the voice again, closer now, and sounding softer and more familiar. Jennet breathed a sigh of relief as she realised she knew this man.

"Tom! Oh thank goodness it's you!" she exclaimed.

Tom chuckled in response and moved nearer to her. By now it was very dark outside, the only light coming from within the alehouse a few steps away. Even in the dim light, Jennet could see Tom's bright blue eyes, looking at her intently.

"It's been a long time...again," he said, with a smile. "How are you? And might I ask what on earth you're doing out here at this late hour?" he added, glancing at the raucous alehouse.

"I am well, thank you. It was Anna's wedding today. Do you remember her, my niece? The celebrations are still going on inside,

I just came out to take some air," Jennet replied, trying her best to sound earnest. She didn't want Tom to think she was a drunk.

"Hmm," replied Tom, clearly unconvinced. "You looked fast asleep to me. Don't worry, your secret's safe with me, we've all drunk a little too much at one time or another. A wedding is the best excuse; no one minds a little drunkenness after a wedding."

Jennet didn't answer him, her embarrassment overcoming her ability to speak. The pair stood there for a few moments in silence, which would have been awkward but for the noise coming from the alehouse. In the end, Tom cleared his throat.

"Where's William?" he asked.

"Still inside," replied Jennet, nodding towards the alehouse door, "and unlikely to come out of there before sunrise. When I left him he was fast asleep."

"Well you can't sit out here all night," said Tom firmly. "Would you like me to take you back to your cottage?"

"Would you mind?" Jennet replied. "I don't much like walking by myself in the dark."

"Nor should you," Tom said. "You never know who's lurking about. I will gladly see you home safely, Jennet, it would be my pleasure."

The pair headed away from the alehouse on foot, Tom's horse trotting obediently alongside them. Tom offered his arm to Jennet, who looked at him hesitantly.

"Sorry, it's just you look a little unsteady on your feet," he said innocently.

"Oh! What must you think of me!" she exclaimed, partially covering her face with one hand and accepting his arm with the other.

"I could never think badly of you, Jennet, you know that," replied Tom, his sincerity evident. "In truth, it's just nice to see you at all. We live so near to one another really, yet I never seem to see you."

"I work a lot at home, so I don't spend very much time in the village," Jennet said, trying to sound matter-of-fact.

"Oh?" replied Tom, clearly intrigued. "What work is this?"

"Wool," Jennet answered him. "Carding and spinning, in the main. Although I've just lost my carder to a husband today, so I may have to think again about how to earn my living."

"Surely you can still do this work, perhaps you will not do so much of it, but nevertheless, you can work alone, can't you?" asked Tom, after a moment's pause.

Jennet drew a deep breath, unsure how to frame her response. She exhaled slowly, contemplating her words.

"Yes, but…" she began.

"You don't want to work alone?" he asked.

Jennet shook her head, which was silly; it was so dark Tom could not have seen the gesture. They walked in silence again for a few moments. Behind them the sounds of the alehouse trickled away into a murmur, making their silence increasingly less bearable.

"No," she said finally. "I don't really want to work alone. I think, sitting in my cottage working by myself for all those hours on end, will make me feel sad. I will miss Anna, I will resent the silence, and I will dwell on things too much," she blurted, regretting the words as soon as they fell clumsily from her lips. Tom Lister didn't need to know about her woes, real or imagined. She bit her lip hard, preventing herself from saying anything more.

"Ah, I see," replied Tom, not appearing fazed at all by Jennet's outburst. He paused for a moment, evidently considering his next words to her. "Well," he said in the end, "if you decide to give up your work and want to work where there's more company, I am sure I could find something for you at Westby. Well, my good lady could find you something; she deals with those matters. But all I need do is ask her. Just say the word and I will ask."

"Tom, that's very kind. I'm not sure it's such a good idea, though. But thank you, it is a very kind offer," replied Jennet hesitantly. She didn't wish to offend Tom, but she couldn't imagine accepting his offer. Jennet Preston, working at Westby Hall again; it would cause a scandal.

"Why is it not a good idea?" Tom asked. Again he was so direct;

so self-assured. Jennet found his confidence and authority breath-taking, almost irresistible.

"Tom, surely you must understand why…" Jennet answered him, her protest fading away as he stopped walking and turned to face her.

"Jennet Preston, you are a married woman of many years, and I am a married man. We were mere children when we…" he paused, searching for the words to continue. "Were we not children, when we declared our love? It was many years ago, anyone still gossiping about that has little else to talk about. I am also the Master of Westby; I have a large estate, and house, and a wife with a number of children who need care. For all this I need to employ local people, those whom I trust. You are one such person, so if it would suit you to come and work at Westby again, then it would suit me also, that is all I am saying."

Jennet looked at him dumbly, unable to articulate her concerns against the strength of his argument. He was right; it was many years ago, it was old news.

"Besides," Tom continued, grinning cheekily in the moonlight which had emerged from behind a dark cloud. "My wife knows nothing of you, other than she knows you stayed with us a few years ago, when you were unwell," he coughed, as though realising he was likely to be treading on painful territory. "And don't worry about my mother! She no longer lives at Westby. She has remarried since my father died and seldom visits."

"And Anne Robinson?" prompted Jennet. "She will remember the whole episode well, I think."

"The old cook's daughter?" asked Tom with a dismissive chuckle. "Most likely she does remember, yes. But I wouldn't worry about her either. Her mother's dead now and she isn't well-liked by the other staff so there are few who would bother to gossip with her. Just think about it Jennet, and when you have, let me know your answer."

Jennet nodded in response and, taking Tom's arm once more, continued along the road with him until they reached her cottage.

It was so dark here, the trees around them obscuring the moon. Jennet blinked, trying to make out Tom's face so that she could bid him good night.

"Thank you for walking me home, Tom," she said graciously. "It was so nice to see you as well."

"What do you think about too much?" Tom asked.

"What do you mean?" asked Jennet, taken aback by the directness of his question.

"You said before that you fear being alone because you will dwell on things too much. What will you think about?" he pressed.

Jennet didn't even know how to begin to answer his question. She couldn't quite believe that he had asked it in the first place. If he wasn't Tom Lister, if he was just an ordinary man, she would have been tempted to swipe her hand across his cheek for his impertinence, or at least she would have chastised him for having the audacity to pry into her feelings. Even William, her husband, never dared to ask how she felt.

"You can't ask me that, Tom. Surely you understand, there are parts of my life which I would rather not think about, let alone talk about," she replied pleadingly.

"Do you think about me?" he continued, his determination unwavering.

Jennet hesitated. She had never been able to resist talking to Tom, she had never been able to lie to him, even when they were children, and she couldn't now. Even after all these years of barely seeing each other, his power over her was captivating, irresistible.

"Yes," she replied simply, her voice wavering slightly as a solitary tear rolled effortlessly down her cheek.

Tom stepped closer to her, so close that although Jennet could barely see him, she could feel his breath on her face. Touching her cheek with his hand, which was smooth and strong in equal measure, quite unlike the rough touch of William's hand, he wiped away her tears with a single movement of his thumb.

"I think about you too, Jennet. I have never stopped thinking about you," he whispered.

Jennet felt the bristles of his beard brush against her lips as he leaned in to kiss her; a firm, desirous kiss which Jennet allowed herself to respond to, surrendering to years of denied emotions, expressing her deeply buried passion for this man. She wrapped her arms around his neck and he responded, placing his hands firmly around her waist, drawing her in and holding her tightly as their lips parted. Jennet rested her head on his broad shoulder, breathing him in, the delicious, overpowering smell of him which made her feel quite giddy and drunk all over again. This time, she wasn't frightened or hesitant even; after all these years, she knew what she wanted. She had always known, and now it was time to admit it. Releasing Tom from their embrace, Jennet gently took him by the hand, and led him inside her cottage.

16

The Prestons' Farm, near Gisburn Village
June 1606

Jennet looked up from her spinning wheel, arched her back and let out a slow, considered breath. Since Anna's departure to married life just over a fortnight ago, Jennet had watched her wool work grow into a paradoxical activity. On the one hand, without Anna's assistance, there did not seem to be enough hours in the day to get a sufficient amount done, but on the other hand the hours upon hours she did spend spinning and carding seemed to drag on endlessly as she sat by herself in the silence of her cottage. There was no idle chatter from Anna to make the time pass by more easily, only the company of her own thoughts which merely served to distract her further. Sitting at her wheel or with her carding brushes in her hands, Jennet would begin to work and as she worked her mind would wander, until she realised after some time that she had stopped working and lost herself in her train of thought completely; at this she would chastise herself and force her mind to focus on the task at hand. This pattern continued throughout the day until, driven half-mad by herself, Jennet breathed a sigh of relief when the two men wandered through the door, weary and filthy from a day in the fields.

In truth, it wasn't that Jennet wanted to run from her thoughts as she had so often done before; it was that she couldn't help but indulge herself in one thought in particular. Tom Lister: that night she had spent with Tom Lister. How she had led him into the cottage with such confidence and conviction, and how he had had to run back out moments later to retrieve and tether his horse which, in his haste to follow her, he had abandoned outside. How they had laughed at his error as he undressed her with care and attention and how, after caressing and kissing each part of her, he had gently pushed himself inside her in a way she had never known before. How, afterwards, they had fallen asleep in each other's arms, waking just before dawn to say a hasty, whispered farewell before William returned or someone else from the village spied them both in the light of day. Jennet smiled to herself as she recounted every tiny, minor detail of their night together; the delicious smell of Tom's skin, the way his blue eyes danced in the candlelight when he looked at her, the tender and loving way he kissed her for the last time before sneaking off to find his horse and head back to Westby. Jennet didn't believe that it was possible to feel more happiness than she had felt that night; it was perhaps the happiest she had ever been. She had held on to that joy ever since, a joy which was marred only by the sense that she should feel guilty yet, no matter how hard she tried, she simply could not feel any shame. She knew that in the eyes of God she had committed a sin; she had lain with a man other than her husband and she should fear for her immortal soul. But, she told herself, she loved this man, she had always loved him and if God was love, as the priest had said many times over in the pulpit on Sundays, then perhaps God would forgive her sin, if he knew it was for more than wanton lust.

If there was one thought which Jennet did wish to avoid, however, it was the decision she needed to make concerning her employment. She knew that the solitude of her wool work would not serve her well in the long run; if she didn't drive herself mad with her racing thoughts of Tom Lister, she would almost certainly grow miserable and lonely in the silence, especially once winter came and extinguished the warm sunlight which acted as a comfort for now. She had consulted Elizabeth on the matter just a few days ago, on her first visit to Malkin Tower since Anna's wedding and that night with Tom Lister. She had told Elizabeth how she felt about her work now, and had cautiously told her of Tom Lister's offer of employment. She had framed her words carefully, suggesting to Elizabeth that she had merely seen him outside of the alehouse and had a conversation, during which he had mentioned that his wife was looking for more maids. Elizabeth, as though sensing an untruth, had narrowed her eyes suspiciously at Jennet and had questioned her tale of this casual encounter. What was Tom Lister doing there? Did he say anything else, did he do anything else? Jennet had looked at her friend as earnestly as she could manage and had speculated that he had perhaps been alerted to the raucous noise coming from the village and, as the landlord, had come to take a look, as was his right. His meeting with Jennet was a chance encounter, a completely innocent conversation between two old friends in which he had enquired after her health and offered her a position in his house, nothing more. At this explanation Elizabeth had seemed satisfied and Jennet secretly breathed a sigh of relief. She had desperately wanted to tell Elizabeth that she had lain with Tom Lister, and about how wonderful it was and how much she loved him. Elizabeth was her dearest friend and the only person in the world who might understand a little of how she felt, the only person who might not stand in judgement of her. But Jennet also knew that Elizabeth had always unwaveringly cautioned her against any involvement with Master Lister; she had always urged her to remain faithful to William and to work hard on her marriage and to try to have more children with him. She knew that the news of her night with Tom Lister would only be met with disappointment from Elizabeth, and Jennet could not bear to disappoint her friend.

Jennet had left Malkin Tower that day, resolved to accept Tom's offer. Elizabeth, for all her misgivings about Tom Lister, had agreed that it was a good offer and that, given how she felt about her current work, Jennet would perhaps be foolish to turn it down. She simply urged Jennet to tread carefully, to keep her head down and not get herself into any trouble. For all you know, that man is looking for a lover whilst his wife seeks a maid, Elizabeth had cautioned. Jennet had nodded in response and promised to be careful, feeling very deceitful as she did so since she knew, in her heart, that she hoped to be both. She knew it was a dangerous game to play, she knew that if caught it would be her, not Tom Lister, who would be disgraced all over again. She knew, too, that despite Tom's assurances, all the eyes of the village would be upon her as she headed to work at Westby each day; people had long memories and did not forget a scandal easily. There would undoubtedly be rumours. Despite all this, Jennet could not resist. She had thought of nothing but Tom Lister for these past two weeks; she just had to be near to him. She had to feel that happiness again. At least this time, if she was caught and disgraced, if William discovered her secret and cast her from their cottage, if God did condemn her and damn her soul to hell, then it would have been worth it, to know such love, to feel such joy.

Convincing William had been much more difficult. Buoyed by her conversation with Elizabeth, she had approached the subject with him the evening after her visit to Malkin Tower. Jennet winced as she recalled the web of deceit she'd had to spin to convince him. She had been honest with him about how lonely she felt, how she missed Anna and craved some female company. She'd insisted that she could earn more as a maid at Westby Hall than she could carding and spinning by herself. That was all true, but that was where the honesty had ended. She never mentioned to William that she had seen Tom on the night of Anna's wedding and that he had offered her work. She didn't dare tell him about that; she knew that it would only serve to make him rightly suspicious. Instead, she suggested to him that it was her idea, that she thought the work and the company of other maids would suit her, and that she was merely suggesting making an enquiry with Mistress Jane Lister. She was careful to emphasise that she would seek work, well paid work, with the lady of Westby Hall and she made sure that she didn't mention Tom's name at all.

Nonetheless, William had looked uncomfortable with the idea, "I don't like you anywhere near that place, Jennet," he had said. "It was bad enough having you stay there after you lost the child. Knowing that you were so close to...well, you know who I mean. The thought of you working there, well that's another matter entirely."

In the end, William had relented, as he so often did. Jennet promised him that she was simply seeking employment as a lady's maid, and she reiterated the same promise that she had made to Elizabeth, that she would steer clear of Master Lister. Jennet recalled how her stomach had heaved at the recitation of this vow, as though she had swallowed the deception in her words and the bile of her deceit burned in the pit of her belly.

Now, sitting in her cottage, distracted once again from her work, Jennet flexed her weary hands in her lap and looked out of her window. Outside, the sun was high in the sky; it was a beautiful summer's day, perfect for the short walk to Westby Hall. Jennet fidgeted on her stool, feeling restless and contrived. She was deceiving everyone who cared about her so that she could pursue this love for Tom Lister; she was committing so many sins in the eyes of God, and yet she still could not resist. Jumping up from her stool, leaving a pile of half-completed spinning behind her, Jennet ran out of her little cottage and headed up the dusty lane.

The walk to Westby Hall was filled with nerves and excitement. As she left the prying eyes of her village in the distance, Jennet could almost feel herself skipping along, her heels kicking up the dust on the dry, rain-starved road. The last time she saw Tom, when he had gently kissed her goodbye as he crept out of her cottage, he had told her to come to Westby and ask to see his wife if she did decide to accept his offer. He had assured her that he would mention the matter to Mistress Jane, so that Jennet's visit, should it occur, would not be entirely unannounced. Jennet knew, therefore, that she may not see Tom today; that instead she may only get to have the gruelling, probing interview which was usually carried out by ladies of rank before choosing their staff. She recalled the one delivered by Tom's mother, Mistress Alice, immediately before Jennet was employed at Westby the last time. Jennet remembered how she had shrunk from the formidable woman's interrogation like a timid mouse, a little girl. This time she would not shrink; she was more experienced now, and older, older in fact than Jane Lister herself. She knew she was capable of undertaking a position at Westby, all she needed to do was convince the Mistress of Westby and she would be a step closer to Tom.

As she approached the big, familiar doors of Westby Hall Jennet paused, ringing her hands on her apron as though to calm her nerves and prepare herself. Drawing a deep breath, Jennet knocked loudly on the great wooden door. After a few moments, the door swung open.

"Yes?" answered a man, his tone abrupt.

"Good afternoon, I wondered if I might ask to see the Mistress, if she is at home?" said Jennet politely. Taken aback by the man's unfriendly manner, she stammered a little over her words. He made her feel instantly uneasy; he carried such an air of authority for a man in service that Jennet assumed he must be the steward.

"I was not told that my Mistress was expecting a visitor this afternoon. Might I ask what business you have here?" asked the steward, his tone still harsh and a touch condescending. Jennet tried not to prickle at his rudeness; she had always disliked those in service who acquired the superior air of their masters.

"I have come to enquire about a maid's position in the house. I believe the Mistress is expecting me," replied Jennet, rather relishing the mixture of surprise and disdain on the steward's face as he realised he wasn't privy to this information. An aspirational servant never liked to feel left out; having an intricate knowledge of his household and the confidences of his masters were the armour he needed to clamber ever further up the ladder of service and maintain the highest position once he got there.

"I see, very well," he replied, beckoning her to come inside. "I will have to see if my Mistress is receiving visitors at present. You may wait here."

The steward left Jennet standing in the porch, from where she could peer into the hall, the largest room on the ground floor. It had changed little since Jennet last set eyes upon it almost eight years ago, its dark wood and high ceiling still impressive, still a statement of the power and influence wielded by the Listers in this corner of the land. Once, as a girl, Jennet had found Westby Hall captivating. Now she found it intimidated her, reminding her that Tom Lister was so much more than a man she had fallen in love with; he was wealth, he was authority, and potentially for Jennet, he was danger.

"My Mistress will see you now," barked the steward, returning to Jennet and interrupting her thoughts. Jennet nodded at the man, a brief thank you, and followed him through the familiar myriad of rooms, corridors and stairs until finally they reached the Jane Lister's chamber.

The steward opened the door and led Jennet inside. Jennet was immediately struck by the delicious smell of flowers, the richly embroidered coverlets draped fashionably across a large bed, and the fine oak furniture. This room had belonged to the last Mistress of Westby, Tom's mother Alice, last time Jennet had set foot within it; yet she did not remember it being so richly or tastefully decorated. Unlike the rest of the house, this room had greatly altered. There, sitting in the middle of her finery, her sewing placed carefully to one side, was Jane Lister. Jennet bowed her head slightly and respectfully as Jane summoned her to come closer.

"Sit down, Jennet," Jane instructed her, gesticulating towards a chair. Jennet sat down and took a moment to study this woman, in many ways her rival. Immediately her eyes were drawn to Jane's swollen belly; she was clearly heavy with child. Apart from that, her delicate frame betrayed the possession of a lovely slenderness between pregnancies, and her face, though beginning to show some marks of ageing around the eyes, was pale and pretty. She wore a warm smile upon her face which showed off her high cheekbones and shining blue eyes. Jennet's eyes wandered back to Jane's belly. Tom had mentioned his children to her several times, but Jennet realised she had never made any further enquiries. She knew that he had a son, also named Thomas, who was his heir, and she knew from hearing the talk in the village that there had been several others born since. Now, sitting here, seeing this attractive, refined lady before her with her large proud belly, Jennet felt jealous and wondered exactly how many children Tom had seen fit to put within her.

"What can I do for you, Jennet?" probed Jane gently.

"Mistress, I believe there is a position here for a maid, and I would like to apply," replied Jennet, still barely able to lift her gaze from Jane's stomach.

"Ah, I see. My good husband did mention he had spoken with you about the matter. Yes, I am looking for another maid," she paused to pat her belly. "This child will arrive in a few more months and as my family grows larger, I feel the strain upon my maids grows also. Another pair of hands will go a long way to ease their burden."

Jennet nodded. "How many children do you have, Madame?" she couldn't resist asking.

"This one will make seven," Jane answered with a proud smile. "For now we have four sons and two daughters." She beamed again, with the assurance of a woman who knew she had done her duty. "I feel this child shall be the last, but you never do know, I said that when I was heavy with Mary and yet, here I am, expecting another."

Jennet smiled in response; a forced, grim smile. This lady was so pleasant, so amiable. She had a handsome, gentle husband and a small army of children. She had everything which Jennet did not have.

"So, when can you take up the position here?" Jane pressed. "Have you other employment presently?"

"I do, Madame," replied Jennet. "I take in work from a wool merchant in Colne. I will need to complete this work and send him word that I shan't take any more from him. I could start two weeks from now, if that would be suitable?"

"That would do just fine, Jennet," replied Jane kindly. "It's settled then. I have my husband's word that you will make a fine and reliable attendant, I need nothing more than that. He holds you in quite a high regard, Jennet, you have a lot to live up to, I fear."

"Yes, Mistress, thank you," Jennet replied, bowing politely as she headed swiftly towards the door. She felt dizzy and sick, as though it had all suddenly become too much for her. The sight of lovely, trusting, pregnant Jane, speaking highly of the assurances from her husband that Jennet would be a good maid. If only she knew what had really passed between Tom and Jennet, she would not be so commending.

Rushing downstairs and back towards the porch, which was thankfully now attended by a groom rather than that unbearable steward, Jennet's mind raced over her deceit, and over her own foolishness. She had spent these past weeks assuming that the love she felt for Tom Lister was completely mutual, that their night together was an expression of a childhood passion for one another which had never been extinguished. Now, having seen his lovely wife with her pretty smile and blooming belly, she began to doubt. What if mere lust had brought him into her cottage that night, what if, seeing the drunken state of her, Tom had seen fit to take advantage of the situation and the feelings he knew Jennet had for him? Halfway down the lane, out of sight of Westby Hall once more, Jennet vomited; her body's reaction to her nauseating thoughts. She would still take up the position at Westby, but she would now heed her friend Elizabeth's advice. She would not trust Tom, and she would tread very carefully.

17

Westby Hall, Gisburn
August 1606

Jennet looked out of the nursery window on to the floral Westby gardens, on what was a fine summer's day. Outside the children were playing, loosely supervised by two of the other maids who, away from their mistress's watchful eye, appeared to be indulging in a little gossip. Jennet watched as the smallest ones, John, Francis and Mary, chased each other around in circles until they all fell about on the ground, laughing. Little Mary usually fell over first; she had only just turned three years old and could often be clumsy on her feet. Jennet watched as Mary fell down hard and her older sister Anne, a serious and diligent child of nine years old, scraped the little girl off the floor in a motherly fashion and scolded the other two for playing too roughly with her. Jennet chuckled to herself; it was incredible how the innocent joy of children could be so infectious, how it could lighten her spirit in a moment.

"Is Anne playing mother again?" asked Jane, looking up from her sewing.

"Yes," Jennet replied. "She does amuse me."

"How are we for linen?" Jane asked, placing her sewing down in front of her and arching her back slightly. Jennet had observed how uncomfortable and restless her mistress had grown over the last week or so. She seemed both tired and impatient, as though her pregnancy fatigued her and she could wait no longer for it to be over. In an apparent effort to keep herself occupied before she went into her confinement, she had decided to oversee all the preparations for the baby's imminent arrival and had tasked Jennet with assisting her.

"I think what you have is sufficient, Mistress," replied Jennet dutifully. In truth she had never seen so much linen; cloths for swaddling, cloths for napkins, cloths which apparently were just cloth for the sake of cloth, either too big or too small to serve any obvious purpose.

"Thomas has said that we may call the child Jane if it is a girl," said Jane, as though pondering the thought out loud rather than talking directly to Jennet, who was sat back on the floor now, trying to create order from a chaotic mountain of linen.

"I think that's rather nice, don't you?" asked Jane, this time clearly addressing Jennet. "To have a child named after yourself. The Listers always name the eldest son Thomas, as well you know, so I suppose it's rather fitting to have our youngest daughter, if it is a girl, named after me. This will be the last baby, I think. It surely must be, for I fear I am getting too old for all of this," added Jane, gesticulating at her burgeoning belly.

"My friend Elizabeth named her youngest daughter after me," blurted Jennet. She looked up from the linens to meet Jane's inquisitive gaze and instantly reddened at her boldness. Jane was a talkative mistress, that was certain, but Jennet had not yet properly assessed whether she liked much chatter in return and thus far had kept conversational responses restricted, but polite.

"How interesting," answered Jane, clearly pleased by her new maid's sudden engagement with her. "Is she a friend from Gisburn?"

"No," replied Jennet, clearing her throat. "Blacko. Young Jennet will be six in October. It's hard to believe, I remember the night she was born like it was yesterday."

"You were there?" asked Jane, incredulous, as might be expected. Women such as Jane Lister were only attended by midwives and physicians during childbed, and perhaps their mother or the odd trusted maid, but certainly not friends.

"Yes, she wanted me to be there. I didn't deliver the child, though, I have no skill in that regard. Her mother assisted her there," replied Jennet.

"Ah, I see. Well I suppose that is to be expected if…" Jane allowed her sentence to trail off, unfinished, as she looked back down at her sewing. Jennet knew what she was about to say, though. It is to be expected if no midwife or physician can be afforded. Clearly, Jane Lister did know a little of how the world worked for the women far beneath her, she just allowed herself to forget it most of the time.

"Has Master Lister said what the baby will be called if he is a boy?" asked Jennet, desperate to change the subject slightly, and hoping that the question was not too bold.

"Leonard, after one of his brothers," replied Jane, still attending to her sewing. She made a disapproving, deflated noise with her lips. "I do not care for it, but my opinion carries little sway when it comes to the naming of our boys. Let us hope for a girl," she said, looking up from her sewing and flashing Jennet a mischievous smile.

"I will pray for it, Madame," replied Jennet.

As Jennet exited through the servants' door of Westby Hall that evening, she smiled to herself. It was a beautiful evening; calm and peaceful, the sun allowing itself to settle gently on top of the rolling hills, its orange glow illuminating the lush green countryside. She headed down the lane towards home, feeling happy; it was wonderful to be working amongst a busy household again. As a young girl, all those years ago, working in the Westby kitchens, she did not really appreciate it, having come from a bustling home herself. Now, as someone who had experienced solitude, who returned every evening to a silent home only periodically occupied by two men who invariably came home, ate, and went back out to the alehouse, she appreciated the merry chaos of a house filled with children's footsteps, laughter, and song.

The Mistress was good to her, too. Jane Lister was pleasant and kind; she expected hard work but her gentle disposition meant that she inspired it rather than having to demand it. It was easy to work hard for someone who treated her maids kindly, who phrased her instructions as polite requests rather than orders, and who clearly liked to indulge in some friendly chatter with them all. Jennet felt a wave of guilt wash over her as she thought about her nice mistress, her open smile and her swollen belly. It would be easier if she was not likeable; it would be easier if she was unkind and ugly, her humour sour and her looks long departed. But she wasn't; she was sweet and generous and clearly devoted to her husband and her children. Tom, despite all this, had looked elsewhere, if only for one night; together he and Jennet had done Jane a grave, terrible wrong. Jennet had to bury the memory of what she had done, the treasured, delicious thought of her night with Tom, deep within her mind whenever her mistress looked upon her with those bright, pretty eyes.

As she continued down the lane, her mind began to wander helplessly over Tom; his eyes, his smile, the way his beard bristled her mouth as he kissed her, the way his bare shoulders glistened in candlelight. She shook her head, trying to suppress her thoughts. She had managed to avoid Tom for the past few weeks since commencing work at the great house. At first she had been worried about seeing him constantly, about how that might weaken her resolve to heed Elizabeth's warning to be careful, how she might surrender once again to her feelings for him at a mere glance from him. As the weeks had passed, however, she realised that need not have worried. Her position in the house, as it turned out, was mostly consigned to her mistress's rooms and the nursery, fulfilling duties for Jane Lister and her younger children. She saw little of the older boys, Thomas and Richard, as they were mostly with their tutor or their father, and she saw virtually nothing of Tom, except for distant, fleeting glimpses of him. He was a busy man, Jane had told her, often out on his estate or on business with other gentlemen. Their eldest son, young Master Thomas, was to marry in the coming months and much of their time was being spent with the Hebers and their daughter, also called Jane, who was to be his bride. Jennet had shuddered inwardly at this news; it reminded her of Tom's own marriage arrangements to his Jane all those years ago, and what had passed between Jennet and him immediately prior to it. It was like history repeating itself, but then she supposed that was what the great families did; repeat history over and over again to sustain their own glory.

As Jennet turned a corner on the lane and the humble, sporadic dwellings which formed Gisburn came back into view, she could see three horses approaching, along with a groom on foot. As they grew nearer, Jennet realised the riders were Tom and his two boys, presumably returning home to Westby after a day of business. Jennet inhaled sharply, willing herself invisible. She wished she could run and hide; however, she knew that she would have already been seen. She carried on walking, casually fiddling with the green bushes growing along the lane as though to distract herself and avoid Tom's gaze.

"Jennet Preston! I thought it was you. Good evening!" said Tom, tugging his hat politely to greet her. "Boys, this is Jennet Preston, one of your mother's maids and an old friend of mine. Jennet and I have known each other since we were children. How are you enjoying your work, Jennet? I trust my wife treats you well?" Tom asked, smiling at her.

"Yes, Sir," replied Jennet deferentially. "I enjoy the work very much."

Tom looked at her, apparently bemused by her guarded tone. He looked back at his boys, who were both intently studying this new and unfamiliar servant with identical gazes, at once superior and childlike.

"Boys, why don't you head back to the hall with Caxton. I'll follow you shortly, I'd just like a moment to speak with Jennet first," he said, giving them both a reassuring smile. At his instruction, the boys headed obediently up the lane, young Thomas glancing behind him once as his father climbed down from his horse. Jennet thought that he looked suspicious; he wore the scowl of a young man denied some piece of knowledge. Clearly, this young man was not used to being left out of things.

"I have been desperate to see you these past weeks, Jennet," said Tom, once the boys had turned around the corner and were out of sight. "I had hoped to see plenty of you once you were working for Jane; however, other matters have kept me away from the house."

"Yes, so your wife has said," answered Jennet, matter-of-fact and impassive. "Young Master Thomas is to marry, I believe."

Tom chuckled. "My wife never could keep her own counsel where her maids are concerned. I see she had taken you firmly into her confidence as well."

Jennet smiled in response. Tom looked at her, a frown passing over his face.

"What's wrong, Jennet?" he asked. "Are you unhappy?"

Jennet shook her head vigorously, as though trying to prevent herself from speaking her mind. "I can't be your…whatever it is you want me to be, Tom. I am grateful for the position, I truly am, and I am enjoying working for your wife and your children; they are all truly lovely, you are blessed. I want to stay at Westby. But this…whatever this is, I just can't do it. I can't look at your wife, her kind face and her belly full with your child, and know that we are…it is wrong."

Tom gave Jennet an understanding look, and let out a gentle sigh. It was as though he was completely unsurprised by what she was saying, as though he expected it, in fact.

"You wouldn't be my Jennet if you didn't care about doing what is right," he said after a moment. "You've obviously grown to like my wife and I would be a man not worthy of you if I did not admit that I care for her too, of course I do; she is a wonderful person and the mother of my children. But I do not love her, not like I love you. As I have said to you before, all those years ago, Jane would not have been my choice. You would have been my choice. Perhaps I am selfish, perhaps I am wrong, but after all these years I still cannot keep myself away from you," Tom said, gently taking hold of Jennet's arm and looking her squarely in the eye. "Tell me, do you love William?" Tom asked.

"I care for William…" replied Jennet weakly, bristling slightly at the mention of her husband.

"Exactly, Jennet. We both understand what it is like to be in marriages without love, marriages which were chosen for us. We both know what it is like to be in love with someone else. We cannot leave our marriages but we can still be together, if you will trust me. This is not something I do, Jennet. I am not the sort of man who betrays his wife with other women. I have been good and loyal to her. I am all she expects me to be. But you are not just any woman, you are my Jennet. I love you," he said again, touching her face tenderly.

"But you must still lie with Jane!" protested Jennet, pushing Tom's hand away. "You must! She is with child right now!" The vehemence of her protest surprised even herself.

"Yes, Jennet," replied Tom, his tone factual but slightly exasperated. Tom had this way of making her feel like a child, an innocent who did not entirely understand the world she inhabited. "We all have duties to perform," he continued, "although I haven't lain with her since I was with you, and if it bothers you so much, I will not lie with her again. I think she will perhaps be glad of it, in truth. Every time I lie with her she ends up with child, and she is tired of it, I can tell."

"Do you mean it, Tom?" asked Jennet, earnestly.

"Yes, Jennet, I mean it," Tom answered with a slight sigh. "If you will come to me. Come tomorrow, to my rooms. Make up an excuse, any excuse, to slip away. Say you will come," he pleaded.

Jennet sighed as she looked at Tom's eyes, which were honest and desperate in equal measure. She could hear Elizabeth's pleas ringing in her ears, be careful, as though her dear friend might personify her own conscience, might give voice to her better judgement. She could see kind, trusting Jane Lister clutching her sewing, an amused smile on her pretty face, her belly big with child. Then she thought again about the night she had spent with Tom, wrapped in his arms inside her little cottage. Her love for him that night had consumed her completely, and as she looked at his earnest blue eyes again now, all those powerful feelings flooded back. She nodded her head, pushing Elizabeth's warning and Jane's image away as she forced a trailing strand of hair back behind her coif.

"Yes, I will come," she replied.

18

Malkin Tower, Blacko Hillside, Forest of Pendle
September 1606

Jennet approached the familiar door of Malkin Tower with some trepidation. It was a calm early autumn afternoon, the leaves were beginning to curl on the surrounding trees and the sky, though overcast, was peacefully grey, without a hint of rain. Jennet realised that the last time she had visited Malkin the sun had still been high in the blue, cloudless sky, giving off a blistering heat. It had been a good number of weeks since her last visit to see her dear friends. As she knocked on the rickety old door, as she had a thousand times before, she hesitated, wondering how well she would be received.

"Jennet, my lass, is it really you? It is good to see you!" Demdike exclaimed as she opened the door to her unexpected visitor.

"Mother," replied Jennet, embracing the old lady fondly. "I am sorry it has been so long. Is Elizabeth at home?" she asked as Demdike beckoned her inside.

"Yes, yes, though you're lucky, she's not long been home. James and Alison are out, but Elizabeth and young Jennet are here," answered Demdike, leading her to their humble kitchen.

"Elizabeth, my dear," said Demdike, addressing her daughter, who was standing over the hearth with her back to the door. "We have a visitor."

Elizabeth turned and let out a surprised gasp. "Jennet! Jennet. Where have you been? It's been so many weeks! I have been wondering about you."

"I'm sorry Elizabeth. I've been needed so much at Westby, that I have barely had a day off in weeks. The Mistress has just given birth to her seventh child, a little girl called Jane, and the house has been so busy, there has just been so much to do…" Jennet allowed her explanation to trail off, as she realised that Elizabeth's face was instantly forgiving. "Anyway," she continued after a moment, "in the end I simply pleaded for a day's leave, so that I could come and see you all. How are you? How are the children?"

"Little Jennet is fine," answered Elizabeth. "Sweetheart that she is, helping me around the home," she added, patting Jennet on the head as the girl beamed proudly at her namesake. "James is fast becoming a man; he has started to bring in a wage, doing the odd labouring work here and there. It's not much, but it all helps. Alison is…difficult," she concluded after a moment's consideration.

"Oh?" asked Jennet, intrigued. Alison was growing into a woman, it was true; but Jennet could only recall a sweet, charming child, much like her little sister. She wondered what had changed since her last visit.

"It's my fault, perhaps," said Elizabeth, sounding a little exasperated. "I think that I have not offered her the solace that a mother should give."

Jennet frowned, confused by the cryptic explanation and Elizabeth's evident guilt. "Well, Alison is at a difficult age," replied Jennet lightly. "We can all remember being fourteen, can't we?" she asked with a slight chuckle, trying her best to soothe her friend.

"It's more than that, Jennet," replied Elizabeth with a curt directness that made Jennet bristle. "Alison has become aware of certain truths about her life and, well, she seems to feel very angry.

She barely speaks to me. She spends hour upon hour out, roaming the country doing goodness knows what."

"What truths?" Jennet asked, intrigued by the source of Alison's anger.

"Well, her father's death, to name but one," replied Elizabeth, "and I'm afraid that is my fault, for I told her far too much about it all, filling her young head with stories about Chattox and Bessie Whittle. She feels such hatred towards that family, and who can blame her, but Mother and I are worried that she will try to provoke them. Over the past few years we have all done a very good job of avoiding them entirely, I just hope that Alison does the same."

"I see," replied Jennet, "but I don't understand why she isn't speaking to you? Surely if she feels that she has been wronged by Chattox and her family, she must see that you are also a victim of their misdeeds?"

Elizabeth gave a twisted smile. "Oh, she has an entirely different reason to be angry with me. Thanks to the mischief of some local boys, Alison recently discovered that John was not Jennet's father. You should have seen the rage she came home in, the day she found out. I suppose again, it's my fault. I didn't want Jennet to be marked out as different from the rest of us so, like her brother and sister, her surname is Device, as you know. James and Alison were just children when she was born and they have grown up assuming that they all shared the same father, and I have never told them any different. You should have heard some of the names she called me that day," remarked Elizabeth, visibly shuddering. "To have your own child stand in judgement upon you, that is not a nice thing," she added.

"Oh, Elizabeth," said Jennet, embracing her friend sympathetically. "You're her mother, in time she will come around, I'm sure."

"I hope you're right," replied Elizabeth, giving a grim smile. "Anyway, enough about my troubles, tell me all about life in that big, grand house. I do envy you sometimes, working in such a place."

Jennet smiled and without hesitation the stories about working for the Listers tumbled forth. As they sat around the hearth at the centre of the Malkin kitchen, Jennet related tales about the children, about how little Anne Lister took charge of the younger children in such a grown up manner that it amused everyone in the house. How John and Francis liked to get up to mischief together, as boys do, usually involving mud, sticks and sometimes even dead mice or hares, much to the horror of the maids! How little Mary was the darling of the nursery, with her tight blonde curls and her petted, quivering lip whenever she fell and scraped her knees. Jennet told them about her mistress, Jane Lister; how she was kind and friendly to her maids, how she was still so young and pretty looking despite having had so many babies now, how she never looked tired even though she professed to be tired always. The two women and the young girl listened, attentively, clearly amused by the stories, relishing the insight into the domestic life of the wealthy and powerful.

"And what about Master Lister," Demdike asked in her usual shrewd tone. "Do you see much of him?"

Jennet shrugged, trying her best to seem evasive. "Not really," she replied. "I mostly work for the Mistress and the younger children. The two older boys, Thomas and Richard, are usually with their tutor or their father, who is mostly out on the estate or elsewhere, or working privately in his rooms. He has his own servants and grooms; he has no need of his wife's maids."

Demdike and Elizabeth both looked unconvinced. Little Jennet, losing interest in the conversation now that it no longer contained stories about other small children, ran off to play, leaving the three women alone.

"Jennet," said Elizabeth, frankly, "you have never been very good at telling a lie. In fact, you're pretty terrible at it. I could tell when you visited in the summer to tell me all about the position you had been offered, that you were holding something back. I didn't pry then but, as your friend, as someone who worries about you, I am going to ask you about it now. Is there something between you and Thomas Lister?"

Jennet looked down at the floor. Elizabeth was right; she couldn't lie, not to them anyway. Drawing a deep breath, she looked at her friends, who were both staring earnestly at her.

"Yes, you're right, there is something between Tom and me, and there has been for some time," she replied, exhaling sharply as she did so. She proceeded to tell them both the whole story, about how she had first lain with Tom on the night of Anna's wedding and how, since last month, she had been visiting him in his private rooms as regularly as was possible without arousing suspicion. She loved him, she told them, she always had, and he loved her. They weren't children anymore; they both knew what they were doing. If the world was a fair and just place where parents didn't choose marriages for their children, where rank wasn't so important, they would have been married. But the world isn't fair, Jennet declared, and therefore they both must take whatever happiness they can find with each other. After a few minutes, she looked at the two faces in front of her, both with their mouths open, jaws dropped, aghast. Jennet fell silent.

"You are a foolish girl," said Demdike. "At your age, you should have more sense. Men only take what they want, especially men of rank! It will not be love for him, you are their maid. He is taking his pleasure with you and probably countless others. Promises, empty promises of love, they are as old as time when a man is trying to get a woman to go to bed with him! This will end badly, mark my words, and it will be for you rather than him. You should have learnt that a long time ago, Jennet. When you were a young lass, all it took was a kiss from him and the suggestion that you might have lain with him to ruin your reputation for years, just think what will happen when folk find out that he really has been bedding you this time."

Jennet looked at the old woman, shocked. She looked at Elizabeth, who was still open-mouthed. "What about you, Elizabeth?" she asked. "Do you agree with your mother? Am I a fool?"

"Jennet, you have to admit that what Mother says makes a lot
of sense. We only say this because we care about you. You are
risking everything; your marriage, your position at Westby, and for
what? A mere promise of love which any man can give easily. And
what if you get with child? What will you do then?" Elizabeth
replied. She tried to maintain a softer, more diplomatic tone than
Old Demdike, but nonetheless her words bit at Jennet's
conscience.

"Is it so impossible to believe that Tom may simply love me?"
she demanded, her sense of objection rising up in her belly as she
spoke. "He is not any man, and I am not any woman to him. You
know the history between us, you must see that. I hesitated to tell
you both about this because I knew that this would be your
reaction."

"Aye, you know that it's wrong, Jennet, that's why you didn't
want to tell us. You know, in your heart, that you are both doing
wrong, to William, to Jane Lister, and to Master Lister's children,"
retorted Demdike, who was still refusing to mince her words about
the matter. Jennet had never been on the receiving end of the old
woman's sharp tongue, and it stung like a nettle on a hot summer's
day.

"If that is how you feel, I think I shall take my leave," replied
Jennet, wincing as she rose from her seat.

"Oh Jennet..." started Elizabeth, taking hold of her friend's
arm. "Mother's words are harsh, I know, but it's only because we
care. You once cautioned me about taking the wrong path, that day
when you caught me with Richard Sellers, you tried to warn me,
and you told me to be careful. I didn't listen to you straight away,
but I listened in the end. God knows, I had less to lose with
Richard Sellers than you do now with Tom Lister, so please, think
about this, please heed our words. Be careful," she pleaded.

Jennet looked straight at her friend, then at Old Demdike, both
of whom were looking at her, waiting for her next move, her next
words. Jennet opened her mouth as though to speak, then closed it

again, sighing as she did so. She moved towards the door, Elizabeth following behind her.

"There is nothing else I can say," said Jennet, without turning around. "I bid you both a good day."

The rickety old door of Malkin Tower slammed shut behind her as Jennet left her friends in a stunned silence. Hot tears of humiliation streamed down her burning cheeks as she ran carelessly down the hillside and back towards the road home. She had always known that Elizabeth and Demdike would not approve of her relationship with Tom Lister, but Demdike's words in particular had been so harsh that they had burned her like fire. The way the old woman had spoken about Tom Lister had shocked Jennet; it was clear Demdike could see no good in him, nor any man for that matter. Even dear, sweet Elizabeth had found herself unable to sympathise with Jennet. Could she not understand that she was in love with him? Did she place no faith in love at all? Jennet clenched her fists as she reached the road, her upset turning to anger. Friends were not friends at all if they could offer nothing but condemnation, if they could do nothing other than call her a fool and dismiss her feelings. As Jennet marched along the road home, the clouds gathered overhead, darkening the sky and releasing the occasional heavy droplet of rain. Quickening her pace in anticipation of the imminent downpour, Jennet resolved that today would be her last visit to Malkin Tower for a long time, and perhaps forever. She did not need friends. She did not need anyone, except Tom. She had only ever needed Tom.

19

Westby Hall, Gisburn
November 1606

Jennet stretched out in front of the glowing fire, curling her toes into the luxurious feeling of the fur rug beneath her. She looked over her shoulder coyly at Tom, who was lying behind her, his gentle fingers caressing her cheek and her hair which she had freed from her coif.

"I love your hair when it is loose," he remarked. "I wish women did not wear these things on their heads. It hides such beauty, especially yours."

Jennet giggled like a girl at his compliment and looked back at the warm fire. It was difficult to feel any guilt about the web of deceit they had both spun so that she could be there this evening when Tom was being so lovely and attentive to her. Tonight was the Mistress's first trip away since the youngest child, Jane, had been born in September. Now that the baby was settled with her wet nurse, Tom had insisted that Jane have some time away from the children. Jane had elected to visit friends near Whalley, although she was anxious about being away from her little ones in the nursery for too long and had planned to be away for only one night. Nonetheless, as soon as plans were made, Tom had seized the opportunity to make his own with Jennet, and so the trail of lies had begun. Summoning Jennet as she had passed along the corridor outside his rooms last week, he had told her of the Mistress's trip away. Thankfully, he said, Jane had planned to take another of her maids with her, leaving Jennet at Westby with the others to attend to the children and the household in her absence. Almost giddy with excitement at the prospect of what he was planning, Tom instructed Jennet to tell William that she would be required for an overnight stay at Westby, due to the Mistress being away. Jennet had done as she was told and, once her work was finished that day and the young children were all tucked up in their beds, she had made the pretence of going home, but instead had slipped unseen to Tom's private rooms. Meanwhile, Tom had dismissed all his servants for the evening, telling them he needed to be left in peace to work through his various papers. Now, there they were; together, and in complete peace.

"I wish we could always be like this," said Jennet, thinking aloud.

Tom looked down at her, his eyes agreeing. "I know, my love. As do I," he replied.

He leant down and kissed her, pulling her close as he did so. It was a lingering embrace; no hurried, snatched kisses tonight. Tonight they would be together properly, in a comfortable, warm house and a proper bed, as though they might be man and wife. Jennet closed her eyes and pretended for a moment that she, and not Jane, was the Mistress of Westby. She pretended that she had the fine clothes and the nice manners, the kind smile, the warm heart, and the entourage of beautiful children. She screwed her eyes up hard, indulging herself in her fantasy. She did not want to open her eyes, for if she opened them she would know again that she was not the Mistress of Westby, but merely Jennet Preston, wife of William. If she opened her eyes she might find that she wasn't at Westby at all, by the fire with Tom Lister, but at home in her cold, slightly damp cottage, with William and his brother John both snoring close by.

"What are you thinking?" asked Tom, interrupting her thoughts.

"Nothing," replied Jennet, daring to open her eyes at the sound of his voice.

"You are so mysterious, Jennet. You always were; you give very little away to people, do you know that?" asked Tom, chuckling lightly.

"I was just looking at the fire. It reminded me of all the bonfires I have seen this month. I still cannot believe that someone tried to kill the King last year," she said hastily, allowing the first thought that came to her mind to spill clumsily from her lips.

Tom looked at her quizzically. "What a thought to have on an evening such as this!" he exclaimed. After a moment's pause his face grew serious. "It is not in the least bit surprising, I'm afraid. There are those who are so steadfast in their adherence to the old ways that they would do anything to bring every person in this land back into the Pope's flock. They are swimming against the tide, however. If they must hold to their faith they should do so in private; from what I hear the King is not an unreasonable man, I am sure he would not seek to root out those Catholics who do not act against him, who pay their fines if they will not conform," said Tom, bristling slightly. Jennet could tell he was thinking about his mother.

"Anyway," he said finally, after a few moments' silence, "do not worry your beautiful head about such matters."

Jennet smiled, feeling that familiar girlish self-consciousness that she always felt in his presence. No one else made her feel that way, only Tom. These days, she mostly felt her age; her knees and back regularly pained her and she was weary most of the time, in mind as well as body. One look at William's drunken face as he stumbled in from the alehouse late at night was enough to make her feel ancient, as though the best of her years were behind her, as though she was condemned now to face old age. With Tom, however, she felt young again; with him she was agile, attractive, ageless.

"Do you wish we were fifteen again?" she asked him, thinking aloud again.

Tom looked down at her, his mouth smiling and his eyes quizzical again. "Why ever should I wish that?" he asked, laughing.

"So that we could start from the beginning and do everything all over again. So that we could…do things differently perhaps," Jennet struggled to explain herself.

Tom looked grim. "I doubt anything would be different, Jennet, even if we did start again. I would still be the heir to the Lister estate, and you would still be Jennet Balderston. We would still be in love with one another but what would that have mattered to anyone apart from us? Circumstance would have always divided us. A bride would have always been chosen for me, if not Jane, it would have been someone else. Perhaps a better man might have been chosen for you; I regret that you were married so hastily because of me."

"William isn't a bad man," Jennet protested. "I think that at one time he really did love me. The problem was that I could never love him, and when we both realised that he gave up on me, I think. Still, he is never cruel, he's just indifferent. I can live with indifferent."

"Do you still lie with him?" Tom asked.

Jennet blushed in response. "Tom! What a question!" she said, laughing and pushing him away playfully. In truth she did not know how best to answer; it had been a long time since she had lain with William, both of them having given up on this marital duty when children no longer seemed likely. But despite their intimacy, Jennet felt inexplicably coy about answering such questions, and decided instead to avoid the question entirely.

"Well! You asked me the same question about Jane once, or don't you remember?" Tom retorted.

"Yes, I remember," replied Jennet, relieved that Tom had chosen not to press her for an answer to his question. "I was jealous, I will admit it. I am still jealous Tom, your wife is beautiful."

"She is," answered Tom, suddenly lifting Jennet and carrying her over to his bed. He began to undress her from her remaining garments, skilfully removing her shift whilst kissing every part of her. Just as Jennet was about to close her eyes and allow herself to be consumed by his touch, Tom stopped abruptly to finish his sentence. His usually bright eyes were dark and serious. "But Jane isn't you, Jennet," he said.

Jennet woke the following morning as the dim winter light trickled lethargically into the room. It took her a few moments to realise where she was; then, as recollections of the night before came flooding back to her she smiled and glanced at Tom, who was snoring softly beside her. She snuggled back down into the cosy bed and, studying Tom's peaceful, slumbering face, she reflected on how happy she felt. Indeed, if she was to die today, she would die happy, knowing that she had felt true love, true joy, and knowing that someone else loved her back just as completely. Nothing else mattered. This bed, right now, was their sanctuary, and the rest of the world could wait. Jennet traced her fingers delicately over Tom's face; his eyes, his cheek, down to his beard and soft lips. Her touch roused him, and he opened his eyes.

"Good morning, my love," Tom said sleepily. "What time is it?"

Jennet shrugged, as though wishing to evade the question. "I wish it was early, but I fear I must leave you soon. They will be expecting me in the nursery."

Tom reached over to his table to look at his pocket watch and gasped in horror. "We have slept too long, Jennet, you are already late. We're fortunate that my man hasn't come in yet, goodness knows, on any other day I would chastise him for his tardiness. You must hurry, Jennet."

Jennet rushed out of bed and put on her clothes as quickly as she could, reflecting as she did so that a woman's clothing was not conducive to swift and efficient dressing, as there were so many layers and items to put on. Indeed, she thought, if a woman's adultery was ever discovered, it was probably the fault of her clothing. She wondered how many adulteresses had been caught in the act of redressing by a servant with poor timing, or had left incriminating items behind in the rooms of their lovers in their haste to avoid discovery. Tucking her hair carelessly behind her coif, she quickly and firmly kissed Tom on the lips and headed for the door of his room.

"Try to avoid being seen, Jennet," Tom cautioned her, his tone irritatingly parental. Jennet bristled; she did not need reminding of the consequences if they were caught.

Jennet carefully and quietly opened Tom's door and slipped outside into the corridor. Checking left, then right, then left again, she made certain that there was no one lingering around outside before making her way back towards the side stairs. From there she would turn back on herself and head back upstairs towards the Mistress's rooms and the nursery, to give the impression to anyone passing her that she had just hurried in through the servants' entrance. She was almost at the end of the Master's corridor when she heard a dreaded voice call from behind her.

"Jennet Preston, is that you? What are you doing?"

Her heard pounding, Jennet swung round to see who was calling her. On seeing that it was Anne Robinson, her heart sank from the back of her mouth where it had been residing in her fit of panic, to the pit of her stomach. Of all the people to catch her in such a compromising situation, it had to be Anne Robinson. It was ironic; Anne worked mostly in the kitchens and the dairy these days, and Jennet counted herself fortunate to have had few encounters with the unpleasant woman since coming to work at Westby. Today, however, it seemed that Jennet's luck had run out.

"I'm going back to the nursery shortly, Anne," replied Jennet, trying to sound innocent as Anne approached.

"Yes, but what are you doing here? These are Master Lister's rooms," insisted Anne, speaking to Jennet as though she might be some foolish apprentice who had lost her way.

"I know that, Anne. I am merely on an errand up here, nothing that need concern you," Jennet replied, turning her back on Anne and walking away so that Anne might not see her reddening face.

"You think you're better than everyone else here, don't you, Jennet Preston?" Anne called after her.

Against her better judgement, Jennet stopped walking away and slowly turned back around to face Anne. "Excuse me?" she asked, incredulously.

Anne walked back up to Jennet, coming so close that Jennet could almost feel the vile woman's breath on her face. "You think you're above us all," she spat, her voice a mere hiss, "but the truth is you're nothing more than a whore."

"How dare you speak to me like that!" Jennet fumed.

"Oh, don't come the innocent with me," retorted Anne, apparently enjoying herself, "you think no one's noticed that you disappear from your duties without explanation? Do you think no one's suspected that you've been coming over to this part of the house, to whore yourself with the Master? It's all the maids giggle about all day long. That's clearly why you're back here again, so that the Master can take his pleasure with you whenever he feels like it. It's that obvious, even the Mistress must know by now."

Jennet could feel the colour rising again in her cheeks. Her mouth was dry, her throat tight; she was speechless. She could hardly deny it, it was all true. She had deluded herself that she had been discreet, that no one would ever find out. She had been sneaking around, telling lies, when all the time the whole house had known what she was up to, and the only person she had been lying to, was herself.

"Is something the matter?" said a voice a little down the corridor. It was Tom, fully clothed now, looking down the hall at them both, wearing a stern expression on his face.

"No Sir," replied Anne obediently, looking down at the floor, her voice now soft and polite.

"Well then, back to work Anne. Jennet, I assume you're away from your duties in the nursery to see me? Thank you for coming up so swiftly, I wanted to speak with you before your Mistress arrives," said Tom, his lie effortless.

Anne looked at them both, clearly unconvinced. Curtseying briefly and, Jennet thought, insincerely, Anne marched off down the corridor and back towards the kitchens. Jennet looked at Tom, dumbstruck and in complete disbelief. Tom looked back at her and, without saying a word, gestured back towards his door. Jennet obediently followed him back up the corridor and back inside his rooms. Tom shut the door, quietly but firmly, leaning on it for a moment as though to prevent any further intrusion.

"She knows, Tom," said Jennet, still in shock. "She knows everything. They all do."

"She thinks she knows something, Jennet. She has no proof. What did you say to her?" Tom asked.

"Nothing, Tom. I swear it. You came out of your rooms and interrupted us before I could answer her accusations," replied Jennet, feeling defensive.

"Alright, well that's fine then. Leave her accusations unanswered, Jennet, whatever you do, say nothing. This will all be fine," answered Tom, in a tone which sounded to Jennet like he was trying to convince himself as much as he was trying to convince her.

"How can you say that, Tom?" asked Jennet indignantly. "How can you possibly believe this will be fine? How long until Jane finds out, if she doesn't know already? And how long until someone tells William? What will we do then?"

"Jane doesn't know," replied Tom firmly. "Believe me; I would know if she had heard rumours. The maids will take care not to speak of this in her presence, Anne included. They know that they would be speaking against me and would risk losing their positions in this house. As for the rest, well, if William hears a rumour and asks you, simply deny it. Tell him that it is predictable gossip given our known history and that there's nothing else to it. As I said, Jennet, no one has any evidence of anything."

Tom went over to his large desk and opened the top drawer, removing from it a small, delicate looking necklace of gold and pearl. Jennet gasped, it was the most beautiful thing she had ever seen.

"My love, this was for you," said Tom. "However, given this morning's developments I think the wiser choice would be to give it to my wife as a token of my affection following her first trip away since coming out of her confinement. I'm sorry; it really would have looked beautiful around your pretty neck."

Jennet nodded, agreeing with Tom's pragmatism but at the same time disappointed that she would not be the recipient of such a beautiful gift. She shook her head slightly, trying to expel the covetous thoughts from her mind. Such finery was never meant for women like her; it hardly matched well with her plain clothing and besides, if William had found it, how on earth would she explain it?

"So," Tom continued, interrupting her thoughts, "if anyone asks where you've been this morning you may simply tell them that you were helping me to choose a gift for your Mistress. You see, and Anne was a witness to me innocently summoning you first thing this morning!" declared Tom, apparently very pleased with himself at having covered their tracks so perfectly. Jennet reflected that she would have been shocked by his ability to lie so effortlessly, if she wasn't so grateful for it. She nodded passively.

"I think it takes a long time to choose the perfect gift for a man's wife," said Tom, gently pushing Jennet towards the wall of the room. "All the options have to be carefully considered," he continued, burying his nose and his lips into Jennet's neck and undoing the ties on her shift with his hand. "I think such a decision could take all morning," he finished, frantically lifting her skirts.

As he pushed himself inside her, Jennet reflected that Anne, for all her harsh and spiteful words, was right about one thing: Tom would take his pleasure with her whenever he wished, and he knew that she would never stop him. She thought too about how assured he was that his servants would never dare speak against him; he knew the power he had over them, just as he was certain of the hold he had over Jennet. If Westby Hall was a castle, Jennet thought, Thomas Lister was undoubtedly the king.

20

Anna Singleton's Cottage, near Gisburn Village
January 1607

Anna Singleton waddled uncomfortably over to the table where her aunt was sitting, nursing a cup of small ale. She sat down slowly and deliberately on her stool opposite Jennet, sighing heavily as she did so. Jennet glanced at her, a look which was both sympathetic and amused passing across her face.

"The time will pass quickly enough," she assured her. "Soon your child will be here and you can stop feeling so wretched."

Anna shot her aunt an unconvinced look. "I feel like the last few weeks have been an eternity, Aunt. I feel larger and more awkward every day. It is nearly impossible for me to get all my work done here, yet still it must be done, it is expected…" she said, her voice trailing off.

Jennet chuckled. "These are normal complaints from a woman so heavy with child! It will all be over soon, and I am here for you. From now until the baby arrives I will call as often as I can, I will help as much as I can," Jennet replied, trying to reassure her niece.

Anna smiled. "That is kind, thank you. Surely you're too busy at Westby Hall?"

Jennet fidgeted uncomfortably on her seat at the mention of

Westby, trying to suppress the memories of the raucous, drunken Christmas festivities which had just passed. After spending Christmas day at home and serving a Christmas feast for William, John, Anna and her husband Thomas, Jennet had worked at the hall on almost every one of the feast days leading up to Twelfth Night, much to William's displeasure. Jennet had not minded; if anything she had revelled in the celebrations, even if these had to be enjoyed from a servant's perspective. The Listers' home, filled with guests in their finery, with good ale and wine and wonderful, delicious food, had been an exciting spectacle that she had not enjoyed since she was a young girl working in their kitchens. Then, Mrs Robinson had been protective, keeping her away from the revelry as much as possible. This time, as a grown woman and the Master of Westby's lover, she had allowed herself to enjoy it. She recalled the rosy complexion of Mistress Lister as she feasted with her friends and family and drank a little too much wine. She remembered the children complaining as they were put to bed; even Anne, who was usually so compliant, wanted to stay downstairs and enjoy the feast for a little longer. She thought about Tom, how his eyes danced in the candlelight, how in a drunken stupor he had stolen her away from the servants' corridor and taken his pleasure with her in the cold dairy, a place so forbidding on a freezing winter's night that they could be certain of there being no intrusion.

"No, not at all," replied Jennet, shaking her head vigorously, resisting her thoughts. "It is quieter at the house after Christmas. Besides, the Mistress knows you are about to have your child, she will understand," she added.

Anna nodded. "Thank you Aunt, it will be a comfort to have you here."

Jennet looked at Anna quizzically. "Anna, is everything alright? Are you well?"

"I'm fine," Anna replied with a sigh. "I'm just a bit frightened about childbed. I have seen how you have suffered, and I just worry…" Anna said, her voice trailing off once again. Jennet could see that the girl was genuinely distressed, despite her apparent composure. She stood up and walked over to her, placing comforting, motherly arms around her shoulders.

"My child, you are not me. You are young, and healthy. All will be well, you will see. I will be here, and we will get help from the village, there is plenty of experience amongst the women here," replied Jennet, trying to reassure her.

"Would Demdike come, do you think?" asked Anna suddenly. "I remember you telling me how she delivered little Jennet safely for Elizabeth."

Jennet winced at the mention of Demdike and the Devices. She had not seen them since they exchanged cross words all those months ago. She had not gone anywhere near Malkin Tower; she had been true to the vow she had made to herself the day she left there with tears streaming down her cheeks. She had pushed all thoughts of that family to a deep recess of her mind and in truth, whilst preoccupied with her work at Westby, not to mention with Thomas Lister, she had quite forgotten them. Now, Anna had reminded her and she felt suddenly and inexplicably guilty.

"I'm not sure, Anna. She is very elderly and frail; I fear she would not travel well. I wouldn't like to ask her. As I said, there is plenty of experience in the village," replied Jennet, trying to be both tactful and evasive. She didn't want Anna to probe any further about Demdike and her family.

"Very well," replied Anna, a frown passing over her pretty face. "You hardly ever mention your friends in Blacko these days, Aunt. You never used to say much about them, but nowadays I never hear anything about them! Are they well?" she asked.

"Yes, yes of course they are," Jennet lied. "I just see little of them nowadays, that's all. As you said yourself, I'm often busy with my work at Westby Hall. I get very little time off," she added.

"Yes, my father says your work takes you away from the cottage for many hours," Anna replied. "In truth, and just between us, I don't think my father and Uncle William like it very much. I think that in your absence they must fend for themselves more than they would like to," added Anna, giggling mischievously.

Jennet smiled and nodded in response. "Men never like to have to look after themselves, Anna. You must now know that, you are a married woman yourself."

Anna groaned in response. "Oh yes! They are very good at wooing you with gifts and sweet, whispered words! But as soon as the priest blesses your marriage…" Anna allowed her voice to trail off once again. Jennet couldn't tell if she was unable or simply unwilling to vocalise her apparent frustrations.

"Are you happy, Anna?" she asked, deciding to probe further.

"Of course, Aunt," Anna replied, without hesitation. "But how quickly do the nice words and tender affections give way to reality, once you marry? It's all hard work and duty, really. Perhaps if women knew this they would choose not to marry."

"And do what instead, Anna?" asked Jennet, slightly incredulous. "There are no monasteries or abbeys left for women to enter! Besides, I think most women do know what it's like really, you included. If you can't remember your parents' marriage then you must surely recall mine; if William and I are not an example of the reality of marriage then I do not know what is," she added, her tone slightly bitter. "I think women simply hope that their marriage will be different," she said finally, "and they are disappointed when they discover that it isn't."

Jennet looked at her niece and saw a familiar look on her face. It was the look she had always worn as a child when chastised; upset but humbled. Jennet softened as she remembered Anna's delicate condition, and resolved not to upset her any further. "I'm sorry," she said. "I fear I am just a bitter old woman, these days. Of course your marriage is better than mine, Anna. You chose Thomas yourself. You married him because you loved him and not because your family said you had to."

"You really don't love Uncle William, do you?" Anna asked with a girlish innocence that Jennet had not seen in her for some time.

Jennet sighed heavily as she sat back down on her stool. It was impossible to lie to Anna now that she was no longer a child. "I care for your Uncle William," she said frankly, "but I will never love him like you are meant to love your husband, Anna, no."

Anna reached over and touched Jennet sympathetically on the hand. "That's sad, Aunt Jennet. It's sad that you will never know love. I know there are many who say it doesn't matter, but I think it does. I think everyone should know love."

"I never said I didn't know love, lass!" Jennet blurted before she was able to stop herself. She fell silent, willing her words to have fallen on deaf ears, praying that Anna would not ask for an explanation.

"Do you mean Master Lister?" Anna asked slowly, unsure whether to venture into this hitherto uncharted emotional territory. "Only I heard talk once, in the village, about you and the Master of Westby Hall."

"Oh yes?" asked Jennet, feigning indifferent surprise. "And what did you hear?"

"Only that a long time ago, before you married William, you were sweet on each other, and that there was a scandal. I didn't wish to give the gossip any credit so I didn't ask what the scandal was, although I suppose I could perhaps guess…" Anna said, her voice trailing off. Raising her eyes from the floor, she looked squarely at Jennet, trying to judge her response.

"That old gossip!" Jennet exclaimed, secretly relieved that the talk of the village was old news. "I didn't lie with him, if that's what you're thinking. I was chaste the day I married your uncle. Not that it matters. I learnt the hard way that it isn't what you do that matters, but what folk think you have done. People's thoughts, their idle gossip, their spreading of rumour; all of it is enough to ruin any girl's reputation," she said bitterly.

"I suppose God knows," replied Anna. "God will know that you did nothing wrong, Aunt."

Jennet shuddered at the mention of the Almighty. Anna was indeed instilled with a piety for which Jennet could only hold herself responsible. Over the past year Jennet knew that she had distanced herself from God, both in thought and deed. She had long ceased to hold herself to account in the eyes of God for her actions with Tom Lister, and instead of feeling guilty and chastising herself, she preferred to indulge happily in the pleasure of it all, turning her back on those like Elizabeth who expressed concern for her, turning her back on God. As Elizabeth herself had once said, on that rainy day when Jennet had caught her with Richard Sellers, she felt far from God. Jennet had not understood Elizabeth's meaning then, but recently she had come to the realisation that she felt the same. Now, confronted with Anna's devout faith and the remembrance of her own, Jennet felt the weight of divine judgement on her back. She hunched herself over towards the table, as though suddenly struggling with the burden of guilt now laid upon her. The pit of her stomach churned intolerably.

"Are you alright?" Anna asked, concern ringing in her voice. "You look very pale, Aunt. Are you well?"

Jennet nodded, unable to speak, trying to force her back to straighten, trying to compose herself.

"So how is Master Lister towards you now?" asked Anna.

Jennet looked down at the table, trying to avoid Anna's inquiring gaze. Her niece, who in truth was more like a daughter to her, was such a kind and affectionate girl; despite Jennet's admissions about past involvement with Tom Lister, clearly Anna had not even considered that her aunt might be guilty of any wrongdoing now. Jennet continued to look downwards, stricken with guilt, unable to speak for fear that the lies which would inevitably spill forth from her adulterous lips would finally incur the wrath of the Almighty. Her mouth, which had been dry, filled suddenly with a sickly, sweet tasting spittle, and her stomach, which had been churning, heaved so hard that she felt it might move itself into her chest. She ran towards the door, flinging herself carelessly outside, and fell down hard on to the frost-bitten ground. There, upon the cold, hard, derelict earth she retched and choked, vomiting violently until her stomach was completely empty. When she had finished, Jennet sat up and looked out at the bleak winter's day; the hint of snow upon the rolling hills in the distance, the gentle plumes of smoke funnelling from the cottages as the village folk fought the battle for warmth against the freezing cold. Breathing in deeply, Jennet realised that the air was so cold that it froze her lungs, but in some strange way its cooling effects calmed her and the nausea which had consumed her moments ago began to subside. She felt Anna approach behind her, her movements deliberate and careful, for the ground was slippery and the weight of her belly now made her unsteady on her feet.

"Aunt, are you unwell? Come back inside, this cold air will do you no good," said Anna tenderly, trying to take Jennet by the arm and help her to her feet.

"No, lass," replied Jennet, shrugging Anna away from her. "I fear I may be sick, I should take my leave. I don't want you to catch my sickness."

"Are you sure?" asked Anna, clearly concerned.

"Yes," replied Jennet firmly, composing herself. "I'm sure it's nothing, perhaps just the effects of too much feasting over Christmas. My belly isn't used to such fine food, and I think it has taken its toll," she added, trying to appear jovial. "But we must be careful, especially for you in your condition," she said finally, her face becoming serious again.

"Alright, Aunt. I would walk with you but..." Anna's voice trailed off as she gesticulated helplessly at her burgeoning belly.

"I will be fine, lass, please don't worry. I will call again in a few days, once I am recovered," said Jennet, as she bade Anna farewell.

Jennet's mind raced as she walked carefully up the lane towards her cottage, trying to understand what had happened to her back there. For all the aches and pains she felt in her back and legs from time to time, she was someone who seldom succumbed to sickness. She recalled suffering from such violent and sudden sickness only a handful of times in her life, on the rare occasions that she was reeling from the ill-effects of drink, and when she was with child. At this thought Jennet stopped dead in her tracks. She hadn't got with child for almost ten years now, ever since her poor baby boy had left her while she slept. After all these years, she believed that it was impossible, that she was barren, that she was too old and her time for bearing children had passed. Feeling suddenly faint, Jennet staggered clumsily to the side of the lane and held herself up against a tree, its branches icy and bare. What if you get with child? Elizabeth's last words to her rang in her ears; what felt like a wild accusation at the time now sounded like a wise warning from a good friend. The nauseating sensation rose again in Jennet's stomach as she stood there and she retched, tears streaming down her face with the strain and discomfort. If it was true, if she really was with child, then God had seen fit to punish her for her sins in the cruellest of ways. God was giving her something she had always desired but in so doing, he had condemned her to face the consequences of what she had done. Realising the gravity of the situation, Jennet slumped down on to the cold ground and wept, great heaving sobs of guilt and remorse. This would be the end; the end of her marriage to William, the end of her position at Westby, the end of Tom Lister's love. Perhaps it would even be the end of her.

21

St Michael's Church, Bracewell
February 1607

Jennet sat down on a hard wooden pew at the back of the church, next to the Mistress's other maids. She shivered; it was a cold day in February and the old stone church offered little respite from the winter's chill. She watched as the church filled with people, locals from Gisburn, Bracewell and Marton taking their seats at the back and middle of the church near to the servants. In front of them sat the distinguished guests from the prominent local families amongst whom the Listers and the Hebers counted their friends and allies, including the Tempests, who were hosting this wedding and its celebrations in their church and afterwards, at their home, the nearby Bracewell Hall. Further forward still sat the two families, who would come together today through the holy matrimony of young Thomas Lister and his bride, Jane Heber. From her seat she could see young Master Lister standing in front of the altar, looking nervous but dutiful. To his side was his father, his posture proud and self-assured, whilst his mother was seated, looking delicate and beautiful in her fine church clothes, her younger children by her side, sternly chaperoned by one of the older maids. To the onlooker, to most of the local folk watching today, the Listers would be quite the spectacle of wealth and authority; the solid family unit, further consolidating their prosperity and power through a carefully orchestrated match with another local heiress. Jennet touched her belly tenderly; she was carrying Thomas Lister's child, she was sure of that now, but despite the noble blood which would flow through his or her veins, this child could never be a part of the great Lister family.

Jennet had not yet told Tom that she was with child. After that day at Anna's cottage when she was so suddenly and violently sick, she had allowed herself to slip into a sort of denial and with it, her symptoms had disappeared, as though her mind had regained control of her body and was determined to dictate to it, to will it not to be with child. At first her mind seemed to be winning the battle, but as a few more weeks passed and the sickness returned and her belly began to round beneath her shift, she had to finally accept the truth of the matter and set her mind to concealing it from her family whilst she grappled with the grave situation she now faced. Jennet felt helpless and alone, and to make matters worse, she had been unable to seek solace in the arms of Tom since sharing the news with him had proved impossible. She had barely seen him these past weeks; after twelfth night, marriages were once again permitted and since then he had been greatly preoccupied with the plans for his son's impending nuptials. The visits to his rooms had ceased and the only moments which had passed between them since that night in the dairy at Christmastide were fleeting, desirous glances as they passed one another in the hallways and corridors of Westby Hall. Without Tom's guidance, without his comfort and advice, Jennet felt paralysed; she willed the wedding and the no doubt seemingly endless feasting which would follow to be over so that she could get Tom to herself again, so that she could tell him of her predicament and appeal for his help and together they could decide what to do.

Her thoughts were interrupted by the congregation beginning to rise as the church doors opened and the bride entered, escorted stiffly by her father. Jennet had only glimpsed Jane Heber previously; she and her father had been to Westby before, of course, but their visits had been guarded and conducted behind closed doors. As she walked up the aisle, Jennet studied her closely. She was a slight young girl, little more than fifteen years of age, with long dark hair and wide, brown eyes. Her face was young and pretty, and her expression was one of concentration with only a mere hint of nerves. Jane Heber had been raised for this moment in her life, since she was a very young child her future marriage would have been talked about, and today she was finally doing her duty. Her dress was the most beautiful thing Jennet had ever seen, fashioned in dark green velvet with gold thread and adorned with matching jewels and a matching cloak. Her neck was dressed with a large gold necklace which complemented the plunging neckline of her gown, but also drew attention to her chest, which as yet lacked a woman's form. She really was little more than a child, thought Jennet, a very young girl being matched with an equally young man to fulfil family ambitions. Both the bride and groom knew the importance of the transaction taking place in church today; the solemnity and significance of it all was written all over their serious faces. Jennet thought then about Anna's wedding, about how happy she had looked as she nearly danced up the aisle to her beloved Thomas, how her dress, though simple and decorated with fresh flowers rather than fine jewels, sat well on the evident curves of her body. Jennet reflected on how much nicer it was to watch a woman marry for love than a child marry for ambition.

As the marriage ceremony commenced, Jennet's mind continued to wander; in truth she wanted to close her ears to the vows as the words, when spoken, reminded her that she had made the same vows to William so many years ago, and she had broken them so many times now. Like young Jane Heber, and like her Anna, she too had promised to love, honour and obey her husband, and to keep only to him. She too had made these promises before God and yet, when tempted, she had betrayed William. She had betrayed God. The first time had been on Anna's wedding day, of course, but there had been so many more times since then; she had strayed so far from God's path that she wondered if she'd ever be able to return. Jennet touched her belly lightly again, reminding herself again of how she was now being punished for her sin. Her guilt made the colour rise in her cheeks; her cold face grew warm and the pit of her stomach churned, making her feel sick and dizzy. She tried to force herself to focus on the proceedings in front of her. The priest, having led the bride and groom through their vows, was now reciting the familiar prayers, blessing the union and reminding them that they were enjoined in a holy tradition which stretched back to the time of Adam and Eve. Jennet had forgotten that part of the service and now, when confronted with it, she felt a lump rise in her dry throat. She gulped hard, suppressing it, trying to push her guilt away. The priest's words being of no comfort, she forced her mind to focus on anything else; the beautiful winter flowers in the church that day, the way her breath formed clouds in the air when she exhaled. She was relieved when the bride and groom moved to take Holy Communion; at least for a moment the priest had stopped stifling her with lectures on the sanctity of marriage.

Suddenly, as the bride and groom were receiving the body and blood of Christ, there was a loud, strangling cry from the front pews. It was a strange noise: louder than a groan but not quite powerful enough to be considered a bellow; a hollow, pained whine. Jennet thought it was like the sort of noise a horse makes when its shoe slips and it injures its hoof underneath. Immediately everyone in the congregation turned their heads, those at the back like Jennet straining to see its source. There were a few loud gasps from the pews at the front and a number of people rushed over to where the noise had come from, including the bride and groom. In an instant the entire congregation rose to stand, no longer silent and still, now murmuring and shuffling around, everyone trying to find out what had happened.

"What's happening? Did you see anything?" Jennet asked the maid sitting next to her, who simply shook her head in response, the confusion and concern evident on her face.

"It's Master Lister!" someone called out from in front of them.

"Quick! Help the Master!" called another.

Jennet's eyes widened with shock as she absorbed what she had just heard. She saw a group of men, some of Tom's servants and some men she assumed to be locals, head to the front of the church. Jennet rose up on to her tiptoes, struggling to see if the cries from the congregation were true, if indeed it was Tom who had made that terrible noise. Peering over people's heads, she could see a well-dressed man, limp and lifeless; his feet dragging along the ground as two large men swiftly carried him away into the vestry. Jane Lister, the bride and groom, the children, and another man, who Jennet supposed must be the family physician followed closely behind, the priest swiftly closing the curtain behind them all.

"It is Tom," she whispered, as though saying the words aloud to herself might make it any more believable. How could it be true? Tom was not old, or ill. How could he be so suddenly struck down?

"What do we do now?" asked the maid who had been so dumbstruck moments ago. Like Jennet, she too appeared to be reeling from the shock of what had just happened. "Do we just stay here?" she asked, as though she supposed that Jennet might hold all the answers.

"I suppose we must," replied Jennet, trying not to let her distress show. "I suppose we must wait until our Mistress summons us," she added dutifully, trying to let her sense of duty suppress the tears which were beginning to gather in the corners of her eyes.

Jennet fell silent and stood there with the other maids for what felt like an eternity. The church, which had felt so cold earlier, now stifled and suffocated her with the heat that was emanating from so many warm bodies. She felt trapped, wanting to rush to Tom's side, wanting to kiss his lips and his cheeks, wanting to revive him, wanting to tell him that she loved him and that she was going to bear his child. She knew she could do none of these things, for she was merely his lover and not his wife. His wife was in there with him, no doubt standing concerned but aloof over his lifeless body while the physician did his work. Jennet clenched her fists, suddenly feeling angry. Jane could not love Tom like she did, no one could, yet it was she who was with him and not the person who loved him most in the world.

Cries of anguish rose from the vestry. The congregation, who had been chattering anxiously amongst themselves, fell silent. Jennet listened closely; was Tom revived, or was it Jane and the children wailing in their grief because their husband and father was now dead? Jennet held her breath, for fear that the mere sound of inhaling and exhaling might stop her hearing clearly. The cries grew louder and more desperate; deep masculine bellows which reassured Jennet that it was Tom, that indeed he did still live. He was shouting now, so loudly and clearly that the whole church could hear what he had to say.

"Jennet Preston, is she here?" he cried out. "For God's sake, find her and bring her to my side! Take hold of her!"

Jennet inhaled sharply and froze, feeling the eyes of many in the congregation fall suddenly upon her. She could hear murmurs of confusion, people asking each other who is Jennet Preston, and in amongst those voices, the whispers of condemnation from those who knew exactly who she was and what she must have done. Her cheeks burning and crimson, Jennet looked to the floor, wishing that she could disappear, that the hard stone floor could open up beneath her and swallow her whole. At that moment she wanted to run away, but she also wanted to go to Tom's side, to reassure him and comfort him.

"Oh she lies heavy upon me, Preston's wife lays heavy upon my heart. She must be here, bring her to me, please, find her!" Tom's railing echoed from the vestry.

Jennet could take Tom's desperate pleas no longer. Without thinking, she forced her way through the row of maids she was sitting with and ran up the church aisle towards the vestry. Bursting in through the heavy curtains, she was confronted with an upsetting scene. There, laid out on a makeshift bed of robes, was Tom, with Jane and the physician at his side, both looking helplessly at him as he writhed around on the floor, his face contorted with periodic fits of agony. The children were standing a little further back; most were sobbing, and the maid and the priest were trying to offer them some comfort. Jane looked at Jennet; she was pale and aghast, as though struggling to cope with the situation unfolding before her eyes. Without hesitation, Jennet rushed over to Tom's side and took hold of his hand.

"I am here, my love," she whispered.

"Jennet? Jennet, you came," Tom croaked, his voice and strength greatly weakened by his shouting. "Jennet, I love you Jennet. I am sorry."

"What have you to be sorry for?" Jennet asked him, leaning down closer to him, putting her ear to his lips as his voice was becoming barely a whisper.

"I'm sorry that you loved me. I'm sorry that I pursued you, that I could not leave you to be content with your life," he said, whimpering slightly as he spoke. Jennet could clearly see that he was ailing, that something was seriously wrong with him.

"Tom, I could never have been content without you. I have to tell you, Tom, I am with child," she whispered back, tears rolling down her cheeks as she spoke. She did not care who heard. She did not know if he would live or if he would die; she did not know how much time they would have. She had to tell him. "Your child," she added. She looked down at Tom's face, still beautiful to her despite his obvious anguish. His usually bright blue eyes looked distant, almost vacant; it was hard to determine if he had understood what she had just said. "I will bear your child," she repeated, desperate for a response. Behind her, she felt Jane Lister bristle; she had heard.

"I'm...sorry," said Tom, struggling to utter his reply. "I love you," he said again, straining over the words, his face screwed up with excruciating pain. His breathing became laboured, and he squeezed Jennet's hand harder with the effort of it. Then finally, looking into Jennet's eyes, Tom Lister breathed his final breath, releasing her hand as he let go of his life. Jennet, realising it was all over, put her head on his chest and let out deep, heartbroken sobs. In that moment, she wanted to die along with him. She wished that God would strike her down also, so that she would be with Tom eternally, so that she would not be left behind. Her hands clawed desperately at his chest, as though searching for a sign of life, as though the power of her grief might be enough to bring him back. Her efforts were futile; Tom was gone, leaving her to face pain and sorrow alone.

"Get out," came a cold, calm voice from behind her. Jennet looked up. In her shock and grief she had forgotten that anyone else was in the room. Now she was reminded that Tom Lister's whole family, his wife and his children, had witnessed everything.

Jennet turned around to face Jane Lister, whose face was pale with anguish and rage. Jane looked down at Jennet, flaring her nostrils angrily at her as she spoke. "You are a whore and I wish never to see you again. Now get out!" she yelled, momentarily losing control of herself.

Jennet stood up and fled from the vestry. Opening the curtain she was confronted by at least a hundred staring, horrified faces. They had heard everything Jane Lister had just said. Tears streaming down her burning hot cheeks, Jennet ran carelessly down the aisle and out of the church, letting the heavy wooden door slam hard behind her. Once outside, she leant against the church door and wept; great heavy sobs of sorrow and grief. Her Tom was dead. She had nothing, no one left to turn to. She couldn't go home and face William, face what she had done, tell him of her betrayal and plead for his forgiveness. She was too weak; she didn't have the stomach for it. Nor could she go to Anna, for surely even her kind, loving Anna could not bear to hear what she had done, especially right now, with a new baby and barely out of childbed. She had nowhere to go. Wiping the tears away from her eyes, she looked out into the cold, desolate countryside; frost-bitten and forbidding. Without a care for where she was headed, she began to walk.

It was several hours later when Jennet, chilled and delirious, reached the familiar hillside at Blacko. Staggering carelessly up to the familiar old door of Malkin Tower, she threw herself down against it, exhausted. The noise she made must have alerted someone inside, as quite quickly the door creaked open. An incredulous Elizabeth peered down at her.

"Jennet?" she asked in disbelief.

Jennet looked up at her, her tear-stained face puffy and despairing. Elizabeth bent down and instinctively placed an arm gently around her friend, drawing her near. The display of tender affection made Jennet sob ever more, crying so hard that her chest heaved and her body ached.

"Jennet, what's the matter?" Elizabeth asked. "What's happened?"

"He's dead!" Jennet replied, her words sounding more like a wail. "Tom is dead and I am carrying his child. I'm sorry, Elizabeth, I have nowhere else to go," Jennet cried pitifully.

"Oh, my dear," replied Elizabeth, her usual calm demeanour remaining steadfast. "Now, come. Come inside, I've a fire lit. You're among friends now."

Taking her friend by the arm, Elizabeth led Jennet inside to the familiar rickety comfort of Malkin Tower, where Old Demdike and the children were waiting by the fire. As Old Demdike set eyes on Jennet for the first time in months she rose slowly from her seat and walked over to embrace her. No malice awaited Jennet, no judgment, no lectures; only compassion, kindness and love.

"Oh, Mother," was all she could say as she wept in the old woman's arms.

Part Four

1611 - 1612

22

Malkin Tower, Blacko Hillside, Forest of Pendle
October 1611

"Bess! Bess, come quick and inside, it's beginning to rain!" Jennet called from the door of Malkin Tower. She squinted through the sudden, driving torrent of water to see a small figure running hurriedly towards her. As the little girl approached, Jennet ran out towards her and gathered her into her arms, protectively hugging her close as she turned back towards the door, thus shielding her from the rain.

"You will catch your death of cold," Jennet scolded as she felt the child's skin and clothing, all soaked to the bone. "Now come, let's dry you off by the fire."

"Yes Mother," replied the child obediently, her bottom lip protruding in an act of familiar and endearing impertinence. Bess would always do as she was told, but through small displays of defiance she let her mother know if she wasn't happy about it.

"Oh good, she's come in," said Elizabeth as Jennet sat her daughter down by the fire. "You would play out in all weathers," she remarked to the child, with a half-smile.

"Where's little Jennet?" asked Bess as Jennet set about drying her. She had taken to calling Elizabeth's daughter 'little' to distinguish between the child of almost eleven years and her own mother. Sometimes Elizabeth and Jennet joked that whilst their reciprocal naming of their children had been mutually flattering, it could also prove highly impractical; indeed, Jennet's own daughter Elizabeth had quite quickly been given the familiar name Bess to avoid further confusion.

"She'll be in soon, I'm sure," replied Elizabeth gently. "I'll warn you though, she's in a bit of a cross mood. She argued with her grandmother a little while ago and has been out sulking in one of the outbuildings ever since. Don't worry, she will come in soon. She doesn't much like the rain, not at all like you!" she added, rubbing the child affectionately on the head.

The child fidgeted in front of the fire as Jennet dried her and wrapped her in a cloth, chattering away, half to her mother and half to herself, about everything she had seen and done while playing outside before the rain came. She was a lively, noisy child; full of energy and wonder at everything around her. Jennet saw more and more of her father in her as she grew older; not only in her looks, although in this regard she was undoubtedly his child, with his bright blue eyes and dark hair, but also in that steely, headstrong determination that she so often displayed. The thought of Tom made a lump rise in Jennet's throat; it would soon be half a decade since his death, yet she felt herself barely recovered from it, her sorrow buried instead deep within her, only soothed by her beautiful, vibrant little girl.

Bess grew restless as Jennet rubbed her damp hair, releasing the rainwater from the mass of tumbling curls on her head. Jennet recalled her shock and surprise when those curls first began to appear; curls just like the child she had dreamt of, the daughter she had hoped and prayed that she would always have. Now, and for every day for the last four years, she had been there, growing and changing, lightening Jennet's heavy heart with her childlike innocence, reminding Jennet of her love for Tom and consoling her in her saddest moments.

The weeks after Tom died had been the hardest time Jennet had ever had to endure, and on more than one occasion, she had reflected that if it had not been for Elizabeth, her mother and children, she would not have survived it. After fleeing to Malkin Tower on that cold winter's day, she had remained with the Devices for many weeks, too paralysed by a toxic mixture of grief, shame and fear to return to Gisburn and face her husband's wrath or the village folks' condemning stares. Day after day she had sat, flitting between episodes of inconsolable silence and uncontrollable tears. Elizabeth had sat beside her, for hour upon hour, trying to offer comfort, trying to coax her to eat or drink something, reminding her that she had a child in her belly which needed nourishment. At first Jennet had refused, certain that Tom's death was her punishment for her sins, and certain too that this child, like him, would surely perish before she made it beyond her womb. Eventually, as the days passed and the child's fluttery movements turned into demanding kicks, she began to hope that this child was strong, that she may live, and she forced herself to eat. From the child growing in her belly, and from Elizabeth's patience and kindness, Jennet had drawn strength, willing herself to continue even when, in her darkest moments, she wished to be laid still in the cold ground next to her beloved Tom. For whatever reason, this was not in God's plan for her. Instead she would bear this child, Tom's child, and she had to go on for him, she had to carry on for his child.

Then one day, a fine spring day when nature was once again coming back to life, William turned up at the old rickety door of Malkin Tower. His face looked tired and much aged, and was sullen and pinched as he sombrely but calmly asked to see Jennet. Elizabeth allowed him inside and Jennet, upon seeing him, had gasped. In her grief, she had given little consideration to the effect her behaviour would have had upon him; indeed she had given more thought to how her actions had offended God than how they had damaged her husband. Now, standing in front of her, the injury was self-evident and she was immediately guilt-stricken. William stood there, looking upon her, drawing his own sharp breath at the sight of her swollen belly.

"So it is true," he said finally, gesticulating towards her stomach, looking down towards the floor, as though now, when presented with the undeniable truth, he could no longer bear to look upon her.

"Yes," Jennet replied, simply. "It is true. I am sorry, William. I'm truly sorry for how I have hurt you."

"You have no idea!" he replied angrily. "Hiding here in Blacko. You've no idea how unbearable life has become for me, Jennet, how intolerable it is for all of us. Anna cannot decide whether to feel angry at you or weep for you, but mostly I think she misses you. We all do. For all that you have done, we still miss you."

"I know what I have done, William," said Jennet, looking down at the floor to avoid his gaze. "Why are you here, William? What do you want? You cannot punish me any more than I have punished myself."

"I don't wish to punish you, Jennet," replied William plainly. "I have come to take you home. You are my wife, when it's all said and done."

"Home?" repeated Jennet, dumbly. She couldn't believe what she was hearing. Over the weeks since Tom's death she had found it difficult to imagine her future, but whenever she did, she didn't think for one moment that William would feature in it. For a man to take back such a deceitful, sinful woman; surely that was inconceivable?

"I can't forgive what you have done," continued William. "But I can't stand by and leave you and this child you carry to perish as paupers either. I have a duty to you Jennet; I made an oath to you the day we married and it is one that I, for my part, intend to keep," he added pointedly.

"Duty," repeated Jennet. "William, you can barely look at me. How do you suppose that you'll manage to live with me? To live with me carrying and bearing this child?" she added, clutching her belly.

William sighed and, for the first time since arriving, looked her straight in the eye. "Jennet, it seems to me that you have no other choice. You cannot stay here forever. You will come home and we will raise the child as our own."

Jennet, realising the truth in William's words, had returned home to Gisburn just a few days later. He had been right, she had no choice; without him she had no home, and no income with which to feed and shelter herself and her child. She needed him. He didn't need her, however, and it was always a puzzle to her that he had chosen to come to Malkin Tower that day, that he had chosen to take her home when no one in the village would have condemned him for casting her and her child from his life. Nonetheless, William was true to his word, treating Jennet with a reserved kindness, and accepting the child, when she arrived, as if she was his own flesh and blood, growing to love her as a father loves his daughter. The last four years, then, had been a period of peace and calm, with both parents enjoying watching their daughter grow but always avoiding each other's gaze, living alongside each other rather than together, never quite able to repair the damage done by Jennet's betrayal. No one in the village spoke to Jennet, apart from Anna of course, but Jennet considered this a small price to pay. Upon her return William had insisted to anyone he spoke to that the child Jennet carried was his; an obvious lie but one which served well enough to stop folk making any comments or accusations to Jennet directly. They muttered behind her back, no doubt, but this was something Jennet had been accustomed to anyway and had long ceased to care about.

Jennet often wondered why, after all she had done, God seemed to look so favourably upon her. After Tom's death she was delivered safely of her child and back at home with her husband, her only apparent punishment being that William could never forgive her, and of course, the loss of Tom, the grief of which still had the power to make her heart heavy and her body ache, even after four years. Still, considering all that she had done, she had honestly expected to be struck down terribly. Our Lord works in mysterious ways, said the priest in Church, and it was true; God had seen fit to give her so many blessings and yet, from what she had heard over these past years, the poor Lister family had suffered nothing but misfortune and grief. William would not speak to her about them, of course, so what little she knew had been gathered from conversations with Anna who, when she visited Jennet with her ever-growing brood of children, liked to tell her the news from the village.

The year after Tom's death, beautiful Jane Lister had also perished, succumbing quickly to an unspecified malady almost one year to the day after her husband had died. Hearing about Jane's demise had renewed Jennet's guilt. As her Mistress, Jane had always been so kind to Jennet and Tom had never denied her to be anything but a loyal and attentive wife; it must have been heart-breaking and humiliating for her to watch her unfaithful husband die in the arms of one of her maids in a Church, of all places. It was little wonder, Jennet reflected, that poor Jane had succumbed so easily to illness.

Jane's death had left a great burden of responsibility on very young shoulders as their eldest son, Thomas Lister, who had inherited Westby Hall after his father's death, now also took on the care of his orphaned younger siblings. Thomas and his wife, the childlike girl in green that Jennet had witnessed walking up the aisle on that fateful day, had recently had their first child, a son called William. Jennet recalled how the village folk had rejoiced at such good news. Their happiness, however, was short-lived when word came from Westby Hall that the child was sickly and the physician did not know if he would live. For all their wealth and prosperity, Jennet reflected, tragedy and death seemed to follow the Lister family like a plague. Apart from saying prayers for them in Church, Jennet tried not to think about the Listers too much, for if she did, she felt a responsibility for their misfortune that was so enormous it threatened to consume her.

"Little Jennet's come in," said Elizabeth, interrupting her thoughts. Jennet realised that Elizabeth was talking to Bess, who jumped up excitedly and ran off to find her friend.

"You've a lot on your mind today," observed Elizabeth, looking at Jennet. Ever since Tom's death and Jennet's time spent living at Malkin Tower, Elizabeth had seemed to have an intuitive sense of Jennet's mood, if not exactly what she was thinking.

Jennet nodded. "Just the usual," she replied plainly.

"Oh Jennet," said Elizabeth with a sigh. "You torture yourself with it all, you know, and in the end it will serve no other purpose than to drive you mad."

"Perhaps madness is all I deserve," Jennet replied.

"And what about little Bess, what does she deserve, Jennet? A mother who has lost all sanity? Or one who accepts that what's done is done, that she cannot change it, that she now must live as best she can for her child?" Elizabeth retorted.

"You're right, Elizabeth, of course you're right," replied Jennet with a sigh. "I just worry, that's all."

"Worry about what, Jennet? That God is going to strike you down? I'd say that if he was going to, he would have done so by now. I'd also say that if he is in the business of handing out punishments in this life, then he has dealt you your fair share. He's also dealt you many blessings, that girl of yours above all of them. Hold on to those blessings, Jennet, and stop thinking so much about it all," Elizabeth cautioned.

Jennet nodded. There was nothing else she could say to her friend and greatest confidante, no other way in which she could articulate her fears so that Elizabeth might find them rational. Elizabeth's plain and sensible perspective was often Jennet's guiding light, but it could also be a wall which, when hit against, was uncompromising, reducing Jennet to complicit silence.

"Speaking of blessings and curses, Mother and I have a sick cow to treat this afternoon. How long were you planning to stay today? Would you be able to look after Jennet for a while? James is doing some labouring work and Alison is, well, goodness knows where," said Elizabeth, rolling her eyes despairingly at the mention of her eldest daughter.

"Yes of course," replied Jennet. "You seem to take your mother out more and more on these sorts of visits," she added.

"Well need's must," answered Elizabeth flatly. "Mother's skills seem to be more and more in demand again, mainly to counter the work of that witch Chattox, no doubt. But it gives us another income and of course, at Mother's age she can't go alone. She's all but blind now, though she won't admit it."

"So are you just helping Demdike?" asked Jennet. "Or are you taking an interest in learning her craft yourself?"

"Both," replied Elizabeth. "I'm still not sure about doing what Mother does. I don't know if I have the strength for it and besides, I still think it is dangerous work. So I help and learn a little so that I have some knowledge, if I ever need it, but that's all."

Jennet nodded. She knew Elizabeth had always felt conflicted towards her mother's work, appreciating both its merits and its inherent danger. She knew too that Elizabeth grew more uneasy as her two older children, James and Alison, began to learn their grandmother's craft. She suspected this was why Elizabeth had decided to accompany Old Demdike on more of her visits to cure sick animals or administer a remedy for a human malady; so that she could limit the amount of involvement had by her children, and also so that she could keep an eye on Demdike, who was increasingly frail in body and mind.

"Besides," Elizabeth interjected with a wry smile, interrupting Jennet's thoughts. "The way things are going for me at the moment, I may have no choice but to ply my mother's trade."

"What do you mean?" Jennet asked. "I thought you had work at the mill-house?"

"I did," replied Elizabeth with a sigh. "Until that wily old rogue Richard Baldwin sent me home without pay last week. So now, I have only the little work which comes from the Hewits in Colne, which is consistent, but is never enough. "

"Oh Elizabeth," Jennet declared sympathetically. "Did he give a reason?"

"Just that I am no longer needed," answered Elizabeth despairingly. "You see, Jennet, men like Richard Baldwin find it easy to lay off workers like me. I mean, I have no man at home to defend me and well he knows it. If he gives me no work, if he gives me no pay, well what am I to do?"

Jennet considered this for a moment. "Would James not appeal to him on your behalf?" she asked. The question seemed reasonable; James was on the cusp of manhood, earning a wage of his own now, however small and irregular it might be.

"James! He's my boy, not my husband! Besides, he would make matters worse. He can't be trusted to handle an argument well. You recall when he confronted Mistress Towneley at Carr Hall, when she accused him of stealing her turves?"

Jennet nodded in agreement, remembering the incident, which had happened at Easter the previous year. Feeling injured by Anne Towneley's accusations, which were being repeated all around the nearby villages, James had travelled to her home to speak to her about the matter and to assure her that he had not dug for peat on her land without permission. James had sworn to his mother that he had attempted to be reasonable with Mistress Towneley, but that she had been so angry that, upon seeing him, she had chased him from her door, hitting him repeatedly over the back and the shoulders, all the way down the lane. The whole incident had made James a laughing stock, until about one week later, when Mistress Towneley was found dead by her maid. Then the laughter became whispers of the sort which Elizabeth had always feared; of murder, of curses, of bewitchment.

"Anyway," said Elizabeth, shaking her head and shoulders as though to shake away the memory of James's mishap, "unbeknown to me, Mother and Alison have been to see Richard Baldwin, to no avail I might add. If anything I imagine they have made matters worse."

"Really?" Jennet asked, drawing a deep breath, imagining the scene. Demdike, for all her frailty, retained a sharp temper that, when provoked, burst forth from her tongue in a verbal flurry of accusation and insult. She could only imagine what the old woman had said to Richard Baldwin and it made her wince. Alison, her young rebellious chaperone, would have been both unable and unwilling to curtail Demdike's venom. "What happened exactly?" asked Jennet, with baited breath.

"Well, Mother says she started reasonably enough, politely requesting my payment, explaining that it was needed to feed my children," said Elizabeth with a sigh. "But Mother says that Richard Baldwin became angry and shouted at them to get off his property, calling them both witches and calling me a whore."

"So, did they leave?" asked Jennet, anxious even as the story was being related back to her.

"They did, but not before Mother cursed him," replied Elizabeth flatly.

"She cursed him?" repeated Jennet, incredulous. She knew that Demdike had the power to curse as well as cure, but the wily old woman had always been more giving with the latter and careful with the former. Over the years she had repeatedly criticised Chattox for what she suspected was a liberal use of curses and had made it her work to root out the accursed and offer them remedies, just as she had done with Jennet and the bottle of pins all those years ago.

"Yes, Alison was so shocked that she came right home and told me. She said that as Mother walked away she turned back for a moment, looked at Richard Baldwin and then looked sideways, as though speaking to someone who wasn't there and said 'revenge upon him or his'," said Elizabeth, clearly despairing. "I mean, how careless does she wish to be, Jennet? That man had already named her a witch, was she out to prove it? I hope and pray that he didn't hear her or we are surely all for the rope," finished Elizabeth, her voice unsteady with fear.

"You said she looked sideways when speaking her curse, like she was talking to someone?" probed Jennet, intrigued by this odd detail.

"Yes, I have asked her about that. She said it was Tibb; that the dog had appeared again by her side. She said that the instruction was to him, that she wished him to exact the revenge. She hasn't spoken about that dog for years and now she is suddenly seeing him once again? I fear she may be slipping into madness again, Jennet," said Elizabeth, clearly anguished.

"Oh Elizabeth," said Jennet, placing a comforting arm around her friend. They stood silently for a few moments, each contemplating the seriousness and the strangeness of Demdike's behaviour.

"Well, mad or not, I suppose I must take her to see this cow now," said Elizabeth, looking outside. "If we leave it too much later we will lose the light. Are you sure you don't mind staying here with Jennet?"

"Not at all," replied Jennet with a grim smile.

As Jennet watched Elizabeth and Demdike walk slowly down the rugged lane that afternoon, she thought about what Elizabeth had told her. Demdike's behaviour towards Richard Baldwin, if correctly reported by Alison, had indeed been uncharacteristically aggressive and careless. Jennet could only attribute her outburst to Demdike's frail and aged state; the ramblings of an old woman who was both angry and struggling with senility. Still, this made her words no less dangerous: if Richard Baldwin had heard what she said then it would be easy for him to make an accusation of witchcraft against her. Jennet felt the pit of her stomach churn. She didn't doubt Demdike's power to heal. Now she worried that the old woman, for all her aged weakness, also had malevolent gifts at her disposal, gifts which she had stored away for all these years, but which slipped out that day in a feverish moment of rage. Jennet gulped hard, saying a prayer to herself, asking God for help to ensure that Demdike's curse was unsuccessful. If it wasn't, if it couldn't be stopped, then something bad was about to happen to the Baldwin family and after that, Demdike and her family would all be in danger.

23

The Prestons' Farm, near Gisburn Village
March 1612

Jennet smiled as William walked through the door of their home that evening, with his brother following wearily behind. They both looked tired and dirty from a day of hard toil in the fields. Bess, clearly excited to see them both, jumped up from the stool where she had been sitting and threw her arms around them both in turn with her usual enthusiastic greeting. William chuckled and spun her around above his head; it didn't matter how weary he was, he always had time for Bess's merry antics. Putting his daughter down, William walked over to where Jennet was standing, still smiling, and placing his arms around her, kissed her gently on the cheek.

"How are you, Jennet?" he asked, almost whispering the words in her ear, sending a shiver down her back.

"I'm well, William, thank you," replied Jennet, taking hold of his hands affectionately for a moment before letting them go to carry on preparing the evening meal.

Quietly, Jennet breathed a sigh of relief and smiled to herself. For a few weeks now, things between herself and William had been changing. They had grown closer, rekindling some of their affection for one another and behaving more like man and wife again. William had seemed to initiate this, steadily relinquishing his cold and distant demeanour and Jennet had responded, becoming less cautious around him, returning his embraces when offered. It was as though, for some reason she could not explain, they had both decided to lower their guards and to soften towards one another.

Last night, for the first time in years, they had lain together. William had come home from the alehouse early and uncharacteristically sober, and had climbed into bed beside her. Jennet recalled how it had seemed strange and unfamiliar, and how initially all she could think was that the last time she had lain with a man it had been with Tom Lister. At first William's touch had seemed rough and urgent but, as she responded, he became tender and more attentive, and she began to enjoy it. Afterwards, as he lay next to her, snoring contentedly, Jennet had reflected that for the first time in her marriage, she felt like she was growing to really love her husband. It was as though the spectre of Tom Lister, and the intense love she had felt for him, was beginning to lift from her, allowing her to experience happiness again, to enjoy the love of another. She hoped that William, with his renewed affection for her, was starting to forgive what she had done, and that he wouldn't change his mind and start treating her coldly again. That was why she had felt so relieved when he had come home and embraced her; he clearly didn't regret their intimacy.

"I need to speak to you, Jennet," said William, interrupting her thoughts.

"Sounds serious?" she replied, the smile falling from her face as began to worry about what he was going to say. Perhaps he did regret last night, perhaps he was about to say that he realised he could never forgive her and that last night had been a mistake that should never happen again.

"Don't look so worried," he chuckled, gently touching her cheek. "Although I suppose what I'm about to say is a sort of warning, and no doubt you will worry about it. It's about your friends, Jennet, the ones who live on the hillside in Blacko."

"What, Elizabeth?" asked Jennet.

"Yes, Elizabeth, and her mother, and the children, though I believe two of them are children no longer," said William. "I'll be honest, Jennet, I've been hearing some pretty awful stories recently, some vicious rumours about them and I really think you need to hear them. They've always been good friends to you and I think you need to warn them about what's being said."

"Go on," urged Jennet.

"People are calling them witches, Jennet, all of them. Now I know in the past you've told me about Demdike's healing charms, in fact I remember you making us have that awful bit of clay she gave you under our pillows to help us have a child. But this is different; people aren't talking about them curing sick animals and offering potions for maladies. They're talking about curses, about misdeeds, about the sort of thing that could get them all into a lot of trouble. Do you understand my meaning?"

"Yes," replied Jennet, a lump rising in her throat. "Do you know exactly what people are saying?"

"They're saying that Demdike bewitched the miller's daughter who died just before Christmas. Baldwin, I think his name is. Apparently they argued last year and he thinks she cursed him. His daughter fell ill shortly after their quarrel and languished for weeks in a horrible state," William said, his tone grave.

Jennet gulped hard. "Surely this is just hearsay, William? Rumour and gossip? After all, no one can prove that Demdike had anything to do with the miller's daughter's death?"

"No one needs proof of these things, Jennet. An accusation is enough to get the Sheriff involved, and from what I hear about the Sheriff over there, he will be very interested in what folk think Demdike and her family have been up to," William replied, brusquely.

"Yes, you're probably right," replied Jennet. "Although one accusation following a quarrel doesn't make someone a witch," she added, defensively.

"There's more than one accusation against them," said William.

"The story about the miller's daughter has started tongues wagging and more than a few have suggested that the boy, James is it? Well some have suggested that James had a hand in the death of the Mistress of Carr Hall a couple of years ago. Apparently the story is similar: James quarrelled with her and she was dead a week later. But the strangest story of all is the one being told by a man known as Bulcock, Henry I think. He says that his daughter was bewitched by Alison Device and that in his desperation he sought a cure from Demdike, for she was always known to be a healer, but that Demdike refused to treat the girl, cackling wildly in his face and sending him on his way."

Jennet stared at William, open-mouthed. "None of this can be true! What can we do?" she asked.

"Not much," replied William, shrugging his shoulders. "Warn them, I suppose. Then keep your distance, Jennet. If folk think that they are witches, then they may come to think that you are one also. You have the child to think about, so please, be careful and stay away for a little while."

Jennet sighed. She knew William was right; around these parts you were guilty by association, and plenty of those who lived in the village and beyond knew that Jennet was a good friend of Demdike and the Devices. She knew she was already disliked in Gisburn because of her involvement with Tom Lister and that there were those who would relish calling her a witch, there were probably even some who would be quite happy to see her dangling at the end of a rope. Jennet touched her own neck delicately, contemplating the gravity of the rumours that were circulating and the danger that all of them, herself included, might find themselves in.

Jennet's thoughts were interrupted by a loud bang at the door. She looked at William.

"Who could that be?" she asked.

"I'll go," he replied, heading towards the door.

Before William had chance to answer, the door swung open, abruptly and violently, making it rattle on its hinges. Two men stood in the doorway, armed and stern looking.

"This is my cottage!" exclaimed William. "You have no right to enter! Who are you and what do you want?"

"We come on the Magistrate's business, and we have every right," replied one of the men with a self-satisfied chuckle. He smirked twistedly as he looked back and forth from William, to Jennet. "This is the home of Jennet Preston, wife of William, is it not?" he asked, almost teasingly.

William nodded gravely.

"Then, my good man, your wife needs to come with us," said the man.

"Jennet isn't going anywhere unless you explain your purpose first," replied William, his voice wavering, his eyes warily regarding the rapiers attached to both men's waists.

"We have orders from Master Heber of Marton," replied the man. "Your wife's presence is required at Marton Hall for questioning."

"Questioning?" asked William. "Questions about what?"

"I am not at liberty to discuss it, but I have my orders and your wife must come with me. Must I draw my sword in front of the child?" he added, glancing at Bess.

Protectively, Jennet gathered Bess into her arms. The child began to whimper as she too realised that something serious was unfolding. Jennet kissed her daughter's head, burying her nose in her beautiful curls, overwhelmed by the urge to cling to the child forever, to stay with her and not let her go. Sadly, Jennet realised that she had no choice; these men were armed and following orders, they came with threat and authority and would not leave until they had what they had come for.

"Don't worry, Bess. I will be back. These men just want to ask me some questions, that's all. I love you," she said, trying desperately to reassure her daughter, slowly and gently letting her go.

William looked at Jennet helplessly as she walked towards the two men and surrendered herself into their custody.

"Let's go and clear this matter up, then," she said to the two of them bravely, forcing herself to look backwards at William and Bess, who were stood together, Bess clutching her father's leg, looking pale and frightened.

The two men took her by the arms and led her up the lane. As they got a little further from the cottage, the smirking one turned to Jennet and heaved her up on to his horse. "You won't be back tonight, you know," said the man with a grim chuckle.

"I know that," replied Jennet, settling down obediently on the horse's back, trying to stifle the tears which were welling up in her eyes.

They arrived at Marton a little while later, just as the spring sun had set and the dark clouds of night time had gathered in the sky, obscuring the moon. As the light had faded along the road to Marton, Jennet had grown more frightened, as though the loss of light equated to her loss of hope, as though the dark itself presented its own threats which she should now fear, along with these two brutish men and whatever awaited her at Marton Hall. The smirking man, upon whose horse she rode, didn't speak to her as she sat behind him. He was a forbidding, repulsive figure, strong and ugly, to be both feared and reviled in equal measure. Jennet wished she did not have to sit so close to him but was frightened to move in case she should fall from the horse. About halfway along the road, as the light became little more than dim splinters spread clumsily across the sky, the man had abruptly stopped his horse and climbed down, lifting Jennet down after him, with neither care nor explanation. Before Jennet could speak a word he had lain her down on the ground and, after placing his sword at her throat, he had forced himself upon her. Too frightened to move or speak, Jennet had lain there, frozen, while the repulsive smirking man had grunted and groaned on top of her, then held her down while his skinny, silent companion took his turn. After they had finished, the two of them laughed as they dragged her to her feet and hauled her back on to the smirking man's horse to continue their journey.

"Some witch you are," the smirking man said, without turning back to look at her. "What good are spells and curses if you can't stop a man taking his pleasure on you?"

"I think she enjoyed it," the skinny man said, clearly taunting her. "You see? Not a tear in her eye. Like a wench at May Day!"

Both men laughed raucously. Humiliated and in great pain, Jennet had merely sobbed silently, wishing privately that she did have the power to curse, so that she could damn these men to a horrible suffering, the kind she had never wished upon anyone before. At least the men's nasty jibes had served to confirm what she had already suspected, that the questioning at Marton Hall was about witchcraft. Oh, Demdike, thought Jennet as the horse galloped furiously towards the forbidding candlelit spectre of Marton Hall, what have you got us all into?

The horse whinnied and stopped abruptly at the front door of the hall. The smirking man lifted Jennet down roughly from the horse. Weak with fear, her legs buckled under her as the man hauled her over towards another man who was standing there, clearly awaiting her arrival. He was tall and grandly dressed, with an air of arrogance and authority that in Jennet's experience, only the wealthy and powerful dared to possess. His dark eyes narrowed as they set themselves upon her, forcing Jennet to gulp nervously and look down at her feet. Even in the dim light outside the hall, she recognised this man as Thomas Heber, Master of Marton Hall and father of Jane, the young Thomas Lister's wife. There was no doubt; this was the dark haired and grand-looking man who had walked his child down the aisle on that fateful February day five years earlier.

"You're late," said the man sternly, addressing the two brutes who had escorted Jennet as their prisoner.

"We had to stop on the way over, Master. The ride was hard and we needed a little relief," the smirking man said, flashing a disgusting smile at Jennet, making her stomach lurch.

"No matter," replied Thomas Heber. "Bring her inside and we will begin."

The two men escorted Jennet through the grand entrance, and the main hall, and up the stairs to Master Heber's rooms. They led to her a room filled with dark furniture and books and forced her on to an uncomfortable-looking stool. As Jennet looked around her, she reflected momentarily that the room was not unlike the one which Tom Lister had used for dealing with his private and business matters. The thought of Tom made her eyes well with tears. How she longed for his protection now.

"Do you know why you are here?" Thomas Heber asked, addressing her directly for the first time.

Jennet shook her head in response, "No, Sir," she replied, her voice shaking with fear.

"Your Honour," said Thomas Heber, his temper clearly short. "You will address me as Your Honour. Do you know who I am?"

"Yes, Your Honour," replied Jennet, terrified.

"Well you will do well to remember it. If you know who I am, then you will also know that you have been brought here on a serious matter, a serious charge," Thomas Heber said, walking away from her and opening the door as he spoke. A man, who had clearly been waiting outside, walked in. Jennet didn't recognise him; in fact she was fairly certain that she had never seen him before. He was a pale, thin man, his clothing slightly dirty, perhaps from a day in the fields. He shuffled uncomfortably across the room to where Jennet was sitting.

"Is this she?" asked Thomas Heber, pointing instructively at Jennet.

"Yes," replied the man glumly, barely glancing at her as he spoke.

"The witness has confirmed it," said Thomas Heber, looking sternly at Jennet. "You will remain here, under house arrest, until your arraignment in York. Do you understand what that means?"

Jennet shook her head. "No, Your Honour," she replied.

"It means that you have been charged with a crime, Jennet Preston, and that you will stand trial for it, once the next Assizes commences in York, just a few weeks from now," Thomas Heber replied, his eyes dark and serious but the corners of his mouth twitching. He was enjoying himself now; he was clearly relishing wielding his power as the Justice of the Peace.

"Your Honour, what crime am I supposed to have committed?" Jennet asked with as much courage as she could muster. She looked again at the man who had acted as witness and tried to understand what crime he could possibly have seen her commit. She didn't know him, of that she was certain, so how could he possibly know her to accuse her of anything? Jennet's stomach lurched again as it dawned on her that she already knew the dreadful answer to her own question. William's words rang in her ears: if folk think that they are witches, then they may come to think that you are one also.

"The grave crime of witchcraft," Thomas Heber confirmed. "Of bewitching to death the infant son of this poor man here, of the devilish murder of Thomas Dodgson by your own cunning hand."

"Your Honour, I beg you to listen, I have never seen this man or his poor son in all my days!" Jennet implored, her voice reeking of desperation.

Thomas Heber was deaf to her plight. "Take her downstairs, and be sure to lock the door and keep guard all night," he said, instructing the two brutish men, who at once lifted her from the stool and led her away.

"I beg you, Your Honour, I beg you! I have committed no crime!" called Jennet as the two brutes hauled her out of the room. The pale thin man, the witness, looked at her angrily as she was led passed him.

"You are a whore, Jennet Preston, the devil's whore!" Thomas Heber called behind her, his tone sneering and triumphant. "And I will see you hang for what you have done."

24

Marton Hall, Marton
March 1612

Jennet flung her bowl angrily at the wooden door as the servant slammed it shut. She watched for a moment as the pottage it had contained slid like thick mud down the door and settled on the ground.

"I don't want any food!" she yelled. "I just want to go home. I want my home, my husband, my daughter. My precious Bess…" she whimpered, her voice breaking. Placing her head in her hands, she wept. Her sobs were heavy, angry, grief-stricken.

She had been locked up at Marton Hall for several days now, detained in a room near the servants' quarters. The room itself was tiny, so small in fact that Jennet could only assume it had been used for storage, perhaps for food. It was certainly cold enough to have housed food, with a hard, freezing stone floor and walls which were almost icy to the touch. Through her tears Jennet shivered, pulling her shawl tighter around her body as she hugged herself for both warmth and comfort. Whatever its previous purpose, this room had obviously been cleared out in readiness for her stay, with a makeshift bed put together from old sheets and straw, and an old pot to serve as her toilet placed carefully in the corner. She shivered again as she recalled all the little cold storage rooms at Westby Hall, the memories of stealing herself away with Tom at Christmastime, when the house was busy and nowhere else was private. She had never minded the feeling of the icy wall against her back when Tom was taking his pleasure with her; indeed, she had barely noticed it. Right now, it was all she could think about; how the cold made her body ache, how she longed to be warm.

Over the past few days, she had thought a lot about Tom. She thought about their meetings in the grounds at Westby, all those years ago when he was not much more than a boy and she was a young maid. She thought about the time he had kissed her in her parents' cottage; that wonderful, treasured first kiss. She thought about how intently he had looked at her, concern and affection radiating from his face, as she lay in bed at Westby, recovering from the loss of her child. She thought about the first time she had lain with him, and all the times after that. She thought about how much she had loved him, and how much she missed him, even now. It was as though being locked in this dreadful, barren room, in captivity but free from distraction, had forced her to face her grief once again. Every time she cried, she realised, it was as much for the loss of Tom as it was for the grief of being separated from her family, and for the hopelessness of the situation in front of her.

Jennet's mind returned to her current predicament. She could feel the anger rising within her once again. Since her captivity at Marton Hall had begun, her reaction to her bewilderment and helplessness had been rage. She had been over it hundreds of times in her mind, yet still she could not understand it. Who was this man, this father of Thomas Dodgson, who had accused her of something so awful? Why did he think that she had killed his son? Could it really be that her friendship with Demdike and the Devices had tarnished her reputation so much that this man, this complete stranger, had seen fit to attribute the death of his son to some imagined misdeed of hers? It just didn't make sense, and the more that Jennet couldn't understand it, the angrier she became. Clenching her fists, she pulled herself to her feet once again.

"Let me out of here!" she yelled, banging on the door. "Let me out! I need to see Master Heber! I need to ask him about all this. I need to understand!" She continued to bang on the door, so hard that it made her knuckles hurt. She shouted so loud that she made herself hoarse. "Let me see Master Heber!"

After a while, just as she was about to give up, Jennet heard someone tap lightly on the door. Startled, she instinctively backed away, her anger giving way to fear. For the past few days she had yelled often and in a similar manner, and yet no one had ever come in response. Now, she felt afraid. She was a prisoner, after all; she doubted that whoever had answered her cries had done so to offer her any comfort.

"Please, you must stop shouting," said a whispered voice outside.

"Who's there?" replied Jennet warily.

"I'm a maid here," the voice replied. "I daren't tell you my name, sorry. There'd be trouble enough for me if I was caught talking to you. I must ask you again, please, you must stop shouting."

"Why?" asked Jennet. "Why must I? I am held here, against my will, accused of something I did not do. All I have is my voice, my protest."

"The men who work for Master Heber, the ones who guard you, they are not kind," replied the maid, her voice laden with caution. "I fear they would harm you, if you anger them."

Jennet shuddered as she remembered how the two brutes had forced themselves upon her. "Don't worry, they've already done their worst," she replied.

"Oh, no," replied the maid, her tone sympathetic but still guarded. "I am sorry for you. No woman should have to endure that, no matter what they're accused of."

There was a heavy silence for a moment. Jennet could sense that the maid was still there, but she could think of nothing else to say to her. Yes, she had been treated brutally. Yes, she was locked up awaiting trial for a crime she did not commit. All of this was true; saying it aloud would make no difference.

"Do you have a husband?" the maid asked eventually.

"Yes," replied Jennet. "William. His name is William."

"Is he a good man?" asked the maid. "Does he treat you well?"

"He is a wonderful man," replied Jennet, realising the truth in her words as she spoke them. Without warning, tears began to spill down her cheeks once again. She bit her fist hard, struggling to stifle her sobs. She missed William and Bess so badly that it made her ache, and the reminder of it was almost too much to bear.

"I'm sorry," said the maid. "I didn't mean to upset you. I don't know why I asked you that! I suppose I'm just curious about you, we all are. Master Heber says you're a witch."

"Yes, although I don't know why. I didn't kill that poor child," Jennet replied quietly, her voice beginning to weaken. Her earlier outburst had made her feel tired, and she felt faint from lack of food since she had so far refused to eat anything offered to her.

"I must go now," said the maid. "I will send you some more food later. Please, try to eat. You must keep your strength up. You must take food when it is offered," she added.

"Thank you," replied Jennet. She was grateful for the maid's kindness. "I have a daughter too. Her name is Bess. I miss her terribly." She suddenly felt determined to continue their conversation, realising that she was comforted by the maid's presence at the door, by her apparent sympathy, pity even. Now she felt like talking, and she didn't want her to leave. "Don't go," she pleaded.

"I'm sorry, I must," insisted the maid. "God bless you, I will pray for you and your daughter."

Jennet's heart sank as she heard the maid's footsteps along the corridor. She was all alone again, left in solitude to confront her thoughts, her memories, and her fears once more. Placing her head in her hands, she began to weep again, silently this time, her body shaking with the effort. The maid's kind blessing rang in her ears; she would pray for her, for all the good it would do. What was the point in prayer, if it would surely fall on deaf ears? Clearly, God had forsaken her! This arrest, this false accusation, this captivity was his punishment, the punishment she had long been due for the sins she had committed, for all the pain she had caused. She had been lustful and adulterous, she had betrayed her husband and although it was several years ago now, God had not forgotten. Now, just as she had begun to put Tom Lister behind her, just as she had come to terms with her grief for him, just as she had begun to feel loving and contented with William once more, God had seen fit to remind her that she was not forgiven. She was damned, and Edward Dodgson and Master Heber were merely God's agents, carrying out his work. There could be no other explanation for it, nothing else made sense. Jennet shuddered with cold once more, then straightened her back as though a stiff posture might strengthen her resolve. If this was God's will, then so be it. She would submit to her fate willingly, she would welcome the death which was surely waiting for her at the gallows, if that was his plan. After all, she thought as she lay down on the cold ground, it was all she deserved.

When Jennet lifted her head again, it had grown dark. She sat up, feeling disorientated and confused, and realised that she must have fallen asleep. Wrapping her shawl tighter around her shoulders, she tried to recall her dreams, but realised that there had been none. Her sleep had been so heavy, so all-consuming, that there had been only darkness, only black. Now, sitting in that little room with no light other than the dim moonlight which was trickling in through a small, high window, Jennet longed for the warmth and comfort of a candle. She was also hungry; achingly, painfully hungry and she wished now that she had not flung that last offering of food away. It would be another long night, she realised. The anger which she had felt so keenly earlier had dissipated now, replaced by self-pity and fatigue. She was about to lie back down again, to wallow in her despair, when there was a noise outside the door. Hopeful that it was the kind maid from earlier in the day, Jennet sat upright as the door opened and a shadow entered with barely a sound. Jennet struggled in the darkness to see who it was, and they did not carry a candle.

"Who's there?" whispered Jennet, her voice hoarse and thick with fear.

"You need not worry, I won't hurt you. I've come to cheer you up," replied the shadow with a small chuckle. Jennet gasped, instantly recognising the voice of the smirking man who had brought her to Marton Hall and had guarded her ever since. Instinctively, she backed up against the icy wall.

"I don't want anything from you," she called out as he approached her. "Please, leave me alone!"

"I said I won't hurt you," repeated the man. "But if you scream you'll alert the servants and that will make me angry. This should be our secret, witch. No need to tell anyone else."

"I'm no witch," replied Jennet, her heart pounding hard in her chest. Suddenly she felt determined not to submit to this man's will, to stand her ground. "Why must it be a secret? Surely if I'm a witch then your master won't care what you do to me?" she asked.

Her words seemed to stop the smirking man momentarily in his tracks. "You are a witch," he spat after a moment. "You're a witch right now, trying to trick me with your cunning words!"

"It's no trick," Jennet replied quickly, her wits returning to her. "Maybe I am a witch. Maybe you're right. Maybe I want you to take your pleasure with me; I am wicked after all, am I not? I am a sinful instrument of the devil, your master said so. They say I killed a child, don't they? What might I do to you, then?"

She sensed the man back away then, as though thinking better of his intentions. He wanted a terrified, cowering victim, she realised, not a woman in league with the devil, versed in the dark arts. Until now she had only understood the danger of being called a witch but now, for the first time, she understood that such a reputation was also a source of power. Briefly her mind conjured the image of Old Demdike, a woman who had spent a lifetime treading the fine line between trading on her reputation for cunning knowledge and until recently, avoiding the danger of being called a witch. Right now, Jennet realised that this man's fear of witchcraft was the only thing keeping her safe from another brutal assault, and suddenly she saw a way to ensure that he never came near her again.

"I know words which would turn your insides putrid and make them pour from your mouth," she said through gritted teeth. "If you touch me again, I will utter them against you."

With a gasp, the man fled from the room, slamming the door shut behind him. Despite her exhaustion, Jennet let out a small chuckle before collapsing back down on her heap of sheets and straw. She was about to shut her eyes when she heard the door open again. She sat up to see that the door was just slightly ajar.

"You dealt with him, then," said a familiar voice. It was the kind maid this time. "I am glad for you, he's a nasty one."

"Yes," said Jennet simply.

"Shall I bring you something to eat now?" the maid asked.

"Please," Jennet replied.

"I heard talk that you're to leave for York tomorrow," said the maid in little more than a whisper. "I'll bring you as much food as I can. You'll need your strength for the journey," she added, her voice still low but serious. She knew as well as Jennet that York meant gaol, a real prison filled with disease, filth and rats, not this little room where at least a straw bed was provided and food was offered.

The maid slammed the door shut, leaving Jennet to reel over her words. The victorious feeling of a few moments ago when she had sent the smirking man running scared had been short-lived and had all but disappeared now, replaced instead with a nauseating mix of fear and despair. Her move to York meant that her trial must be imminent and, she was certain, that the gallows would follow quickly thereafter. Instinctively, Jennet got down on her knees, clasped her hands together, and closed her eyes. She knelt there for some time, praying silently, asking God to care for her family, and to help her to face her accuser, her judges, and ultimately her death. When the kind maid returned a little while later and pushed a bowl of food through the door without a word, Jennet was still praying, and even when the door slammed shut again, she still could not be disturbed. She felt like a figure made of stone; whilst ever she remained still she was solid, but if she moved, she knew she would shatter on the floor into a thousand pieces. If she wobbled even a little, all the fortitude she had collected within herself through prayer would melt away, to be replaced once again with fear. So she remained there for most of the night, silent and unmoving, asking God for strength, for comfort, but never for forgiveness. She knew she could never bring herself to ask for that.

25

York Assizes, York Castle, York
6th April 1612

Jennet was led from her dusty, murky cell up to the courtroom. As she was taken, chains still rattling relentlessly at her feet, she managed to get a glimpse of the city of York through the small castle windows. She screwed up her eyes, unaccustomed to daylight after so many days locked up below ground, and peered down at the city which she realised she lived quite close to, and yet had never visited. So many people and buildings, so many market stalls and horses, so many noises and voices – its curiosity served, at least momentarily, to distract her from the dreadful fate she was sure she was about to encounter.

She had been locked up now for what felt like an eternity, first at Marton Hall, in that small room near the servants' quarters, then at York for what she thought had been about ten days and nights, but in truth she had lost all concept of time and could not be certain how long she had been there. She looked down at herself despairingly; her clothing was filthy and smelling putrid, her throat was dry and her belly so empty it had ceased to groan for food, for this would be a superfluous use of energy which it could ill-afford. Since her arrival at York she had barely slept, barely been fed, and had barely been offered something to drink. She was starving and exhausted. She recalled how she had railed against her captivity at Marton Hall, screaming and shouting and weeping with anger and anguish, throwing food and drink back at the servants in disdainful protest. She remembered the kind maid who had brought food and urged her to eat a last meal on her final night at Marton Hall. She thought about that bowl of food, and how it was still sitting untouched the following morning when she was led out of that cold room and on to a cart bound for York. Now, she wished more than anything for someone to put a cup of ale to her lips and to offer her some bread to eat. Her lack of nourishment made her feel weak and she stumbled wearily over her chains.

"Get up! Move!" barked one of the guards escorting her.

They entered a grand-looking chamber through a heavy wooden door. Jennet felt the eyes of the entire room set upon her. She tried not to hang her head for fear that it might be interpreted as an admittance of shame. In the end, however, her embarrassment defeated her and she walked to the front of the room, looking at the floor all the way. As she approached the front of the room she looked up and saw a man sitting in front of her, dressed grandly and wearing a stern expression. To his side sat a group of men who looked a little more ordinary but who, for the most part, were still well-dressed for their day at the Assizes. Jennet presumed that these must be the men who would make their judgement of her. She gulped nervously.

"Jennet Preston!" declared the grand man who sat at the front. "You have been charged with a most serious offence, that of bewitching a young infant, Thomas Dodgson, son of Edward Dodgson, of Bolton-by-Bowland, and causing his death through your cunning and wicked practices. We will now hear testimony from the child's father and the only witness, Edward Dodgson, after which there shall be an examination of said testimony and a decision made by the jury as to the question of your guilt. At no time must you, the accused, speak, unless a question is directed toward you. Do you understand?"

Jennet nodded nervously, frightened by the towering and forbidding presence of the law man in front of her. The judge beckoned Edward Dodgson to come forward. Jennet glanced at Edward Dodgson; he looked pale and nervous, as though it might be he who was on trial.

"Edward Dodgson, please tell the court what happened to your son," the judge instructed.

"My son Thomas was born on the tenth day of September 1610," began Edward Dodgson, his voice shaking with nerves. "He was our first child, and he brought me and my wife great joy. He was a contented child and slept often, until one day in April last." Edward Dodgson paused.

"Go on," prompted the judge.

"He became bad tempered, Your Honour, and sickly with it. His face a terrible colour of red at first, then a deathly pallor soon followed. He became tired, weak, and gave up feeding. He was a small child, having lived only seven months of his life, and once he refused the milk his mother offered, we feared he would not be long for this world. We were right, and he breathed his last on the twentieth day of April and was buried three days hence," said Edward Dodgson, his voice breaking at the anguish. Now, having heard his story, Jennet felt immense pity for him; she knew what it was to lose a child, having seen Elizabeth suffer the loss of little Henry, having lost so many little babies of her own.

"Your story is indeed tragic. What makes you certain that the accused, Jennet Preston, had a malign hand in your son's death?" the judge asked.

"They say she is a witch, Your Honour, and this must surely be the work of a witch. How else can a young, healthy child take ill so suddenly and die?" Edward Dodgson replied, his tone indignant.

"Yes, but did you ever see the accused near your son, did you hear her utter devilish chants, did you see her perform any malign rituals?" the judge replied, his tone probing. "Did you quarrel with her, or have any quarrel with her family, or was there any grievance between you which might have given rise to her working some cunning practices against you?"

"No Your Honour, I have never before met this woman. But I tell you that I have it on good authority that she is a witch!" insisted Edward Dodgson.

"You say you have never met this woman, and yet you call her a witch?" asked the judge, clearly incredulous. He glanced at the jury and paused. "Can you reveal this good authority you speak of?" he continued, his tone lowered and more neutral.

"No, Your Honour, I cannot. I can only say that it is well-known that this woman is a witch and that I believe she caused the death of my child," finished Edward Dodgson.

"I thank you for your testimony. You may sit down," instructed the judge. "Good men of the jury, I ask you now to consider your verdict on this matter," he added, raising an eyebrow before looking down at the bench in front of him.

The jury whispered amongst themselves, their heads turned in to face one another so that Jennet could not even try to read on their lips what they were saying. Feeling weak again, she steadied herself on the wooden bar to her side and, glancing upwards to the heavens, she prayed. She believed that it was God's will that she was here, being accused of this awful crime by a man she had never seen. In the lonely isolation of her cell she had convinced herself that this was the final punishment for her multitude of sins; for loving another man, for bearing his child, for bringing so much pain and suffering to William, to Jane Lister, to her children. Now, confronted with judgement, she clasped her shaking hands together, beseeching God to reconsider. Please God, do not let these men believe this man's story, she begged, please let them send me home to my husband and child. A tear rolled down her cheek as she thought of Bess; how she ached to see her dear, sweet girl once again. She looked back at the jury, who had turned to face the room again and had fallen silent. Jennet inhaled sharply and held it there, afraid to breathe.

"Do you have a verdict on this matter?" asked the judge.

"We do, Your Honour," replied one of the men, who rose to

his feet as he spoke.

"And, is the accused guilty or not guilty of the crime of witchcraft?" prompted the judge.

"Not guilty," replied the juror, sitting back down swiftly after delivering his verdict.

Jennet exhaled and panting, fell down to her knees and wept. Thank you God, thank you God, thank you, she repeated over and over to herself. Two of the guards who had escorted her to court now lifted her to her feet and began to remove her shackles.

"You are free to leave this court, Jennet Preston," said the judge, sternly but kindly, and the two guards escorted her out of the courtroom. As she was led past those who had watched her trial she could hear their murmurs about the verdict; however, she had not a care for what they were saying. It didn't matter now. She had been found innocent and after so many weeks in captivity, she was free once again.

The guards led her outside and into the streets of York which were bright, smelly and bustling. Without a word or a second glance, they left her there and went back inside, no doubt to another prisoner and another trial. Jennet sat herself down on a discarded wooden crate and looked out at the street in front of her, realising then that she had no real idea where she was or how she would get home. Moreover, she was weary and hungry, but had no means or money to eat or find shelter for the night. The relief that she had felt at her acquittal moments before disintegrated into tears of confusion, exhaustion and despair. Head in hands, she wept, both for the ordeal she had just been through and the hopelessness of the situation which faced her now.

"Jennet?" said a voice through the sound of her own sobs. Jennet looked up, blinking away her tears, to see William standing in front of her. Her legs, which had felt so weak, suddenly found renewed strength and she jumped up, stumbling towards him and throwing herself into his arms.

"William! My love, I thought I would never see you again!" she exclaimed, enthusiastically kissing him, his lips, his cheeks, his forehead, leaving not one part of his face un-kissed.

"Never leave me again," he whispered into her ear as she held him tightly, gathering her into his arms as though he never wished to let her go.

"How did you know to find me here?" Jennet asked as William finally released her from his embrace. "And where's Bess?"

"She's well, don't worry. She's with Anna. She wanted to come, but this is no place for a child. They told me you would be tried today, but when I arrived, they wouldn't let me in. God knows why. So I have stood out here all day, hoping to get some news of the trial, hoping and praying that I would be able to take you home. And thank God, now I can," William said, clasping his hands together in a gesture which was rare for him, since he was not a devout man.

"Yes, home" replied Jennet feebly, realising the extent of her exhaustion once again.

"Not today, though," said William, studying his wife closely. "You're in no fit state to travel today, Jennet. I have a room at an inn where I stayed last night, we will stay there tonight. Some hot food, some sleep and some clean clothes and you will feel much better tomorrow."

Jennet nodded, too weary to respond, as William took her by the arm and led her through the unfamiliar streets of York to his lodgings.

Several hours later, Jennet awoke with a start, her heart racing in her chest, her head disorientated and confused, her voice crying out into the darkness which was all around her.

"Jennet? Jennet, it's alright," came William's sleepy voice next to her.

Remembering where she was then, Jennet grew calmer, and drew herself closer to William, holding on to him tightly, taking comfort in his presence and rejecting the nightmares which were continuing to circulate in her mind, in spite of her wakened state.

"I'm sorry I woke you," she whispered. "Go back to sleep."

"It's alright," replied William, sounding more awake now, "I would be having nightmares too. You mustn't apologise, my love," he said, kissing her on the neck.

Jennet lay there for a few moments, listening to the sounds of the streets outside. York was not at all like Gisburn at night. In the village everyone would be asleep by now, and the only time it was noisy at this time of night was if there had been a feast, or if someone's baby was crying in one of the nearby cottages. York seemed to be perpetually noisy and Jennet pondered as to whether city dwellers ever really slept. She longed for Gisburn then, with its peace and familiarity.

"Go back to sleep," urged William, sensing she was still awake. "What are you thinking about? The trial?"

"Not really," answered Jennet.

"I am," replied William. "In truth, Jennet, I can think of little else. These past weeks I have worried myself sick for your life, hoping and praying that you would be freed. Now that you are free, I can't stop thinking about how such a monstrous accusation could be made against you, though I have my suspicions."

"The only witness was a man called Edward Dodgson, the father of the poor dead child, who I found out during the trial is from Bolton-by-Bowland, which is why I had never seen him before. I don't know anyone from out that way," she added simply.

"Yes, after you were arrested I asked around, firstly to find out what you had been accused of since those men who took you away that day would tell me nothing, and also to find out who had accused you. Edward Dodgson's name soon cropped up," said William.

Jennet shuddered at the thought of the two men who had taken her away that day and what they had done to her. She knew she could never tell William about that; he would likely hunt them down and kill them both in vengeance for it. She pushed the unwelcome memory of it from her mind. "And?" she asked. "What did you discover?"

"Very little, other than his name and the nature of his

accusation," replied William. "Sorry to ask you to talk about this at this hour, Jennet, but what did he say at the trial?"

Jennet shrugged, "In truth, hardly anything at all. He told the story of what happened to his son, which was tragic and I pity him greatly for it. Then he said that he was certain that I was responsible for his boy's death, because he had been told that I was a witch."

"Told by whom?" William asked.

"That's just it, he wouldn't say," said Jennet, realising the strangeness of it as she spoke. At the time she had been so preoccupied with her own fear and exhaustion that she barely considered how odd it was that this man, who seemed so certain of his accusation, would not reveal his source to the court. Who was Edward Dodgson protecting?

"Well, that confirms it in my mind," said William. "I have long suspected that young Thomas Lister had a hand in all this, and now I am certain. I think poor Dodgson does believe you bewitched his son, because Thomas Lister told him you did."

Believing that she must have misheard him, Jennet turned around in the dark to face William. "Thomas Lister?" she asked.

"Yes," replied William, his tone resolute. "Thomas Lister. Think about it Jennet, the accusation you faced had but one witness to support it, and his only evidence was that 'someone' had told him you were a witch? Now, who do you suppose that someone might be, other than Master Lister? Folk in Gisburn call you many things, believe me, but never a witch, and to be frank, no one else would have strong enough motivations to do something so wicked to you. Thomas Lister, on the other hand, undoubtedly has."

"I know he dislikes me, but, after all these years..." Jennet replied, trying to convince herself that it couldn't be true. The more she thought about it, however, the more it made sense.

"Jennet, it's not so many years, and indeed even if it were a hundred years, I don't think it would matter. His father died on his wedding day, revealing you as his lover before the entire congregation. Then, his mother died a year later, no doubt from the shame and a broken heart. Any man would feel aggrieved, but a man as wealthy and powerful as Thomas Lister, he will want revenge. I began to suspect that he was behind it when I found out you were being held at Marton Hall. Master Heber's a magistrate, I know, but he's also Master Lister's father-in-law. I think someone told Master Lister about poor Edward Dodgson's child's sudden death and he decided to use it as an opportunity to get rid of you, without having to get his own hands dirty. We're just fortunate that the story, in the end, didn't convince the jury. But you've made some powerful enemies, Jennet, and we're going to have to be very careful," warned William.

"What do you suggest we do, William?" Jennet asked as all the pieces of the puzzle fell into place. It seemed so obvious now, so logical, yet when she was locked up she could never have made sense of it all, except to assume that this was all somehow God's plan, his intervention, his punishment. It had never occurred to her that any plotting against her might have come from a more earthly source. It was as though the captive Jennet's mind had been confused, blurred by sleep deprivation, hunger and fear to the extent where it was no longer capable of independent thought.

"Give up our tenure and leave Gisburn," William replied, his tone firm and uncompromising.

"Leave? Are you sure?" Jennet asked, incredulous. People didn't just leave their village and move to another.

"Yes," said William. "We have no choice. If we don't leave, Jennet, Thomas Lister will find another way to get rid of you and next time, he may succeed and you will end up with a noose around your neck."

Jennet touched her neck gently at the thought then, shuddering with both cold and the prospect of death, wrapped her arms tightly around William. As her eyelids became heavy once again, her mind wandered over the English country, as she imagined it to be, with its forests and rolling hills and small stone villages marked only on the landscape by the delicate plumes of smoke trickling gently from little chimneys. As she fell asleep once again she wondered how far she would have to go to escape Thomas Lister's vengeful grasp, how far she would need to travel to keep herself and her family out of harm's way once and for all.

26

Malkin Tower, Blacko Hillside, Forest of Pendle
10th April 1612

Jennet rode her old horse as fast as his weary legs could carry him. He had been a faithful creature for many years now, but he was aged and his body was beginning to tire. Jennet could almost hear him groan as she squeezed him gently with her legs, urging him to go on up the hill to Malkin Tower. Normally she was content for him to trot at a leisurely pace when making the familiar journey to Blacko, and in any other circumstances, given that the poor old animal had just trotted all the way back from York, she would have given him a chance to rest before paying a visit to her friends' home. Today, however, was not a day which could be put off, or upon which she could take her time. Today's visit required urgency.

The journey back from York had taken them two days, on account of both Jennet and her horse's weariness. William had worried for them both and at his insistence they had taken the journey slowly. Fortunately, the weather had stayed fine and dry and the roads, therefore, had not been treacherous, their composition underfoot being moist but not water-logged. Upon arriving back in Gisburn they had gone directly to Anna's cottage, where Jennet had grabbed hold of Bess and squeezed the child tightly, sobbing silently into her beautiful curls for the love of her. The child had cried too, unable to articulate at her young age how fearful she had been; how she had thought that she would never see her mother again and how happy she was to see her now. Once mother and child had been reunited, Anna, her belly once again big with child, had sought comfort in Jennet's arms also, her body shaking uncontrollably with tears of relief. Once they had all cried enough to water a crop, Anna offered food and ale, which was welcomed and much appreciated by the weary travellers. At first the mealtime conversation had remained light, but after a while Anna, true to her nature, could not help but ask the more difficult questions.

"Has Uncle William told you that he believes that Tom Lister was behind all this?" she asked, looking directly at Jennet as she spoke, clearly trying to read her reaction from her face.

"He has," replied Jennet, her tone remaining neutral.

"I can't believe that man would do something so dreadful. I mean, I know he surely thinks that you did his family a terrible wrong, but no one deserves to be accused of something so grave without any foundation," Anna replied, allowing the words which had no doubt roamed around her head for many weeks now to tumble forth clumsily.

William cleared his throat to speak. "Anna, we have come to a decision on the way home from York, and I think it is best that you hear it from us sooner rather than later. Your aunt and I are both now convinced that her ordeal was Master Lister's doing and we fear he may try something else, or something worse, again. We think that the only way to prevent this is…" he paused, collecting his thoughts before proceeding. "The only way to stop him is to leave Gisburn for good."

Anna looked from William to Jennet, and back again, her face aghast. "Leave?" she asked. "You can't leave the village. Where will you go? How will you support yourselves?"

"That is still to be decided," said William firmly. "Although as you know we have family in Giggleswick who I may be able to call upon for some help. I would like to go further than Giggleswick, but perhaps for now it will be far enough."

"But...but I will miss you all so badly!" protested Anna. "Aunt, I've only just got you back! You can't leave me again, not in this condition," she added, gesturing at her large belly.

"Anna, you are almost always in that condition," teased Jennet. "You have borne quite a few babies now; you don't need my help there. As your uncle says, it's settled, we will make our way from the village in the next couple of days. Your father will still be here, your uncle thinks he may stay in the cottage and take the tenure of the land himself."

Anna looked helplessly at them both. "Alright," she replied with a sigh of resignation. "But hadn't you better go over to Blacko to say goodbye to your friend Elizabeth before you run away? Especially considering everything she's going through at the moment, I think you'd be a great comfort to her, don't you?" she added, looking pointedly at William as she spoke.

"What do you mean 'everything she's going through'?" asked Jennet insistently. She glanced at William who was silent and pale, his eyes fixed angrily on Anna. She had clearly given away a grave secret to which Jennet was not meant to be privy.

"Oh, so Uncle William hasn't told you?" said Anna, feigning surprise.

Jennet was sure that she heard William growl at his niece. Sitting there next to him, she could feel the heat of his rage emanating from him. "Told me what?" she asked, growing agitated.

"I don't know all the details, but from what I can gather from the talk in the village, Old Demdike and Alison have been carted off to Lancaster gaol. A few weeks ago, not long after you were taken away, Alison had some sort of argument with a pedlar and he took ill shortly afterwards. Someone made a complaint to the Sheriff, saying that Alison bewitched him, and a few days ago she was arrested and sent to Lancaster, along with her grandmother and a couple of others, I forget their names. I'm not sure why Demdike has been taken also. Poor old woman, sitting in a gaol at her age," said Anna.

"You have no idea," remarked Jennet pointedly. She shuddered, recalling the utter horror and misery of a gaol cell. She thought about Elizabeth, and how she must be beside herself with worry for her mother and child, how distressed she must be that they had been taken away from her and she was unable to care for them. She felt angry with William, then. How dare he keep this from her when she could be offering her friend some comfort! Carefully and deliberately, she turned to her husband who was still sitting there, silent and furious. "When were you going to tell me?" she asked, forcing her tone to remain calm.

"When we were far enough away that you couldn't go there and get yourself involved in it," replied William firmly. "And frankly Jennet, perhaps I never would have told you. Now we will never know." William turned his attention to Anna, his face full of scorn. "Anna, do not look at me or speak to me. If I wasn't in your house, I would send you away. You've done a terrible thing for very selfish reasons."

"She had a right to know!" Anna cried defensively.

"And I have a right to keep my wife out of harm's way," replied William, his tone controlled but seething. He turned back to Jennet. "My love, I know that there's no point in me asking you not to go to your friend. That's why I hoped to keep this from you. Now you know, and there is nothing I could do to prevent you from going, I know that. But I insist that you wait until tomorrow morning, when it is light and you have rested. I also insist that you keep your visit brief and that afterwards we will prepare to leave for Giggleswick."

Jennet eyed William, a look of hurt and disappointment strewn across her weary face. "That was a terrible secret to keep from me, William," she said. "I will do as you ask, because I know you're only trying to keep me safe, to keep us all safe. But I still think that you've done a horrible thing and I'm not sure I can forgive you for it."

Jennet's own words rang in her ears that morning, as her horse pounded up the hill in Blacko. She still couldn't believe that William had tried to keep such dreadful news from her. He had never been able to understand her closeness with Elizabeth and her family; to him, all that they had shared might as well mean nothing. To Jennet, it meant everything. She had been there for Elizabeth when little Henry passed away, when little Jennet was born, when Demdike had taken ill. Elizabeth, in turn, had comforted Jennet through her darkest days following Tom's death, taking her in when she had nowhere else to turn, pleading with her to carry on living when every fibre of her being wanted to give up. Elizabeth was the truest friend she had ever had, and it was unthinkable that she should forget her now. Yet that was exactly what William had wanted her to do, to leave without even saying goodbye.

Jennet clenched her jaw as her thoughts turned again to her husband. She had not spoken another word to William since leaving Anna's cottage the previous evening, and after a restless night's sleep and a kiss on the forehead of her slumbering child, Jennet had set out on her horse at first light. As her tired old horse slowed his pace to a pitiful march as they reached the familiar old cottage on the hillside, Jennet felt a sense of unease. Malkin Tower to her was a home from home, its shabby exterior masking the welcoming, comforting abode of friends which hid beneath its crumbling stonework. Today, however, Malkin Tower looked sunken and shrivelled, as though the building itself had withdrawn into the hillside in a state of fear. Tethering her old horse to her usual tree, Jennet approached the big old wooden front door with a measure of anxiety, and knocked. The door creaked open hesitantly in response.

"Oh, thank God, thank God, thank God it's you!" cried Elizabeth, flinging her arms around her friend. "The last I had heard was that you were in gaol in York, but no one had brought me any word since then. It seems God has answered my prayers and you are safe," she added, throwing her arms around Jennet again, and beckoning her inside.

"I was released yesterday," said Jennet as she entered. "I'm sorry no one brought you any word about me, Elizabeth. I came here as soon as I heard about your mother and Alison. I would have come yesterday but William chose to keep the news about them from me until it was too late to travel."

Elizabeth put up a hand as though to hush her friend. "Jennet, I wouldn't have expected you to come at all, after all you've been through. You should be at home with Bess, resting. But I am glad now that you're here," she added, forcing a grim smile. "Master Lister didn't manage to do away with you, then?"

"William thinks it was Thomas Lister's doing as well," said Jennet thoughtfully.

"Who else could it be? Who else would hate you so much to have you arrested by their wife's father on trumped-up charges and carted off to York before anyone could object?" Elizabeth replied.

"You know an awful lot about it, Elizabeth. I imagine it's been the talk of the villages, then?" asked Jennet. Usually she detested being the subject of gossip but this time she was glad, for it had clearly been the only way that Elizabeth had received any news of her.

"Yes. And the one advantage of having a daughter who chooses to go begging far and wide is that I get to hear all the news from all around," replied Elizabeth. "Well, I used to anyway. I don't suppose I will anymore," she added, her face growing sad at the thought of her poor child.

"What happened, Elizabeth?" probed Jennet. "I know a little about the pedlar; Anna told me that Alison argued with him and that he fell down ill after that, but there must be more to it than that, if your mother has been arrested as well?"

Elizabeth drew a deep breath and the whole story tumbled forth clumsily. Alison, she said, had encountered the pedlar whilst out begging near Colne and had asked him for some pins. He had refused, and had called Alison a few names. Alison, known for her short temper, had responded and the brief conversation had become quite abusive. Eventually Alison turned her back and continued to walk on; as she did so she heard the pedlar make a dreadful strangling noise and turning back, she saw him fall down to the ground. Horrified at the sight of this man taken ill she took his arm over her shoulders and walked him into the nearby village to get help, which she found, and there she left him. She thought nothing more of it until about ten days later when two men, one of them the son of the lamed pedlar and the other the local constable, arrived at Malkin Tower and insisted that Alison go with them to Read Hall for questioning by the magistrate. Alison dutifully went along with them, and three days later the constable came back, this time for Old Demdike.

"I have not seen either of them since," said Elizabeth, her voice full of sadness. "Master Nowell, the magistrate, has since sent the constable, a man called Hargreaves to tell me that Alison and my mother have both been sent to Lancaster gaol and will be tried for witchcraft. He also told me that Old Chattox and her daughter Anne are being held on the same charges. I don't know any more than this," she added, her voice breaking down into sobs.

Jennet held her friend tightly as she wept. She thought about what she had just been told. Firstly Alison had been arrested, then Demdike, then Chattox and her daughter. How had it spiralled from one event with a pedlar into so many arrests? Jennet wondered what Alison had said during questioning; as Elizabeth herself had said only moments earlier, the girl liked to tell stories. Young, silly Alison had perhaps bragged about her grandmother's cunning ways which had been enough for the magistrate to summon Demdike for questioning. Poor old Demdike, frail and close to senility at times, perhaps sensed the gravity of the situation and in an effort to deflect attention from her family, willingly told Nowell all about Chattox and her family. Jennet could see the old lady in her mind's eye, pleading her case to the magistrate, insisting that though she undoubtedly had cunning gifts she used them only for healing whereas Chattox, terrible Chattox mostly used hers for malign practices. It was a line she had repeated for many years, one with which she was comfortable, one which she clung to now in

247

her old age. Jennet wondered if the arrests would stop there or if, as she feared, there would be more to come. She clung to her friend tightly, sensing the danger they were in and knowing that William was right, by coming here she was now involved in it.

A knock at the door interrupted her thoughts. Jennet looked at Elizabeth quizzically as she straightened her back and wiped the tears from her eyes. She was clearly expecting company.

"It's Good Friday, Jennet, or have you forgotten?" she asked.

"Ah! I had quite forgotten," replied Jennet, understanding now. Demdike and the Devices always had a small gathering of friends at their home on Good Friday, and Jennet had been a guest on many a year past. It was an old tradition, Demdike had once told her, which stretched back to when she was a girl, and the old faith was still intact. Many frowned upon it now, but Demdike still insisted upon holding a small feast at their home on this holy day each year. Jennet was surprised that in the circumstances, Elizabeth was pressing ahead with the usual arrangements.

"Mother would want me to," she said, as though reading Jennet's thoughts. "Besides, James and I agreed that we need others around us right now. We need to be with our friends and family, not shut away on this lonely hillside. Will you stay a while, Jennet?" she asked as she opened the door and the first of her visitors flocked in.

"I was supposed to only stay for a little while," replied Jennet, hesitating. She realised she hadn't yet told Elizabeth about William's plans to take her away to Giggleswick. She knew that now was not the right time.

"Please stay," pleaded Elizabeth. "James has caught and slaughtered a sheep, it will be delicious and plenty to go round. We will eat, drink and pray for the safe return of my family. Please stay. I need you here."

Jennet sighed. For all of her defiance towards William she did have every intention of heeding his warning and returning home swiftly so that they could get ready to leave for Giggleswick. She knew, too, that although Elizabeth may find a gathering of friends

248

comforting, it was also dangerous. This magistrate, this Master Nowell, was obviously now watching Elizabeth's family very closely, listening carefully to their testimonies under examination, shrewdly following any line of enquiry which might lead him to more witchcraft, as he saw it. Anyone associated with Demdike and the Devices could now be viewed as guilty and therefore everyone coming to Malkin Tower that day was potentially in danger. Despite all this, Jennet also knew that her friend needed her there and that as she was leaving for Giggleswick soon, this might be the last time that they were together.

"Alright," she said finally, taking Elizabeth tenderly by the hand and giving her a reassuring smile. "You'd best fetch me some ale then."

When Jennet left Malkin Tower later that afternoon, the feast was still going on. It was the best attended gathering at the Devices' home that Jennet could ever remember; it was as though friends and family from far and wide had come to show their support for Elizabeth in her time of need, to let her know that she wasn't alone. Many of the people there were already known to Jennet, such as Elizabeth's brother Christopher Holgate and his family, and Katherine Hewit, the clothier's wife from Colne. Many other faces, however, were new, and Jennet spent a happy afternoon meeting the Hargreaves family, the Bulcocks, and a mysterious lady called Alice Nutter, a woman of such grace and good manners that Jennet felt herself inclined to treat her as though she was her Mistress. It didn't matter for how many years Jennet had known Elizabeth and the Devices; their connections to others in their community never ceased to surprise her.

As she rode away on her tired old horse, Jennet reflected on the afternoon's events. As time had worn on and the ale had flowed freely, many had loosened their tongues, talking wildly about acquiring some gunpowder and blowing a hole in the wall at the Lancaster gaol so that Demdike and Alison could be free once again. Quite uncharacteristically, Elizabeth had burst forth at this jest, railing about how they could do so but she would wish to see Chattox and her daughter left in there, because even after all these years she still felt that they both deserved to rot. Her outburst was met with surprise and nods of silent agreement. For the first time, Jennet realised the esteem in which Demdike was held by so many local people; it was odd, but at previous gatherings, no one had ever spoken openly about the services Demdike provided, about her abilities to heal. Now, in her absence, they lamented the loss of her, telling stories amongst themselves of animals, and people, that she had cured, of acts of kindness she had performed using her considerable abilities. Jennet could have stayed and listened to these tales all afternoon; they fascinated her, but the light outside was growing dimmer and eventually she had to tear herself away.

Elizabeth, intoxicated with ale by this point, had clung to her, pleading with her not to leave, weeping about how she worried for her and telling anyone who would listen about what had just happened to her at the hands of the terrible Master Lister. Although she knew that most people there already knew all about her incarceration and trial in York, Jennet's face had reddened at the attention, and in the end she had stolen herself away, to return to Gisburn, perhaps for the very last time. Jennet gulped hard as she thought about leaving her village, her family, and her friends. She had left Malkin Tower without telling Elizabeth about the plan to leave for Giggleswick. She had gone there today to offer comfort, to show friendship, but ultimately to tell her friends that she must leave. However, when it came to it, she couldn't bring herself to utter the words. How could she abandon Elizabeth now, when she needed her most? Tears of sadness and frustration stung in Jennet's eyes as she urged her horse to pick up his pace along the road home. For these past weeks Jennet's life had been dominated by fear; fear of execution, and then fear for her friends upon learning of their incarceration. Now, for the first time, she felt something quite different. She felt angry; angry with William for asking her leave, angry with the pedlar and his son for accusing Alison of something so awful, angry with Alison for presumably being foolish enough to talk about her grandmother's gifts. Most of all she felt angry with Thomas Lister for taking her away from her family and trying to have her killed, for no greater crime than loving his father. I wish I had cursed him, she thought.

27

The Prestons' Farm, near Gisburn Village
Early May, 1612

"God's death, Jennet, you should have let us leave!" William exclaimed angrily, banging his clenched fist upon the table. Jennet looked at him directly, shock and worry evident upon her face.

"I'm sorry, William, but I won't say you're right. I'm glad we stayed. I had to be here for my friends, I couldn't abandon them," she replied, although in truth her previous defiance was beginning to give way to anxiety.

"Yes, because your remaining here has done them a lot of good," he retorted. "It's all over the villages; they're all in gaol now! Even the little one, she's Jennet like you isn't she? Even she's been taken over to Read Hall for questioning. Damn, Jennet, how long do you think it will be before they come for you? Master Lister must be rubbing his hands with delight at so easy a case to press. He need only whisper in the ear of that magistrate Nowell and he will be over here, looking for you next."

William's words made Jennet shudder. Little Bess, who had been sitting meekly on her stool listening to the conversation, wrapped herself up in her mother's apron, as though afraid to let her go. Jennet patted the child affectionately on the head.

"Don't worry, little one," she whispered.

"She ought to worry," said William. "We all ought to worry. This thing, this act that Alison Device is supposed to have done, it has caused a lot of trouble, Jennet, and everyone who knows that family is being dragged into it. For whatever reason, that magistrate over at Read Hall isn't content just to root out one witch, he wants them all!"

"Please don't call them witches," Jennet protested weakly. "You know none of it is true."

"It doesn't matter what I know. It only matters what the magistrate thinks," replied William. "They will all be tried as witches, possibly they will be hanged for being witches and if you don't get away from here soon, I daresay so will you."

Jennet bowed her head and pulled little Bess closer to her. She tried to deny it but she knew that William was right; with every passing day the likelihood of her arrest increased. She knew he was terrified for her life. She had survived one trial, but what were the chances of surviving another? Over the past few weeks, Jennet had insisted that they should remain in their cottage, that they shouldn't go anywhere, baffling and frustrating William in equal measure. Why, why, why? He had asked over and over again, and yet Jennet could never explain it. At first, after she had been released from prison, she had agreed with William, she had been set upon leaving. But then she had visited Elizabeth, her distraught and helpless friend, and her resolve had begun to ebb away. She knew that she was behaving recklessly, that she risked everything by staying in Gisburn. She knew that she should be frightened, but the more she tried to want to run away, the more she couldn't face leaving. It was like she had become numb, immune to fear, awash with a desire to cling to the familiar; her home, her family, her friends. It was like she was living in a tunnel, able to blot out Thomas Lister, Master Heber, filthy dungeon floors, the looming spectre of the gallows; all the dreadful things which would otherwise have driven her away. In their stead she was able to fool herself that she was out of harm's way, that Demdike's witch bottle, still tucked away within her cottage's walls, could protect her, that perhaps even Edmund Hartley's faithful black dog would come to her aid. It was madness, she now realised. Madness had taken over.

After her visit to Malkin Tower on Good Friday past, she had pleaded with William to stay a while. She had tried to make him understand. She couldn't just leave, she explained. What about Anna, so big with child and so close to her time? What about John, running the farm by himself, shouldn't they make sure he's alright first? What about her friends in Blacko? Her friends needed her, she had insisted. She couldn't leave them now; she couldn't live with herself, it would be the end of her! They would leave, but just not yet. In the end William had reluctantly agreed to stay, although he had insisted that it was just for a short while, that ultimately they must get away from Gisburn. At the time, Jennet hadn't understood why he had relented, but standing there now, looking at his weary face, etched with lines of worry and grief, she began to appreciate the predicament he had faced, to see the situation as he had seen it. He must have thought she was losing her mind, after being on trial for her life and surviving, only to return home and discover that those she cared about so dearly were facing the same dreadful fate. He must have stood there, listening to the ramblings of his wife, knowing that he had to decide: stay a little while longer and risk her safety, or leave now and risk losing her sanity? He must have decided, after much agonising, that he couldn't risk her fragile state of mind. He knew that this resolute Jennet was only half the story. He knew that her delusions of safety, of bravery were the tip of the iceberg, that they masked the turmoil which lay beneath.

For the weeks since her return from her own incarceration, Jennet had barely slept. Every time she closed her eyes she saw old, frail Demdike, rotting in a prison cell, her terrified grand-daughter offering her no solace. She imagined the guards, mistreating them both, taking their pleasure with Alison as Master Heber's men had done with her. On those occasions where she did fall asleep, she would imagine herself locked up with them, filthy and half-starved, being held down on the ground by brutish men, and she would awake screaming. Now she had just learned that Elizabeth too had been taken away, along with James and little Jennet, and she feared for her. Kind, gentle Elizabeth, who had always resisted knowing about her mother's cunning ways because she sensed the danger it might bring, because she was petrified of ending up dangling from the end of a rope. Jennet wondered if Elizabeth had the strength for prison, if she would make it to trial at all. Terrified for her dear friend, she began to weep.

"We will leave today," declared William, ignoring his wife's tears. "Get the child ready, Jennet. We will pack up a cart and tell my brother we are leaving, but we must make haste. Don't tell anyone else that we're going, don't even tell Anna, I'll ask John to speak with her once we are gone. If you tell her now it'll be all over the village in minutes and a send-off is the last thing we need," he added, still angry with his niece for her indiscretion.

Jennet reached out and grasped William's hand. "You were right, we should have left sooner. You agreed to stay even though you knew it was best that we go," Jennet whispered, her voice breaking. Through her tears she struggled to convey to her husband how she knew the sacrifices he had made, the risks he had taken against his better judgment. She struggled to make him see that she understood now, for the first time in their marriage, the lengths he would go to for her happiness.

"Never mind that," he said kindly, placing a reassuring hand on top of hers. "There's still time to get away. If we hurry, we can still get you safely away from here."

Jennet nodded obediently. The fear which should have driven her away weeks ago was beginning to rest heavily upon her now. She knew it was time to go, that there was nothing more she could do for her friends except hope and pray for their acquittal. She bent down to little Bess, and stroked her affectionately on the cheek. "We're going on a journey, sweetheart, and we're going to go soon. Can you help me gather everything we'll need?" she coaxed gently.

Bess nodded and the pair set about assembling their possessions ready to be loaded on to the cart which William had gone to fetch. As she packed, Jennet looked around her small cottage, as though trying to absorb its detail for the last time. As a grown woman, this had been the only home she had known; it had been hers ever since she had married William all those years ago. She thought about the memories her humble walls contained, all the laughter those walls had heard, all the angry voices, all the tears. She remembered all the afternoons spent spinning with Anna, all the meals cooked on her hearth, all the nights she had lain with William, and all the babies she had borne in her modest bed. She recalled the first time she had lain with Tom Lister; that had been in her small cottage also, a magical night when her home had seemed so warm, cosy and protective, enveloping the pair of them so that they might be the only two people left in the whole world. At the thought of Tom a solitary tear rolled down her cheek. She wiped it away defiantly, remembering that it was his son who posed such a danger to her now.

"Let's go," said William, returning with Jennet's horse and a small cart a little while later and frantically loading it up with everything they had chosen to take with them.

Jennet picked up little Bess and placed her in the cart. The child whimpered, sensing the finality of their act. Jennet drew her close. "I will sit with you, little one," she whispered. "Your father can ride. He'll like that, won't he? He hardly ever gets to ride my horse," she teased.

Jennet and Bess huddled together in the cart as William mounted Jennet's horse and urged the old animal to move. The horse strained with the weight of the load.

"If this poor creature makes it to Giggleswick it will be a blessing," remarked William over his shoulder. "I think this will be a very slow journey. We may have to walk some of it, to save his legs."

As they crawled along the road, Jennet looked back at the village for the last time. It was the only place she had ever lived, the only place she really knew, and the only place that knew her, for all her faults, all her sins. Gisburn was her world and now she was leaving it, she was wandering into the unknown. All she knew about Giggleswick was that William was born there, that he had family there; she had never visited, she had never shown an interest. Jennet began to panic a little. What if Giggleswick was unpleasant, what if William's family didn't care for her? What if they knew what a bad wife she had been to their William and chose to treat her unkindly for it?

"What is Giggleswick like?" she asked William, deciding to try to quash her fears.

"It's like anywhere else, Jennet," replied William over his shoulder. "Not that it matters. We won't be staying long. We will need to go further than Giggleswick to keep you safe."

The horse picked up pace slightly as they reached the top of a small incline and the road levelled out. Jennet looked behind her once again, the village now becoming little more than gentle plumes of smoke idling from chimneys. Jennet glanced down the road to see horses behind them in the distance. At first Jennet thought little of this, but when she looked again, she realised that these horses were coming up the road at a considerable pace.

"There's someone coming behind us," she called out to William, "and they're coming quickly. William, what do we do?"

"Nothing," replied William. "We keep going. They may not be looking for us, Jennet; this road can be busy with many folk on all kinds of business. Say nothing when they pass us, just keep your heads down and hopefully they won't notice you. I don't want anyone to know where we are going."

The horses drew nearer. Jennet gasped as she realised she recognised the riders. The man in the middle, on the tallest grandest horse, was Thomas Heber, flanked on each side by the two brutes who had come for her last time. Jennet grabbed Bess and held on to her tightly, trying to shield both of their faces, desperately hoping that these men would pass by them, that their presence on this road today was a mere unhappy coincidence. Her heart pounding in her chest, she closed her eyes and prayed. She heard a horse whinny, and she felt the cart come to a stop.

"Jennet Preston?" said a voice beside her.

Jennet forced herself to open her eyes and look up. This was it; they had waited too long, and now they would never get away. The chase was over and Master Heber was the victor, here to enjoy his spoils. Jennet looked at William, who had now dismounted from her horse. His face was pale with fear as he lifted Bess out of the cart and held her tightly. The child cried out for her mother, a shrill desperate wail which made Jennet begin to weep.

"I think you know why I am here, Jennet Preston, so we may dispense with the formalities," Master Heber said with a menacing grin. "Come on, out of the cart. You must come with us."

Jennet looked again at William and realised that for the first time in her life she was seeing the spill of tears down his cheeks. They stared at one another for what felt like an eternity, as though their gazes could prolong the inevitable.

"A moment, Your Honour," said Jennet bravely. "I know what I must do, but will you allow me a moment with my husband and child first, to say goodbye? I don't know when I will see them again," she said, labouring on those final words as the meaning of them struck her.

Thomas Heber nodded. "Be quick," he said sternly.

Jennet walked round the cart and over to William and Bess. Her legs felt weak and she had to use the edge of the cart to steady her. She took Bess into her arms and leaned into William's chest.

"I'm sorry," she whispered, her voice wavering with tears. "I'm sorry that we didn't go soon enough."

William answered her only with dreadful, mourning sobs. After a few moments it was Bess who spoke up.

"Mother, don't leave me. Mother, please don't go," she said pleadingly.

"My darling I have to go, these men will not have it any other way. My dear, sweet Bess I don't know when we will see each other again. Know this child: I love you and keep you in my prayers always," Jennet said, kissing the child on the head as her body shook with tears. She kissed William too; he was still silent, still pale, and still crying. "I love you, my darling William. I am sorry for all the pain I have caused you. Look after my little Bess," she said finally, before turning back to Master Heber.

Wiping the tears from her eyes, Jennet gave Thomas Heber a hard, cold look, one which might have delivered death on the spot if only she had such abilities. "I hope my suffering eases Master Lister's burden, that it is not all for nought," she said plainly. "May God forgive you both for what you do."

Thomas Heber's jaw hardened. "There is no God for the likes of you," he spat, as his men forced her on to the back of one of their horses and began what Jennet suspected would be the final journey back to Marton Hall.

28

York Assizes, York Castle, York
27th July 1612

"All rise in court!" said the judge as the heavy courtroom doors burst open.

Jennet didn't turn around. Instead she closed her eyes and willed herself to be somewhere else, anywhere else. In her mind's eye she soared, seeing Gisburn, Giggleswick, the familiar Blacko hillside which her dearest friends called home, even her prison cell, which had been her home for so many weeks. Captivity now was her friend, as she had become so accustomed to it. She had grown used to her dry mouth, her dirty clothes, her empty, aching belly. She knew that she could live with sleeping on a hard floor with little to cover her, she could live with shackles, she could live with the violence and cruelty of the guards. She could live with all of it, because at least it all meant that she was still alive. She screwed up her eyes even tighter, willing herself away to somewhere, anywhere, anywhere but here, on trial for her life. As her mind roamed she grew dizzy and her stomach heaved, causing her to vomit all over the floor without warning.

"Fetch the prisoner a bucket!" barked the judge. "Compose yourself, woman," he instructed her harshly.

"My Lord Altham, will I proceed?" asked Master Heber, now standing in front of the bench where the judge sat. Heber looked straight ahead, not turning to look at Jennet at all.

The judge gestured towards Thomas Heber in response, "Yes, do go on," he replied shortly. Jennet noted that this judge was not as pleasantly spoken as the one who had presided over her first trial. Apart from chastising her for being sick, this judge didn't look at her at all, didn't address her, and he hadn't taken the time to explain to her what would happen, as the first judge had. He was even ill-tempered towards Master Heber. Jennet shuddered and shrunk down as Thomas Heber began to address the court. Clearly he was not content to leave justice to the judges this time.

"This woman, Jennet Preston of Gisburn, in Craven, in the county of York, is accused of witchcraft of the most mischievous and wicked order," Thomas Heber paused on those words, allowing the jury to consider them, before turning to address them directly. "Good men of the jury, you will today hear evidence of how this woman bewitched to death Master Thomas Lister, deceased some five years since, and not content at this suffering, sought to cause the death of Master Thomas Lister still living. Mercifully she was only prevented from doing so by her captivity. You will hear, by testimony in this courtroom, that she is a devilish woman, capable of the most bloody murder," he finished, his face solemn, but clearly relishing the theatrical spectacle of his own words.

"Have you witnesses to call?" prompted the judge, keen to press on.

"Yes, my Lord Altham. I call Anne Robinson to bear witness against these heinous acts," Master Heber replied.

Jennet gasped as she heard that name. She hadn't seen Anne Robinson for several years, but as she watched her walk towards the front of the courtroom and approach the judge's bench, she could see that she was mostly unchanged. Her frame was still skinny but slightly hunched these days and her face, though now lined, still bore the same twisted nasty smile that it always had. As

Anne reached the judge's bench she turned and looked at Jennet; a triumphant glance which made Jennet's stomach churn. A whore, Anne Robinson had called her once. What would she say about her now?

"Anne Robinson, you have been a faithful servant of the Listers for many years, is that correct?" Master Heber began.

"Yes Your Honour," replied Anne with an obedient nod. "Just like my mother before me."

"And you knew the accused, Jennet Preston, during her service at Westby Hall?" Thomas Heber prompted.

Anne glanced slyly at Jennet; a look which made Jennet wonder what the maid was thinking about. Was she thinking about that day when she very nearly caught Jennet in Tom Lister's rooms? Was she recalling the words she said to her, the hatred and venom which had poured from her lips in that brief moment of victory, before Tom's quick thinking put an end to her accusations?

"Yes, I knew her well," replied Anne, her gaze still intent upon Jennet. "As a girl she was a kitchen maid when my late mother was the cook, then latterly she returned to service at Westby as a maid for Mistress Jane Lister, now deceased. I always found it odd that she came back. I assumed that she and her husband must have needed the income, but now I think she must have had a far crueller purpose," added Anne spitefully.

"What are your recollections about the death of Master Thomas Lister, the father of Master Thomas Lister still living?" asked Thomas Heber.

Anne's face became solemn and she shook her head. "A terrible business," she began, "Master Lister became suddenly and gravely ill. It all happened so quickly, Your Honour."

"Take your time, Anne," Thomas Heber replied gently.

"He was lying in his bed, crying out, clearly in terrible agony."

"And what did he say? Could you make sense of it?"

"To anyone who would listen he said that we should take hold of Jennet Preston, that we shouldn't let her leave, that she lay heavy upon him. He kept calling these words, over and over, until he sadly breathed his last," said Anne, pausing then for the jury to consider her words.

"And what did you take Master Lister's dying words to mean, Anne?" coaxed Thomas Heber, leading his witness perfectly.

"I believe Master Lister was trying to warn us, Your Honour. I believe that he knew that Jennet Preston had harmed him and that he wanted us to stop her. Unfortunately we didn't understand his words at the time; it was only afterwards that their meaning became clear."

"What do you mean, Anne?" Thomas Heber pressed.

"Well, once the Master's body had been settled on a winding sheet, all those who worked at Westby were welcomed before it, to say goodbye to their Master. When Jennet went forth to say a prayer over him, she touched his corpse. I'm not certain if she meant to touch him or not, but in any case, the strangest thing then occurred," said Anne.

"What happened, Anne?"

"The corpse bled, Your Honour. Fresh, red blood came from his nose, and a little from his ear. I didn't know that corpses could bleed," she added, her voice filled with faux-incredulity.

"A corpse may bleed, if touched by a witch," said Thomas Heber, addressing the jury as well as the witness. "Thank you for your testimony, Anne, you may stand down."

Jennet dug her nails into the wooden bar in front of her as Anne Robinson marched victoriously passed. Her cheeks burned as she became so angry that she thought she might faint. Anne Robinson's evidence, coached and rehearsed to perfection, was a concoction of lies and omitted information. She never mentioned the wedding, never mentioned that Tom died in the church in Bracewell and not at home in Westby. She twisted Tom's dying words and then, to conclude, she had told a completely fabricated story about Tom's poor lifeless body bleeding at Jennet's touch. Jennet began to weep as she recalled that she had touched his corpse, but only to embrace him, to try to force life back into his still, breathless body.

The court muttered and murmured as Anne Robinson made her way back through the courtroom. Jennet could just about make out some of the hushed whispers and it was clear some of them at least were horrified and spellbound by what they had just heard. Taking a deep breath, she tried to close her ears and her mind to their remarks. Their condemnation would serve no purpose other than to terrify her. She had to remember that she was still on trial, that sentence hadn't yet been passed. Perhaps the jury wouldn't believe Anne's story, perhaps they would find it a little too fanciful, too hard to believe. Clinging to this thought, Jennet closed her eyes and prayed for a moment.

"This is all lies!" someone shouted from the small crowd at the back. "You can't believe any of it. Jennet Preston is an innocent woman. She is the victim of a conspiracy against her!"

The entire courtroom swung round, Jennet included, to see Anna Singleton standing at the back, a tiny new-born baby swaddled closely to her chest. Jennet's heart raced momentarily as she recognised a familiar, friendly face. Forgetting herself for a moment, she almost smiled.

Realising she had everyone's attention, Anna grew more vitriolic, shouting so loud it made her baby cry. "Jennet Preston is innocent of the crime of witchcraft! She is the victim here!"

"Anna," Jennet said quietly, her voice little more than a hoarse whimper.

"Have a care for your child," scolded the judge. "Please remove this woman from this court," he instructed his guards standing nearby.

Anna strained to look back at Jennet as she was led away, "I love you," she managed to mouth, before being taken from the room. The brief flicker of a smile faded from Jennet's lips as her dear niece was taken away and she turned back obediently to face the judge.

"Are you ready to call your next witness?" the judge asked Thomas Heber.

"Yes, my Lord. I call Thomas Lister, the son of Thomas Lister now deceased, to give evidence against Jennet Preston," Thomas Heber said.

The court murmured again as Thomas Lister made his way to the front of the room. Most of their mutterings, Jennet noted, were in sympathy, which if they believed what they had just heard, was hardly surprising. Jennet's heart sank as she realised that many in court that day did believe Anne's story to be true; even Anna's outburst had failed to convince anyone. Jennet studied Tom Lister closely. It had been five years since she had last seen him. Considering his relative youth he looked much aged, his hair greying around his ears and his face prematurely lined around the eyes. As he passed Jennet he continued to look straight in front of him, his eyes not straying to glance at her even once. He reached the front of the courtroom, bowing briefly but courteously before the judge and his father-in-law, who gave him a slight nod and a small smile.

"Thank you for coming to address the court today, Sir," Thomas Heber began respectfully. "We have already heard testimony from your loyal maid, Anne Robinson. Are you able to confirm her words about the manner of your father's death?"

"I can, Your Honour. Anne Robinson's words about my father's death are true, he did cry out a great deal against Jennet Preston. I cannot speak to the assertion that my father's corpse bled at her touch; I did not see this happen. However I can confirm that there was blood present around his nose and ears, as Anne has said, and I saw this not long after Jennet would have touched the body. I can surmise, therefore, that what Anne says is correct," answered Thomas Lister eloquently.

"Sir, a man of the law such as myself is bound to ask; if the circumstances surrounding your father's death pointed so strongly to some malevolent act performed by Jennet Preston, why has your complaint not been heard by a court sooner? Forgive me Sir, but your father has been deceased five years since," Thomas Heber asked.

Thomas Lister took a deep breath as he paused for thought,

furrowing his brow as though carefully considering his words. "In truth, Your Honour, for a long time I didn't believe it was true. The anguish of a dying man's words makes them difficult to interpret and I am a reasonable man, I don't fall prey easily to stories about corpses bleeding at the touch unless I witness such things with my own eyes. To my knowledge, my father had always treated Jennet and her family kindly and therefore I didn't believe she had any grievance again him, so I had no good reason to believe she was responsible for his death. Furthermore, I had no reason at all to believe that she was a witch."

"What then, Sir, led you to change your mind?" Thomas Heber pressed.

"There is a trial soon to take place in Lancaster, Your Honour, of what appears to be a coven of witches from the Pendle area. The magistrate there, a good Christian man by the name of Nowell, was diligent in the task of collecting statements from complainants and the accused. Whilst assembling the evidence with which to press his case, he came across the name of Jennet Preston, and on discovering that she was a Gisburn woman, he saw fit to ask me about her. It was then that I learnt the full extent of this woman's satanic activities. It seems she is involved with this coven, and that she attended a witches' Sabbath on Good Friday last, during which she plotted with her fellow witches to murder myself and my uncle, Leonard Lister. I thought then about my father's words, the blood on his body and the mutterings of my servants and I decided that it must be true. This woman must be a witch; she murdered my father, she plotted to murder me and my uncle, she may even be responsible for the death of my poor mother and my dear infant son William, deceased in January past," Thomas Lister finished, casting his eyes down solemnly.

"I am truly sorry for all of your losses, Sir," Thomas Heber replied. "You may step down now. I have no further questions for you."

Jennet clung weakly to her wooden bar as she watched Thomas Lister walk away. She stared hard at him, trying to steal his gaze, as though if she made eye contact with him she might be able to peer into his soul and understand if he really believed all that he said. Did he really think she was a witch? Did he really hold her responsible for these dreadful events? Or was it just that he was still angry that his father had loved her more than his own poor mother? Was it just that he still felt keenly the humiliation of that day in church, when in front of their friends and neighbours, his father died in the arms of his lover? Was he still haunted by his father's anguished cries, echoing through that house of God? Thomas Lister skilfully avoided her gaze and walked steadfastly passed her, as though she might not exist at all, as though she might already be dead.

"If it pleases the court, I will now read a series of depositions collected by Roger Nowell, his Majesty's Justice of the Peace in the county of Lancashire," continued Thomas Heber.

Jennet listened aghast as one by one, the statements given by her friends were read out. Thomas Heber laboured greatly over the evidence of James Device, Elizabeth's son, who had apparently talked at great length about the gathering at Malkin Tower on Good Friday. Jennet closed her eyes, half-listening, half-remembering that afternoon. In her mind's eye she could see James, carving up the sheep that would be their feast, drinking his ale as quickly and fervently as everyone else in the room. The conversation that afternoon had undoubtedly grown wild as the intoxicating mixture of ale and anxiety loosened people's tongues, but the way in which the story was retold in James's testimony painted the gathering in a completely different light. James, if his testimony was truly in his own words, had not portrayed the gathering as a coming together of friends on a holy day, but had told his interrogators about curious rituals involving naming spirits, something which Jennet could neither recall from that afternoon nor understand. He had also told them of plots; plans to free prisoners from gaol cells, plans to murder Thomas Lister. James had talked of Jennet coming to Malkin Tower that day, not to comfort and assist her friends, but to seek help from them in ensuring Thomas Lister's demise, before riding away on a spirit creature which had taken the form of a white foal. Had the charges against her not been so serious, Jennet could have laughed at the picture painted of her poor horse as a magical spirit; the way the weary old thing plodded about it was clear to anyone that it was something of this earth.

Elizabeth's testimony was read out in support of James's, as was little Jennet's; they had all asserted that her purpose that day was to plot to kill Thomas Lister. As the final words were read out, Jennet hung her head in confusion and despair. She wondered how her friends could have been led to say these things against her. Surely they had not turned against her after all these years? Elizabeth, especially, was a true and loyal friend; she must have been out of her wits to have said these things. Perhaps that was it; they had been so frightened that they had assented willingly to any suggestions made to them, to bring the interrogation to an end. Or perhaps they had been misunderstood; James's odd statement about naming spirits certainly suggested to Jennet that his questioner had not always understood his meaning, or else James was being foolishly and dangerously fanciful. Looking back up to face her judge and jury, Jennet realised that she would never know the answer, but nonetheless she had to face the consequences of their condemnation.

"Will the jury now retire to consider their verdict," instructed the judge.

Jennet was led back to her prison cell. Now it was time to wait.

The jury took most of the day to consider their verdict. Jennet, sitting in her cell, grew a little more hopeful, for surely their long deliberation meant there was doubt, and where there was doubt, there was also hope. With each passing moment she also grew more desperate, as she knew that this could still be the end of it all, she could still be found guilty and be condemned to hang. Masters Heber and Lister had built a forceful case against her, and it would not be easily overcome. By the time she was recalled to court, she felt giddy with fear, her head spinning and her legs so weak she had to be carried to her bench by two guards.

"Good men of the jury, have you reached a verdict?" asked the judge without any delay.

"Yes," replied one of the men, rising to his feet as he did so.

"And do you find Jennet Preston of Gisburn in Craven guilty or not guilty of the murder by witchcraft of Thomas Lister Esquire, as contained in the indictment against her?"

The juryman paused only momentarily, but to Jennet it felt like a lifetime. Inhaling sharply she held her breath, terrified to let it go, clinging on to that delicate wisp of air in her lungs just as she was holding on to her life.

"We find Jennet Preston guilty," replied the juryman.

Jennet closed her eyes and released the air which was fighting its way out of her chest, surrendering to it as she gave in to her fate. It was all over. Thomas Lister had won. She would never see William again. She would never see Anna again. She would never see her darling little Bess again. It was all over now.

"Jennet Preston, in accordance with the law of this land, you are sentenced to be hanged by the neck until you are dead. Court dismissed," the judge barked.

Jennet was led out of the court and back towards her cell, tears streaming down her pale and sunken face. As she passed Thomas Lister she managed to catch his eye. He was the victor now, and he looked straight at her, a cold, unforgiving stare which made her heart ache and her stomach lurch. As he looked away again, Jennet spoke to him, uttering her final words in this life.

"I loved your father. Truly, I loved him. May God forgive you, Master Thomas."

29

Knavesmire, York
29th July 1612

It was a curious thing, Jennet thought, knowing that you were about to die. As she was lifted from the cart and up towards the gallows, her legs weak and no longer able to bear her weight, Jennet wondered if this was how Tom had felt in his anguished last moments; frightened, angry, shocked, and yet oddly serene and peaceful, as though the knowledge that life was reaching its inevitable conclusion was somehow a source of comfort.

She had spent the previous day and night in prayer, not sleeping at all, committing her final hours to God just as she hoped now to commend her soul to him. Immediately after the verdict, Jennet had been wracked with guilt, acutely aware of how gravely she had sinned in this life and fearful once again that her execution was God's punishment for her lustful and selfish behaviour. In her gaol cell she had railed against her fate; sobbing uncontrollably, vomiting violently as though to purge her body and cleanse her soul.

Eventually, as she became exhausted, a strange calm had come over her and as she moved on to her knees and clasped her hands together tightly, she knew what she had to do. She prayed for forgiveness, for all the terrible things she had done in her life, for all the pain she had caused. She prayed also for forgiveness for Thomas Lister; he had suffered greatly, she told God, and she hoped now that he would find peace. She prayed for Old Demdike, Elizabeth and her family; if death was to come for them also she hoped that it would be swift and merciful. She prayed for Anna and her children, asking God to keep them safe, and she prayed for William and Bess, begging God to make sure that they both found peace and comfort with one another. At the thought of her daughter she had wept; through prayer she had come to terms with her own fate but she found the knowledge that she would never see her precious child again almost too much to bear. Her tears spent, she prayed then for a quick death, followed by peace in everlasting life. Peace; she felt at peace with God now, even if only time would tell if the Almighty had forgiven her.

As the executioner tested his knot, she thought about William and Bess once more, saying one final prayer for them both. She knew that they wouldn't be there today. She knew that if William couldn't bear to see her tried he certainly couldn't bear to watch her executed, and she knew he would never have brought Bess to watch her mother die. Her eyes darted back and forth through the crowd of faces but she saw none that she recognised, not even Anna who had so bravely come to her trial to voice her objections. Jennet felt glad; she wanted none of those she loved so dearly to remember her in this way.

"Have you anything to confess?" asked a priest, clutching his Bible.

Jennet shook her head in response as the executioner fitted the noose. She had said all she had to say to God, there was nothing else to say now. She gulped hard as she felt the rough rope touch her skin. She closed her eyes, trying instead to imagine a soft blanket, enveloping her and taking her away to the next life. As the box beneath her feet was removed and the rope pulled tight, she forced herself not to struggle, choosing instead to submit, to succumb. Her eyes still closed, her ears indifferent to the jeers and cries of the crowd before her, she began to soar, higher than ever before, back to Gisburn, back to her little cottage, where William and Bess were waiting for her. In her mind's eye she could see little Bess playing outside, her mass of curls dishevelled, her knees muddy, her face screwed up in familiar concentration. Jennet drew herself closer, reaching out for the child as though to touch her, as though to hold her one last time, but she found that she was unable to reach, unable to pull herself down. She could only go up now, her mind light, her body empty, her soul released. In the brightness before her she could see a hand and reaching out for it, she saw then a face, a familiar face, with bright blue eyes and hair as dark as night. Tom smiled as his hands grasped hers, kissing her tenderly on the lips as the brightness around them became the familiar fields of Westby Hall, the familiar bare trees on a cold January day. Tom kissed her again and held her tightly as she closed her eyes one last time and felt herself become free.

The End

Another story of the Witches of Pendle, that of young Jennet Device will be told within the novel *A Woman Named Sellers*.

AUTHOR'S NOTES

This novel is the story of Jennet Preston, who was executed for witchcraft in July 1612, after being tried and found guilty of bewitching Master Thomas Lister of Westby Hall. She did also face an earlier charge of bewitching the infant son of the Dodgsons, of which she was acquitted. Beyond this and her marriage to William Preston of Giggleswick in 1587, very little else is known about her life.

Jennet Preston did live in Gisburn, then in the county of Yorkshire, which meant that she was tried separately from the rest of the Pendle witches. Her solitary trial in York often makes her feel forgotten, as the focus is so often on the main trials in Lancaster. As a historian this was what first drew my attention to her, and as a writer I found the few details we know about her compelling. I found myself asking, how could she have ended up embroiled in all this? Why was she accused of killing Thomas Lister, when there was no evidence of previous involvement in witchcraft? Unlike many of the other Pendle witches, not least the infamous Demdike and Chattox, no one had ever seen Jennet make a picture out of clay and crumble it, or utter a curse; nor did she ply a trade as a wise woman. Why did her friends and family so vehemently insist that she had been framed? Certainly the historical evidence for a conspiracy is strong: two trials for witchcraft in a matter of months, both founded largely on hearsay. The fact that the damning charge against her was that she was seen to make a corpse bleed seems tenuous at best and frankly fabricated at worst. But who would conspire to judicially murder Jennet, and why?

This novel attempts to create a story which answers some of these questions; in doing so I have added a number of fictional elements and characters. We don't know how well she knew the Devices, although we can suppose she was reasonably friendly with them as she was reported to have been at Malkin Tower on that fateful Good Friday. We don't know the nature of her relationship with Thomas Lister, although the supposition that she was his mistress seems a plausible one, given that he is said to have died calling out her name. We don't know if she had any children; her daughter Bess is fictitious, as is her spirited niece Anna.

If this novel has inspired an interest in the Pendle Witch Trials, I can recommend two good books on the subject. These are The Lancashire Witch Craze: Jennet Preston and the Lancashire Witches, 1612 by Jonathan Lumby and The Lancashire Witch Conspiracy: A History of Pendle Forest and the Pendle Witch Trials by John A Clayton. It is also worth reading the only primary sources which exist concerning both Jennet's trial and the trials in Lancaster. These are The Arraignement and Triall of Jennet Preston, of Gisborne in Craven in the Countie of Yorke, and The Wonderfull Discoverie of Witches in the Countie of Lancaster, both written by the court clerk, Thomas Potts.

ABOUT THE AUTHOR

Sarah L King has always loved writing and as a youth she flirted with poetry, some of which was published. In addition, she has always loved History which led to her obtaining a 1st Class Honours degree in the subject from Lancaster University. Now, with her first novel, The Gisburn Witch she has begun a new journey to merge her two passions together and bring some new, interesting Historical Fiction to the world.

Born in Nottinghamshire, England, Sarah has lived in several places but now resides in West Lothian, Scotland with her husband and two children. Her days are filled with trying to juggle her time between writing, working and looking after her children.

For further information please visit her website & blog at http://www.sarahlking.com/

Printed in Dunstable, United Kingdom